THE RED HAND OF FURY

THE RED HAND OF FURY

A Silas Quinn mystery

R. N. Morris

This first world edition published 2018
in Great Britain and the USA by
SEVERN HOUSE PUBLISHERS LTD of
Eardley House, 4 Uxbridge Street, London W8 7SY.
Trade paperback edition first published
in Great Britain and the USA 2018 by
SEVERN HOUSE PUBLISHERS LTD

British Library Cataloguing in Publication Data
A CIP catalogue record for this title is available from the British Library.

ISBN-13: 978-0-7278-8785-6 (cased)
ISBN-13: 978-1-84751-908-5 (trade paper)
ISBN-13: 978-1-78010-963-3 (e-book)

All Severn House titles are printed on acid-free paper.

Severn House Publishers support the Forest Stewardship Council™ [FSC™],
the leading international forest certification organisation.
All our titles that are printed on FSC certified paper carry the FSC logo.

Typeset by Palimpsest Book Production Ltd.,
Falkirk, Stirlingshire, Scotland.
Printed and bound in Great Britain by
TJ International, Padstow, Cornwall.

ONE

10 July, 1914.

Stanley Ince looked out of a first-floor window, down on to No. 2 Airing Court. A group of about twenty or so male lunatics occupied themselves in various forms of activity, or, in the case of most of them, inactivity.

One stood talking to a tree. His head cocked intermittently to listen to the tree's responses. Stanley recognized him as one of the syphilitic patients.

A number of the men paced their own small patches of earth, wearing the lawn brown with their incessant steps. Round and round they went, in ever-diminishing circles, until each reached a point where they came to a stop, turned around and began the pacing again, gradually widening the spiral of their exercise. It was strange how this obsessive practice had recently spread among them, both the males and the females, despite the strict segregation of the sexes.

Two men occupied a bench, each staring straight out in front. He had seen them together before. Stanley didn't like it when they formed bonds like this. A single, isolated madman was bad enough. But when they started to conspire, well, there was no saying where that would end. He made a mental note to keep them apart in the future.

One of the younger attendants tried to engage three of them in a game of badminton, over a makeshift net strung between two trees. It was a fruitless task. The lunatics seemed to delight more in throwing their racquets as high as they could into the air.

Stanley shook his head disdainfully. He was about to open the window and shout a warning to his less experienced colleague when he caught sight of a solitary figure dressed in a gardener's smock, working patiently among the shrubs at the edge of the court. He could not see the man's face but he knew immediately who he was. Timon Medway cut a very distinct figure. It was almost as if there was a line drawn around him, a fine black border that marked him out as . . . as being Timon Medway. Or perhaps it was more accurate to say that Medway emanated some special quality of his own. A kind of dark charisma.

Stanley had never admitted it to anyone. Hardly even to himself. But he could no longer deny the truth. He was afraid of them.

And he was afraid of Timon Medway most of all.

But whenever he was in the presence of any of them, he felt it. His scalp tingled. A cold sweat broke out over his back, trickling down his skin. He could taste the fear on his own breath.

There was only one way to get past that moment. A thump thrown out in passing. A chair leg driven down with force on to a bare foot. A twist and tug of hair. Or a lit match tossed casually into one of their faces.

Then he would be able to go on. To face them with equanimity. With a jaunty laugh even. To lay hands upon them in whatever way was required.

Of course you had to be careful.

Not everyone on the staff shared his approach. Some of the doctors were particularly fastidious.

You could test the water with a harmless jest at the lunatic's expense. If you got an appreciative laugh, you knew that here was someone you could get along with. You could risk a light slap around the chops. Nothing too heavy handed. Delivered with a brisk, jolly quip, to show that it's all meant in fun.

But if, at mere words, the other fellow tenses up, if his eyes challenge you with silent rebuke, then best to leave it at that. And be on your guard with him in the future.

Store up the slaps for later, when you're alone with one of them.

For you will need to buy your peace of mind somehow.

Of all the occupations in the world that he could have chosen, it was strange that he had ended up here, at Colney Hatch, working among *them*.

What was even stranger was how long he had stayed here. It was almost as if, however much he hated to be in their presence, he hated even more the thought of letting them out of his sight.

He could still remember the day he arrived at the asylum, even though it was over twenty years ago now.

It was a beautiful spring day. The trepidation that he had felt on the train turned to wonder at his first sight of the building. It was such a fine, grand edifice, a broad palace of a place, stretching out to possess the gentle slope upon which it had been built. At that first glance, it was impossible to think of it as the home of madness and despair. The sunlight winked along the rows of windows. A sense of rational optimism seemed to emanate from the place. As if all that was needed to cure its inmates of whatever ailed them was a sunny day.

As he had approached the main entrance, walking through the well-kept gardens, breathing the floral scents, his ears pleasantly assailed by birdsong (and not the screams of the mad that he had expected), he almost felt that he would be turned back. That they would tell him there was no longer any need for his services. All the lunatics had been cured and sent home.

He had felt so hopeful that first day. Whatever was contained within that splendid building was not to be feared. This was the modern way to deal with a problem such as madness. To build a fine and well-appointed palace around it. Airy rooms, high ceilings, plenty of illumination. A pleasant aspect, good drainage, fresh air far from the smoke and grime of the city.

Nor had he entered there with any intent to harm the poor wretches who were to be given into his care. Indeed, he was drawn to the work by vaguely philanthropic sentiments. And by a strange and almost overpowering curiosity.

The truth is, he had no experience in administering to the mentally afflicted before that day, having previously worked as a porter in the freight yard at King's Cross. The idea of madness both appalled and fascinated him. He thought too that it would be easier work – physically, that is – than lugging crates about.

If he thought about the type of individual he would be called upon to look after, he imagined a weak and docile imbecile, who could be persuaded and directed by subtle guidance, the application of the gentlest pressure at the elbow perhaps.

All this was before he had clapped eyes on his first lunatic.

He had not counted on the calamitous effect that that would have upon his morale.

For in that encounter, madness ceased to be an abstract idea. It became real, dangerously personal, and frighteningly close.

*   *   *

He remembered the case well.

It was a young man, apparently of good family. His father, who was recently deceased, had been a doctor. It was said that the patient was studying medicine too. His father's death (the rumour was that he'd committed suicide) seemed to have precipitated some kind of crisis in the young man's mental equilibrium. A breakdown. His behaviour had become erratic, frightening to those who knew him. He had been making a nuisance of himself to his landlady's daughter and had threatened a fellow lodger with violence. A delusion had taken root in his mind that he had killed the other man, whom he saw as a rival for the girl's affections. There was no evidence that this was the case.

Some might consider it remarkable that Stanley could recollect so many details of the case. But this was his first exposure to an insane individual. It cannot be surprising that it made an impression upon him.

What struck him most about the young man – what shook him – was how, well, ordinary he looked. If you didn't know, you would never have thought him mad. He had what Stanley would have described as a 'clever' face. His eyes were alert and engaged. Stanley had believed that lunatics could be identified by their 'stark, staring' expression. There was no sign of that in this young man. Perhaps his gaze was a little too searching, as if he was expecting something from you. Was it a sign of madness to expect things from your fellows?

Nor was he raving when he spoke. Admittedly, there was a certain overstimulated brightness to his manner. But nothing that he said went beyond the bounds of rational speech. He was fluent and articulate. A little garrulous perhaps. But rather divertingly so. Stanley found himself hanging on his every word.

'You have caught him on a good day,' one of the old hands observed. 'Most days we cannot get a word out of him. He curls himself into a ball and cowers in the corner. He would not stir for days at a time, even soiling himself as he festers there. Must be he likes you.'

That notion horrified Stanley. It seemed to suggest that there was some kindred spark between him and the young man.

He had believed that the insane were a separate class from himself. Almost a distinct species. Something less than human.

He could have nothing in common with them. And if there were steps that took a sane person into the realms of insanity, they were such immense and unimaginable steps, associated with such outlandish circumstances, that they could have nothing to do with him.

But this boy, it was said he had gone mad purely on account of the death of a parent. That was the sort of thing that might happen to anyone.

And here he was, on the day that Stanley first encountered him at least, clean, presentable, coherent, if a little excitable. How was it possible that he could be this bright young thing one day and a closed-off catatonic depressive the next? If this boy could go so easily from one state to the other, then perhaps anyone could? The barriers that existed between the sane and the insane were not as solid as Stanley had imagined.

Such a realization might have inspired compassion in another man. But in Stanley Ince it had provoked only horror.

Suddenly Timon Medway straightened from his task and turned his face to look up, directly at Stanley. Their eyes met, no doubt about it. Not for the first time, Stanley had the impression that Medway had read his thoughts. The sly ironic smile he detected on the lunatic's lips seemed to confirm it.

'Fucker.' Stanley spoke the word out loud, moving his lips with deliberate articulation. If Medway couldn't read minds, then he would at least be able to read that.

'Ince?'

He turned on his heel to be confronted by Drummond, one of the psychiatric nurses on the male wards. Drummond was a member of the bleeding heart brigade. The type who believed in treating the lunatics with tenderness and brotherly love, and all that rot. He had once caught Stanley punching an inmate on the ear and had threatened to have him dismissed if he ever so much as laid a finger on one of them again.

'Dr Pottinger requires your presence in the waiting room.' Drummond's tone made it clear that if it were down to him, Stanley's presence would not be required anywhere. 'Pick up a straitjacket on your way. We have a new admission and he is somewhat agitated.'

'And Dr Pottinger knows that if anyone can calm him, it is I.'

Drummond made no effort to conceal his distaste. 'You are merely to report to Dr Pottinger with the straitjacket.'

Stanley could not conceal his amusement. 'He sent you to fetch me.'

'Don't push it, Ince.'

'Or what, Mr Drummond?'

'I am watching you.'

'You may not approve of my methods . . .'

'You have no *methods*! You're not allowed to have methods! You're a glorified porter. Your job is to do as the qualified medical staff instruct you.'

'Calm yourself, Mr Drummond. Otherwise, who knows? One day you might find yourself admitted as a patient here. Now wouldn't that be a lark?'

'Get a move on, Ince. Dr Pottinger is waiting for you.'

As he walked away, Stanley exhaled vigorously through his nose in a series of snorts: not laughter, a mockery of laughter, almost silent. But audible enough, he felt, to leave Drummond in no doubt as to his contempt.

At any rate, he ignored the urgency of Drummond's command. He frankly dawdled. It made the powers that be more appreciative of his contribution if he kept them waiting. Besides, time in a lunatic asylum had a different quality to it to time outside. A moment could last an eternity. While ten years went by in the blink of an eye.

The corridors of Colney Hatch were his domain. All six miles of them. He proclaimed his sovereignty with the crisp echo of his footsteps. His shining black steel-capped shoes rapped and squealed against the boards.

The exposed brick walls were painted a chill institutional blue, wan and spiritless. Once it had been thought that the colour had a calming effect on lunatics. Now the walls were always repainted the same colour out of tradition. If it was meant to put them in mind of a summer's day, it failed. Perhaps it worked by sapping their will. It certainly absorbed nothing of their pain, but rather amplified it, resonated with it, turning the corridors into a vast sounding box of misery. The terracotta tiles on the ceiling added a thin, harsh stridency to the notes.

(He had never been convinced that the honeycomb design was a wise decision. If he had a guinea for every inmate who imagined himself persecuted by giant bees, he would be a rich man by now.)

He kept the keys to the store cupboard at the end of a long chain, together with all his other keys in a massive fob. He felt the weight of it in his trouser pocket. The chain was deliberately long, so that he could swing the fob threateningly at recalcitrant lunatics. From time to time, if needs be, he would let the weight of spiky metal strike home. Some of the keys were now crusted with dried blood.

And so the object in question, the lethal claw of keys, never failed to provoke a certain reaction in him, even when he was wielding it innocently as now. It was a kind of awe, a quickening of the heart, accompanied by an icy, empty sensation. As if a blast of wind from some desolate polar vastness had blown away his soul.

It was the feeling a man experiences when he faces up to what he has become and does not like it.

The store cupboard smelled as if it was where they kept the despair. He took a straitjacket from the shelf, releasing with it the more precise odours that it had absorbed over the years in the restraint of troubled humanity. Sweat, mucus, vomit, blood, urine, faeces. He did not think he detected semen. It would be hard even for some of the prodigious masturbators in Colney Hatch to engineer an ejaculation with their hands so tightly tethered. But he wouldn't put it past them.

The semi-muted cries of some self-torturing wretch came to him from the depths of a padded cell. But the howls of the mad were trivial in this place. He hardly heard them any more.

As he moved towards the central block of the asylum, he began to be aware of a second source of screaming. Sharper, rawer, louder than the first. He knew most of the inmates by their screams. But these new screams he did not recognize. He had the feeling that he had heard them once before, long ago. It was not impossible. The mad were never cured, and those who were from time to time released often found themselves readmitted.

He quickened his step, as if hurrying to meet an old friend. But as he reached the top of the stairs, he stopped dead. The screams were suddenly much louder here as they reverberated up the stairwell. And yes, there was something half-familiar about them. The pitch, the timbre, the peculiar ferocity coupled with a brittle fragility, the sharp broken edge of them. It was a long time ago. But he was beginning to be convinced he had heard these sounds before.

The young man he had thought of earlier now came to mind again. Could it really be?

His hand drifted towards the key fob in his pocket, as if for comfort. It was his protective talisman. And, of course, it had a more practical function. The youth had been the first to feel the brunt of it across his cheek.

Not a youth any more, Stanley had to remind himself. More than twenty years had passed. He would be middle-aged now. Stanley couldn't be sure he would recognize the man, not from a distance. Time had a habit of ravaging lunatics more viciously than the sane.

It never failed to impress him how much chaos a single lunatic can generate, how quickly he can fill a room with it. Any room, of any size: the chaos expands around him. Put a single lunatic in the Albert Hall and he will fill it.

This one was all flailing arms and incoherent screaming. Frantic bursts of pacing, going nowhere, as if he was trying to break free from imaginary restraints. Coming to a sudden halt, as if fresh restraints now bound him.

The policeman who had brought him in stood nearby. His work was done, but he couldn't quite tear himself away from the spectacle. For most people, a maniac in full, florid flow was not something you saw every day. There were two other men with him. One had the air of being some kind of official. A plain-clothes police detective, Stanley guessed. His expression was strangely anguished, almost as if he had some kind of connection with the individual at the centre of it all. The other man carried a physician's leather bag.

The doctor was impatient to be gone. 'It is out of our hands now, Macadam. We must leave him to those who are experts in this field.'

The man called Macadam shook his head disconsolately. He

was evidently a policeman after all, for he commanded the uniform: 'Come then, Constable. We've done our duty by him.'

For a moment it seemed that he would address the raging maelstrom directly. But he simply shook his head once more and followed the doctor out of the waiting room, calling out 'Constable!' for the lingering copper.

Two young, inexperienced attendants – useless fuckers – were tiptoeing around the new admission, trying to reason with him. You cannot reason with a lunatic! Rush him, ground him, hold him down, pin his four limbs with a solid man squatting on each. Sit on his head if you have to. That was the only kind of reasoning your average lunatic could understand.

But still they persisted with their: 'Now, sir, if you will just calm down.'

The lunatic alternated between rushing at them and running from them. This was some kind of acknowledgement of their existence at least. Otherwise, the man's ravings bore no relation to what they were saying to him.

'A bubble! A bubble! He was a bubble! And I have popped him!'

It was him, all right.

His hair was matted, and plastered to his head in wet clumps. It could have been sweat or some other liquid. Wiry grey tufts now grew at the temples, which were not there the last time Stanley had seen him. A growth of about five days shadowed his jowls. The rest of his face was smeared with grime and filth. There was a fresh wound on his forehead. His hands were covered in scabs and scratches, and possible bites. A nasty cut on his knee showed through a flapping hole in one trouser leg. His feet were bare and black and bleeding.

But the truth was, if you could look past all the superficial squalor of his appearance, he had aged comparatively well – well, that is, for a lunatic. His hair may have been matted and greying, but at least he still had hair. His face was dirty, but he did not have the emaciated features of the long-term destitute. Whatever crisis had propelled him into Colney Hatch had happened relatively recently.

Though they were soiled and torn now, his clothes were well tailored and essentially of good quality. The dubiously stained herringbone ulster was of a distinguished cut, bespoke by the looks of it. Beneath that he wore a three-piece suit, although his shirt had lost its collar and necktie. In one hand he clutched a battered bowler hat defensively.

The two wet-around-the-ears attendants coaxed him as if it were a knife. 'Put down the hat now. There's a good fellow.'

Roderick Pottinger, the chief psychiatrist and superintendent of Colney Hatch, stood by, watchful and detached as ever. Pottinger was a neat and somewhat dapper man in his early fifties. His grey imperial beard was impeccably trimmed. A white doctor's coat protected his suit from the stains of madness. There was something of the priest about him. He held a clipboard in front of him as if it were a holy tablet received directly from the deity. He put all his faith in clipboards, did Dr Pottinger.

Next to Pottinger was Charles Leaming. Pink-cheeked and eager, the younger man had been at Colney Hatch for only a year or two. His look was avid, hungry almost.

It was said that Leaming had studied in Vienna with the celebrated Dr Freud and had brought some of Freud's ideas with him to Colney Hatch. However, Stanley doubted that Leaming had understood those ideas correctly. His methods, such as they were, were utterly beyond Stanley's comprehension.

Two male nurses were also in loose, ineffectual attendance. Flapping around like panicked chickens.

'Fuck's sake!' muttered Stanley. He strode decisively towards the eye of the storm. He knew that he could change the dynamic of the situation merely by his presence. Lunatics were like dogs, he often thought. They can smell your fear.

'Leave him to me,' shouted Stanley. All heads turned towards him. Including the lunatic's. The flicker of recognition was unmistakable. So, he was not that far gone, after all. Recognition followed quickly by cowering fear. Some bobbing flotsam of memory surfaced long enough for him to grasp it.

Stanley took out the fob and jangled it. Then swung it on its chain.

The lunatic's eyes were locked on the keys.

'You remember me, don't you?' Stanley's cold smile gave his voice a steely edge. 'Because I remember you. Yes, I remember you very well, Silas Quinn.'

* * *

They got the straitjacket on easily enough now. Quinn was subdued by Stanley's presence, utterly compliant. The key fob seemed to mesmerize him.

'Re-*mark*-able!' said Dr Leaming. He spoke with an enthusiastic emphasis. A slight accent could be detected too, which seemed to betray Yorkshire origins, muted by education.

'Oh, me and Silas go back a long way,' Stanley explained, not taking his eyes off Quinn's face. 'You never forget your first loony, do you?'

'Like your first love,' observed Leaming.

'Hardly,' said Stanley. The idea of it!

'There is a special place in your heart for him, though?'

'I'm not sure Mr Ince possesses such a thing as a heart!' That was Pottinger's idea of a joke.

Stanley let it go. He even rewarded it with a burst of his strange, near-silent nasal laughter. 'Lord, but he stinks though! To high heaven! As rank as a sack of dead rats.'

One of the young attendants, a spotty Herbert with bad teeth, started to explain. 'I think he's . . .'

'Shat himself?'

'Yes.'

'Of course. The filthy bastard. That's an old trick of his. Let's get him cleaned up.'

Stanley pocketed the fob and gave a shooing gesture in the direction of the bathroom.

The bathroom had the air of resenting their intrusion. It seemed to want to be left alone to its frigid dampness. A tap with a worn washer dripped incessantly, with a rich variation of tone, from quizzical, to condescending, to startled, to blasé. A row of bathtubs jutted out along one wall, like bystanders at an atrocity. Every one of them was cracked and stained, enamel worn away to a coarse, abrasive texture. They were as neglected as the people who bathed in them.

The neglect spread out from the baths, infecting the walls with a web of cracks. The tiles were the kind of white that reacts badly with electric light to create a sour glare.

At Stanley's direction, the spotty attendant peeled Quinn's layers away, starting with the straitjacket. Quinn put up no resistance. The fight seemed to have gone out of him.

The other young attendant, a lanky, red-haired individual, gingerly took each article of clothing and dropped it in a laundry basket.

'What are you doing that for?' demanded Stanley.

'Shan't we take them to the laundry?'

'Burn them! Burn the whole fucking lot. He won't ever need them again, I shouldn't think.'

'The hat as well?'

'Yes! The fucking hat as well!' Stanley shook his head in exasperation.

They stood Quinn in the showers, stripped and shivering. The skin of his body was as grey as newsprint, except where sores broke out in angry clusters.

'So. Silas Quinn, as I live and breathe. I've been following your career, Silas. You've been doing well for yourself since the last time you was in here. Quite the celebrity. What's that they call you in the *Clarion*? Quick-fire Quinn? Marvellous, the way you managed to make something of your life. Who would have thunk it? Not me, I confess. I'll be honest with you. I didn't think you'd last five minutes on the outside. Thought you would go the same way as your old man. Topped himself, dinnee, if I remember rightly? But look at the state you're in. It's all turned to shit, by the looks of it. Never mind. You've come back to us now. Back where you belong. Back home, you are, Silas. We're your family.'

Quinn let out a small whimper. A bubble of snot formed over one nostril.

Stanley curled his lip with distaste. 'Get the clippers. He's crawling with lice. The fucking dirty bastard.'

He assumed the privilege of shaving Quinn himself. He held the clippers at arm's length and allowed the shorn clumps of hair to fall over Quinn's naked body and on to the stone floor. If a strand found its way on to his apron, he would deliberately nick Quinn's scalp. Whenever this happened, Quinn would tense and wince and let out a brief yelp of pain. For that he was punished with a sharp tap of the clipper head. He quickly learnt to stand immobile, his whole body cowed in a pose of submission.

When he was completely shaven, Stanley turned the shower on and stepped back.

The water was cold. Quinn began to scream. He sank down to his haunches and tried to cover his head with his arms.

'Now, now, Silas. I know you don't like getting clean, but we can't have you going around like that. We got standards in here, you know. The inspectors come round and see you like that, they ain't gonna be very pleased now, are they? They're going to give us a right bollocking.'

Stanley held to the notion that the shock of the dousing had the capacity to rouse the lunatics from their mental disarrangement. It hadn't happened yet but there was a first time for everything.

'Stop making such a fuss, will ya! A bit of cold water never did no one no harm!'

Stanley killed the shower. Quinn huddled himself into a ball. A kind of braying came from him, half shrieks, half sobs. His trembling was more than shivering now. It was the final quaking of a system before it breaks apart.

Stanley gave a nod in the direction of the baths. The two attendants signalled their uselessness with confused frowns.

'Run a fucking bath for him! Hot! Make it hot. Can't you see the poor fucker's freezing his bollocks off there?'

The two useless articles almost tripped over each other in their haste to placate him. The problem was that the first bath lacked a plug. As did the second and the third. Eventually, they tracked down a plug and, between them, got a bath running. Steaming water thundered into the tub.

Stanley pursed his lips as he looked at Quinn. 'Some of those sores look very nasty to me. We're going to have to wash him with carbolic soap, we are. And we'll have to give him a good scrubbing to make sure we get all the fleas off him. It would be negligent of us not to.'

'Shall I get the things, Mr Ince?'

Stanley deigned to give the briefest of nods. 'And get him a suit while you're at it.'

The spotty attendant scuttled off.

'Stand up now, Silas. You're going to have a nice hot bath. You'd like that, wouldn't you?'

But Quinn only kept up his braying. If anything, it became more distressed.

'Stand up, I said. You don't want to make me cross, do you? You remember what happens when I get cross.' Stanley's hand went to the pocket where he kept the key fob.

Although Quinn didn't see the gesture – his head was turned to the wall – he must have known what Stanley's words portended. He rose, quaking, to his feet. His posture, however, was bent over and cringing. His perseverated braying resolved into half-articulate sounds: 'Ubble, ubble, ubble!'

Quinn kept his eyes closed, and Stanley was thankful for that. The sight before him provoked only disgust, which he could handle. With Quinn's eyes open, and the challenge of confronting them, it would have been different. It would have meant the resurfacing of that first visceral fear that had lodged in Stanley's soul like a cancer all those years ago.

The spotty attendant returned, carrying a three-piece suit made from brown corduroy, together with a grey calico shirt, undergarments and a threadbare towel. He placed these items on a wooden shelf and held a block of red carbolic soap and a scrubbing brush out to Stanley, which he ignored.

'Come on, Silas. It's time to get in the bath.'

Quinn screwed up his eyes, as if refusing to look at the bath would make it go away.

There was no way round it. Stanley would have to touch him.

His distaste hardened into hatred. The only way he could bear to lay hands on any of them was violently. He put a hand at the back of Quinn's neck and squeezed, guiding him forwards with his arm held rigidly straight. In some part of him he had always believed that madness was catching.

One of the other attendants grasped him under the arms from behind while the other lifted his legs and hoisted them over the rim of the tub. All the while, Quinn's body writhed as if an electrical current was being passed through him. His arms flailed. His head shook violently from side to side in desperate refusal.

Water splashed over the side as the attendants let go. Quinn's eyes snapped open in shock and his body became rigid. He began to scream.

'Ub-buuuullllll!'

'Did you check the temperature, you moron?'

'I thought you meant it to be hot, Mr Ince?'

'Don't you know the regulations? This is on you if he's burnt.'

In panic, the red-headed attendant opened the cold tap as far as it would go, stirring the water to spread the coolness.

As the water cooled, Quinn became physically agitated again. His legs pumped like he was riding a bike and his arms swirled and thrashed about him. Water went everywhere. Quinn's cries of 'Ubble! Ubble!' grew high-pitched and frantic.

'Keep his head out of the water, for Christ's sake. We don't want him drowning.'

Stanley leant over the bath. 'You see how I'm looking after you, Silas?'

He had done it. The thing he feared most of all. He had looked directly into the lunatic's eyes. He had opened himself to the madness.

It was important not to flinch.

To escape the fear himself, he must make the other afraid. That was how it worked. Stanley held out a hand behind his back. 'Gimme the carbolic soap. And the scrubbing brush.'

'Bubble! Bubble! Bubble!' screamed Quinn.

It was not always necessary to inflict pain. Sometimes the idea of pain, their fear of it, was enough to render them compliant.

'You're safe now. Nothing can hurt you here. As long as you're a good boy and do as you're told. We'll keep you safe here. For the rest of your life.'

He dipped the block of carbolic soap into the water, then vigorously lathered the bristles of the brush.

Stanley left it to the others to dry Quinn. He did not respond to their commands, but he suffered them to manhandle him in such a way that they could get the job done efficiently enough. When they wrenched up one of his arms to dry his flank, he held it at right angles without demur until they manually pushed it down again.

The same went for dressing him. He was turned about, his feet lifted into the well-worn but essentially clean linen underpants, which were pulled sharply up to his waist. His passivity was total as he was dressed in the rest of the asylum uniform.

The scrubbing had not just killed any vermin on his skin. It had broken his will.

Quinn's expression communicated nothing meaningful. His lips moved constantly as he muttered his endless nonsensical monologue, about the man who was a bubble, and how he had popped the bubble. His unfocused gaze skittered about. From time to time it seemed to snag on something, a point that no one else could see.

At last they had him in his uniform. Shaven headed, carbolic scented, cowed and cleansed.

Whatever had happened to Quinn in the intervening years – whatever heights he had scaled, fame he had achieved, triumphs won, enemies overcome – he was returned now to the helpless, vulnerable, unreasoning wretch that he had been the first time Stanley had seen him.

Stanley Ince stepped back, like an artist admiring his creation.

TWO

Six weeks earlier.

Harold didn't like the way the bear was looking at him.
Sitting there in its grubby white coat. Stuffing its drooling
snout with cold, dead fish, the blood staining its chops
as it relentlessly crunched down on its disgusting meal.

It envied him, he knew it. Why wouldn't it? It had been wrested
far from its home, to be gawped at by the world and his wife.
And with only raw dead fish from a stinking bucket to feed on.
Not to mention having to defecate in the same place as it dined.
Even a bear must object to that.

He could feel its hostility and its envy.

Now and then, he could even hear the bear's evil thoughts.
Naturally, the animal was not capable of verbal thought.
Which was how he knew that it was the bear's thoughts he
was hearing. They came to him as unpleasant vibrations and
strident screeches that he felt in his solar plexus. And even
though they were wordless, there was no doubt about the malice
they bore.

Oh, it was a sly one all right. Pretending to be absorbed in the
fish, or from time to time breaking off to consider the long claws
of its toes with perfect complacency.

It seemed to be saying to him, 'It would be an easy thing for
me to rip you apart, you know.'

Harold noticed how it turned its head in every direction except
towards him. *Sly! Very sly!*

He looked around to see if anyone else shared his suspicions
and his outrage. But no, the other visitors to the Mappin
Terraces at London Zoo seemed perfectly enchanted by the bear's
demeanour.

Could they not see how it wished them all harm?

The polar bear was man's enemy. The only thing that had
prevented war between man and polar bears was the accident

of geography; neither had very much interest in the other's territory.

But the zoo authorities had made a fatal mistake in bringing this beast to London and placing it in the midst of the civilian population, without any form of military supervision. Not only that, they fed it and kept it alive, with only a low railing and a shallow pit to protect the public.

The bear could easily climb out and run rampage. Go berserk, in fact. A teacher had once told him that the word berserk had something to do with bears. Wasn't it to do with warriors who fought like bears, ripping their enemies apart with their teeth and bare hands? Who fought without arms or armour, protected only by the bestial rage that possessed them.

He seemed to remember it came from the Norse. Or was it Russian?

He couldn't remember exactly what the teacher had said now. The lesson had been given in the context of his own behaviour at the time. Apparently he had gone berserk himself, and old Mr Beesley couldn't resist the opportunity for a lesson in etymology.

The bear looked peaceful enough now. At this moment it was holding its toes, as if it had only just discovered they were attached to it. Feigning simplicity, Harold had no doubt. It liked to give the impression that it was some kind of arctic Buddha. It was fat enough. A deceitful smile played about its chops. But Harold knew what was really going on. It was trying to hide its envy with a smile. But it lacked the control over its facial muscles to pull it off: the bear was not a good actor.

It pretended to be a simple creature, content with a bucket of fish and a pond to swim in. But it did not know that Harold could hear its malign thoughts.

He had the measure of that bear, all right. He knew how, despite its demonstration of placidity, deep down, it hated all humans. And Harold especially. Perhaps it had an inkling of his power as a bear mind-reader and feared him as its natural master. All creatures hate that which they fear.

Did it expect them all to bow in homage to it? Or to pay it tribute of some kind? To throw it iced buns or a freshly sacrificed child?

It must have sensed that it would never receive such obeisance from Harold. And hated him all the more for that reason.

No, he would never bow to it. On the contrary, he would teach that bloody polar bear a lesson!

He would wipe the deceitful grin off its face.

But most of all, he would silence the din of its thoughts crashing into his head uninvited.

Harold began to pull at his clothes. He was hardly conscious of what he was doing, or why.

The clamour of the bear's ill will left little room for thoughts of his own.

First his jacket came off, discarded carelessly on the ground behind him. Next he tore away his waistcoat, and then the shirt, which was ripped apart with the force of his undressing. He would meet the bear on equal terms, without the trappings of civilization or even basic humanity. If anything he would become more bear than the bear. He would not have it said that he had an unfair advantage over his adversary.

As Harold kicked away his shoes and stepped out of his trousers, the bear's rage filled his head with its noise. It seemed it had found a way to transmit the screams of the human females, whom it was bent on attacking as soon as it was at liberty.

Harold was completely naked by the time he scaled the railings to the enclosure. The polar bear maintained its show of serenity, but he could tell it was rattled. It had cranked up its mental assault, amplifying the sounds of women screaming in his head.

Still the bear feigned interest in its toes. It seemed to have sated its appetite for dead fish.

Harold held on to the horizontal bar of the railings. It was about a ten-foot drop to the terrace where the bear was. The strain began to tear at his fingers and arms. He would have to let go soon. His arms were about to pop out of their sockets. But the pain was worse when he let go. It ripped across his thighs and torso and snagged at his penis as his body scraped down the concrete wall.

He landed heavily, feeling the kick in his ankles before toppling over on to his side.

He screamed himself back into his rage before clambering to his feet.

The stench down in the enclosure was ripe. He could smell the raw fish, of course, warming in the sun. And then there was the smell of the excrement produced by a diet consisting solely of raw fish. On top of that there was the animal smell the bear produced to mark out its territory.

Harold breathed in all this but it did not intimidate him.

He felt an instinctive repulsion.

He stretched out his arms and extended himself to his full height as he faced up to the bear. His mouth opened and his throat vibrated with a howl of primal rage. The roar drowned out all other sounds, silencing at last the violent screeches and clangs and screams transmitted by the bear.

The bear broke off consideration of its toes and looked up. Its expression was mildly curious, though there was perhaps an air of being inconvenienced that might have given a more perceptive intruder pause for thought. For a second or two it seemed to be engaged in some kind of calculation.

In the end, it decided to overcome its natural indolence to defend itself. It rose on its hind legs, to its full massive height, towering over its adversary. It gave an answering growl, an effortless bass rumble that suggested untapped resources of power and violence.

But Harold was deaf to such alarm signals. He rushed towards the sound. He kept up his own roar, but to any ears other than his own it must have sounded puny by comparison.

He held his hands tensed open in front of him as if he fully expected to tear his foe apart.

The bear watched him approach with a kind of bemused indignation and, at the last possible moment, merely batted him away with its unfurled claw, as a man might swat a bothersome insect.

The man's body sprawled with everything akimbo as it flew through the air. The skull struck the concrete first, with a sickening crack. The man fell as limp as a crumpled sack and lay unmoving.

The bear's nostrils twitched. In the scent of fresh blood it detected the promise of an unexpected variation from the monotony of its diet.

THREE

S ilas Quinn sat at his desk in the attic office of the Special
Crimes Department in New Scotland Yard. The ceiling
sloped sharply along one side. It looked like a segment
of the room had been cut away. Quinn always had the sense
that they were being hampered by their environment. The missing
space seemed to represent the missing pieces in whatever
investigation they were pursuing. If he could solve the case, he
would restore all the corners of the room. But that never
happened. Which left him dogged by a sense of permanent failure.
On top of that, the three of them invariably banged their heads
if they rose too sharply from their desks. And it was in the nature
of police work that one was often called upon to rise sharply from
a desk.

Outside, a light spring shower intensified into a thorough downpour, noisily slung against the window panes by a loutish squall.
The temperature in the attic room dropped perceptibly.

Quinn's herringbone ulster and bowler hat were hung on the
coat stand by the door, the shoulders of the ulster speckled
with damp. More than just items of clothing, they were the
accoutrements of his office. The props, almost, of his *dramatis
persona*. When he put them on, he manifestly became the great
detective he was reputed to be. But the truth was Quinn no
longer believed in his own myth, if he ever had. He felt that
all the success he had achieved as a detective had been down
to nothing more than good luck. More and more these days,
when a new case came in, he found himself entirely stumped
as to how to proceed. He allowed his subordinates – Sergeants
Inchball and Macadam – to suggest competing plans, and he
would alternately favour one and then the other. It was no way
to run a department, he knew.

He refused to read the newspapers any more, because it was
in the newspapers – especially in the pages of the gutter rag *The
Daily Clarion* – that his reputation had been forged.

Just to look at a front page was enough to bring Quinn out in a flush of humiliation and shame. Should he not have been proud of his celebrity? Of his soubriquet of Quick-fire Quinn? No. It was a profound embarrassment. It mocked the dead, and made light of the risks his men faced at his command. As if policing was just another branch of the entertainment industry.

He knew better than anyone at what price his spectacular success rate had been achieved. How many people had died. Some of them, it was true, were violent criminals, whose deaths few would mourn. But there had been other deaths along the way too.

And for all his supposed investigative genius, he had not been able to stem the tide of death. In fact, he had the sense that death was marshalling its forces and building momentum as it led them all towards some great tour de force.

Quinn could not shake off a sense of impending catastrophe.

All his days seemed to be shaped around death. It was only to be expected. He was a murder detective. Death was his occupation. He could not get the stench of it out of his nostrils. The colour of it haunted his dreams.

The last straw had been the death of Miss Dillard, the lonely inebriate spinster who had lodged at the same house as him. It was strange how her death had affected him more than any other recently. He felt that he bore a greater share of responsibility in it than the others. Not simply that he had failed to save her life, but that he had caused her death.

And suicides always upset him.

So many deaths, of so many people. And he was the one thing that connected them all.

'Penny for your thoughts, guv?' The enquiry came from Sergeant Inchball. But Quinn felt the solicitous gaze of both his sergeants on him.

The idea of sharing his thoughts frankly appalled him. And yet it seemed that something was expected of him. They would not let him be until he gave some response. 'We must be vigilant, Inchball.'

'Vigilant, you say. What are we looking out for in particular, guv?'

Quinn angled his head with slow deliberation. It was a gesture designed to convey supreme acuity of thought. Quinn wondered if it was enough to satisfy Inchball. He suspected not. Inchball was your bullish, blunt breed of copper, the sort who insisted on calling a spade a spade. Enigmatic, ambiguous gestures rarely cut it with him. And long silences invariably made him fidgety. Quinn sensed this one had probably gone on too long already. 'For anything . . . unusual.'

Confusion drew in Inchball's eyebrows. The man couldn't help it, but there was always something belligerent about his expression.

Macadam was arguably more sensitive to the nuances of a situation. And he tried now to deflect what threatened to be a dangerous turn of the conversation, to rescue Quinn with an exercise of his initiative.

'You mean something like this, sir?' Macadam had the day's papers spread out on his desk. 'A very unusual case. It's in all the papers. You must have seen it?'

'No.' Quinn's answer came a little too quickly. He wondered if they had noticed his wince of dismay at Macadam's mention of *the papers*.

'A young man, mauled to death by a polar bear.'

'Well! What's to investigate?' cried Inchball disdainfully. 'It's the bear what done it, you said so yourself.'

'No, no, but the circumstances of the death are very unusual. The man entered the bear pit willingly, and – I should say – naked. That is to say, he took off his clothes before he jumped in. And he ran at the bear, as if inviting his own destruction.'

'A madman, obviously,' said Inchball.

'I agree with Inchball,' said Quinn. 'I don't see what there is for us to investigate here.'

'Perhaps not,' conceded Macadam, a little dejectedly. 'But you have to admit it is *unusual*.'

'Are you suggesting that we should prosecute the zoo authorities for not sufficiently safeguarding this man from his own desire for death?'

'No, no. I just wonder what made him do it, that's all.'

'What makes anyone do anything?' From the way Inchball barked out the question, it was clear that he neither expected nor wanted an answer. 'Especially if he's a nutter, as this geezer obviously was. I mean, what did he have against polar bears?'

'I can't help feeling that there's something more to this,' insisted Macadam. 'I have noticed that there is a mood among the young today. A death wish.'

Quinn forced himself to engage in the discussion. 'It seems to be a simple case of suicide. If you discount the more outlandish circumstances of the death.'

'But, sir, haven't you often said that it is the outlandish circumstances of a death that are the very things we should not discount?'

Quinn could not remember having ever said such a thing. He suspected it of being an original thought of Macadam's, to which he hoped to lend authority by attributing it to his superior. 'Did I say that?'

Macadam became evasive. 'Well, I may not have remembered the exact words.'

Quinn shook his head impatiently, animated by a sudden energy. 'We need something more concrete. What are the Irish up to these days?'

'The usual,' cried Inchball bitterly. 'But tell me, guv, are we now to be an adjunct of the War Office? Are we military intelligence now? Because if that's the case, nobody told me.'

'In these times of heightened tension and uncertainty, we must respond to whatever call our country makes.'

'Do you think it will come to war, sir?'

Quinn was taken aback by the question. 'In Ireland?'

Macadam helped him out. 'It's a bloody mess there, I'll grant you. A powder keg about to blow up. The unionists are willing to go to war with Great Britain, in order to remain part of Great Britain. It makes no sense, I know. Meanwhile the nationalists are amassing arms to fight the unionists, which would place them on our side in an Irish Home Rule war. Except the British Army would never fight the loyalists, as was proved at Curragh. So the nationalists are really amassing arms to use against us, to ensure that we push through with Home Rule. Then again, if there is war against Germany, the likelihood is that both Irish factions will fall in line and fight with us.'

'Let's hope that happens then,' said Inchball brightly.

'No, no. That would be the worst possible outcome!' objected Macadam.

'It's doing my head in, I tell you,' said Inchball. 'So who are we to keep an eye on? The unionists or the nationalists?'

Quinn looked to Macadam for guidance, but his expression was as expectant and trusting as Inchball's. 'We must watch them all.'

'Right you are,' said Inchball, with an uneasy glance to Macadam.

'Particularly the known troublemakers.'

Inchball vented his feelings with an oath: 'Bloody Micks!'

'I tell you who I worry about, sir,' said Macadam. 'The pacifists.'

Inchball let out a wheezy guffaw. 'The pacifists! You ain't got nothing to worry about there! Pacifists! They don't exactly go around blowing things up, do they? It's against their principles.'

'Even so, I worry about the damage they do to the nation's moral fibre. Sapping the martial spirit. I wonder if it wasn't their influence that led this young man to do what he did.'

'What a load of tosh! Have you ever heard such rot, guv? I mean, from anyone other than old Mac here?'

Quinn was finding it hard to keep up with his sergeants' squabbles. He couldn't remember in whose favour he had intervened last, and to whom therefore he owed favour now. The important thing was to keep them occupied. 'You're right, Macadam. We must keep an eye on the pacifists. Compile a dossier on all known pacifists active in the city. Bring it to me as soon as it is complete. You, Inchball, your brief is to watch the Irish.'

'Where do I start?'

'I shall leave that to your discretion.'

'In that case, I'll go to the pub. It's as good a place to watch the Irish as anywhere.' Inchball's shoulders heaved in appreciation of his own joke.

FOUR

Cedric looked down and gasped.

Shooting stars passed beneath him. He had never seen a single shooting star in his life before, and now, tonight, he couldn't keep count of how many there were.

He'd obviously been looking in the wrong place until now. Everybody knew you had to look up if you wanted to see stars, shooting or otherwise. And yet, here he was, looking down at them.

An endless procession of shooting stars passed by. In fact, two processions, each passing the other in parallel transit. It was strange how every star he saw followed the precise path of the one in front of it. He had never known they moved like that. It must be something to do with gravitational pull and orbits. He tried to work it out, but it only made his head ache.

Another thing he had not known: shooting stars travelled in pairs. Perhaps he was seeing double? He tried to focus on one pair of stars, trying to force the twin blobs of light back into one. The effort made his headache worse.

The stars were moving backwards, shooting their tails out in front of them. It wasn't what he would have expected at all.

They were big, too. Bigger than the stars he usually saw when he looked up. Wherever he was, he was closer to the stars than he had ever been.

Ever since he could remember, he had tried to picture the universe. Even as a small boy. It was always the last thing he did before going to sleep. He would lie there, staring up at the swirling blackness of his ceiling, watching it open up into an immeasurable vastness. He would feel his bed break loose from his bedroom floor and soar. He would have to close his eyes to keep the vertiginous panic at bay.

He would already have said his prayers: kneeling by the bed before he got in, eyes tightly closed, murmuring the words with quiet intensity. God bless Mother. God bless Father. God bless Nanny. God bless Granddad. Godbless Granny. God bless Grampa . . .

They had to have different names for his mother's parents (Nanny and Granddad) and his father's (Granny and Grampa), so they would know them apart. And so God would know who to bless. But he always asked for them all to be blessed, so what difference did it make?

He had believed in God back then. That was before God had abandoned him. It's hard to believe in a God who abandons you. Who takes your parents and leaves you in a filthy madhouse, full of screaming lunatics and men like Stanley Ince to look after you.

But maybe the seeds of his atheism had been sown before his time in Colney Hatch.

In his childhood, he had imagined God to be as he was depicted in his Sunday school Bible. The white-bearded old man in the sky, appearing between parted clouds. But even back then, the universe he imagined was resolutely Godless.

All that vast expanse opening up in his mind, and yet he could find no space in it for God.

Higher and higher his imagination would soar. Above the earth's atmosphere. Out into the solar system. And then beyond that, into the galaxy.

He would reach a point beyond the galaxy, beyond the stars, a place of utter emptiness and desolation. He would begin to panic. His breathing would become short and rapid. His loneliness here was oppressive. And the thought that this emptiness went on forever infected him with a physical terror.

His young mind needed to put some kind of limit on the infinite. So he would imagine a kind of solid construction existing around the universe. A cube made out of some jet-black, diamond-hard substance. This would calm him. But then he would realize that there had to be something beyond the cube. Either that, or the cube would need to be infinitely thick itself. And he was caught in the same trap again.

The infinite would overwhelm him once more.

And if infinity was solid, then there was definitely no space for God.

Perhaps he had always suspected it. But he had clung to the

hope, willing himself to believe as he shifted his scrawny behind on all those church pews over the years. There had to be a God. So many grown-ups told him there was.

He had longed for a sign that would prove God's existence. He had even tried making very specific requests in his prayers, to see if God was listening. Nothing covetous – he knew that was a sin – just a polite, earnest plea for God to show Himself in some way. *Please God, if Thou art there, please move the curtain slightly.*

And lo! The curtain stirred!

But he knew his bedroom window was open and the stirring could easily be explained by a draft.

Looking back now, he wondered if the reason he had said his prayers so conscientiously was to drown out the silence that he knew was there behind everything.

His young dreams came to be haunted by a precocious sense of utter loneliness. He would wander through deserted streets, lost and alone in strange, uninhabited cities. In these dreams, he would stop as he heard his name called out, only to realize it was just the wind blowing through the empty spaces. There was an ache where the memory of his parents ought to have been.

He was sixteen when he heard the first voice. He wondered if it was God, speaking to him directly at last. But the voice put him right on that.

'Don't be fucking stupid.'

More voices came to join the first. The voices of a tree, a squirrel, a lamppost, countless strangers, and even notable figures from the newspapers. But all of them steadfastly refused to be identified as God.

The voices were not always with him. When they were, it was terrifying. They drowned out his own thoughts and urged him to do things he didn't want to do.

But sometimes it was worse when they were silent. He always had the sense that perhaps they were still there with him, watching him silently, storing up information that they could use against him. They always knew his most humiliating secrets. Or if they had gone away, it was only to plot some fresh evil with which to torment him on their return.

He always knew they would be back.

He could invariably feel their impending return. Almost smell it. Cedric would feel the approach of the voices in a build-up of pressure in his head. That pressure would spread throughout his whole body. At some point he would realize that the pressure consisted of *them* – a chorus of voices, first whispering, then rising to a clamour of competing malice.

He made his first suicide attempt at nineteen. His admission to Colney Hatch came soon after that.

It was there that he met Dr Leaming. Dr Leaming had told him that the voices were nothing to be afraid of. They were not external entities – not the things they pretended to be, still less demons who possessed him. They were part of him. He created them. They were nothing other than his own thoughts, to which he had given a separate identity, because of their unwelcome nature. But they were not his enemies. They did not mean him harm at all.

He simply had to learn how to control them. And the way to do that, according to Dr Leaming, was to engage with them. To talk to them, in other words.

But every discussion he tried to initiate with his voices ended with their screaming vile abuse at him, until he gave in and agreed to do whatever they commanded. His voices always won.

And after his voices finally coaxed him on to the top of the East Wing tower (from which he had to be forcibly removed before he had a chance to obey the rest of their instructions and throw himself off), Dr Leaming was directed to consider a different therapeutic approach.

Cedric tried to remember how he had got from Colney Hatch to a place where he could look down on shooting stars. They must have let him out of the asylum. He had no memory of that. Perhaps he was cured. It was certainly a long time since he had heard the voices. Yet he could not believe he was free of them.

He could not say how long he had been walking the streets of north London. At some point, the blackness at the edge of the universe had come down and possessed the city. Somehow it must have acted as a bridge, bringing him to this unexpected vantage point. It was a blackness so thick you could walk upon it.

As the stars passed beneath him, disappearing under the bridge of blackness, he felt it: that brimming of pressure in his head that normally presaged the return of his voices. But instead of the voices, he found that he could hear the thoughts of the stars beneath him. Being stars, their thoughts were not verbal. They consisted of a clanging, clashing stridency.

A chill went through him. He had believed the stars to be neutral to the affairs of men. So far above the Earth were they, that it was absurd to think they concerned themselves with anything mundane. And yet, hearing that sound left him in no doubt of their concentrated malevolence towards humans. Were they gathering their forces for some kind of attack? It could not be ruled out.

Cedric realized that he had been brought to this place for a reason. No man had ever come so close to the stars. No man before him had ever been granted access to their thoughts. It was up to him to stop them.

The only weapon he had against them was his humanity. He must find a way to wield it.

The stars must have discovered his intentions. They were closing in on him now. They shot by behind him, their angry thoughts a deafening roar.

But he was not afraid. And the way to defeat them, he realized, was to show them that he was not afraid.

He stripped away his clothes and dropped them into the blackness. Then climbed upon a parapet that ran along the bridge that had brought him here.

The cold wind that blew at the end of the universe caused all the hairs on his body to stand on end. He swayed for a moment in the wind, then leant into it. The universe took over, pulling him towards the shooting stars below.

FIVE

Quinn turned his key and opened the front door carefully. It was half past five on a bright afternoon in early summer. The kind of day on which, if you knew nothing about the countless tragedies that had occurred in all the days preceding it, you might be hopeful for the future.

It was not an indulgence Quinn allowed himself. In fact, the fine weather only made him feel more anxious, in a general way. He had often been struck by the absurdity of the pathetic fallacy. As far as he was concerned, the weather was indifferent to the sufferings of mortals. He was immune to the charms of a sunny day and, unlike Sergeant Macadam, he had never had his spirits lifted by a change in the weather.

Let it shine, let it rain, it was all the same to Quinn. His trusty ulster served him equally on all days.

He closed the door behind him with all the tensed control of a cat burglar.

This was where he lived, and yet he still did not feel as if he belonged here.

His fellow lodgers had only recently, after the death of Miss Dillard, discovered what he did for a living. They had begun to look at him in what was evidently a new light. Even those two young coves who worked at the Natural History Museum, Timberley and Appleby, seemed to treat him with uncharacteristic respect. They no longer quipped about him behind his back in Latin. The Latin remarks he overheard passing between them now were tinged with a sombre excitement. It irritated him that they kept up this public school game. But now it seemed they were hiding their comments from him not out of mockery, but awe. Not to put too fine a point on it, they thrilled at the sight of him.

It was naturally bewildering for them to discover a celebrity in their midst. Especially one who had earned his fame by his dealings with notorious criminals and death.

Once or twice they each separately tried to engage him in conversation about his work. It seemed that they had independently conceived the ambition of writing detective stories and were intent on plying him for 'info'.

He was understandably anxious to avoid them as he came in.

For different reasons, he was just as anxious to avoid his landlady, Mrs Ibbott. She oppressed him with her solicitude. She seemed to be labouring under the entirely false apprehension that he had, after all, entertained tender feelings towards the deceased Miss Dillard. It was certainly true that his emotions concerning Miss Dillard were complicated and troubling. A part of him wished that he had been able to alleviate some of the distress that led ultimately to her suicide. God knows, he had tried. But what efforts he had made were made out of his sense of their shared humanity. There never could be any *romantic* aspect to it.

If anything, his reasons were selfish, shameful even. He suspected that he only helped her in order to feel better about himself. And she punished him by killing herself.

That'll teach him.

It is always unnerving coming back to a house that has recently been visited by death. Hard to shake off that sense of something missing, however tenuous or oblique one's connection to the deceased. Absurdly, he felt himself overcome by a strong sense of wanting to avoid an encounter with Miss Dillard herself.

Even after her death, he had not been able to shake off the sense that there was something between them, something that needed to be addressed.

It was all to do with her expectations regarding him, of course. Expectations that he had been scrupulous not to encourage. But she was a lonely woman of a certain age, who took her consolation in the gin bottle. He now knew that she habitually went without food in order to fund her alcoholism. It was inevitable perhaps that certain fancies might take root in her inebriated mind. He suspected she had seen him as something of a kindred spirit, a shy loner aching for someone, anyone, of the fairer sex to show him a little tenderness, or even just interest.

He was not good with women, he knew that. He seemed to have the knack of encouraging the wrong ones and driving away those to whom he genuinely was attracted. She was right in one respect, Miss Dillard: he was lonely. He ached for the consolations of a physical relationship.

Was this what she had been offering him? And what he had rejected?

And then, to add insult to injury as it were, he had patronized her by secretly offering to pay the arrears she owed to Mrs Ibbott. Word had got back to Miss Dillard. She had been mortified. There was no other word for it. He had repaid her love with pity. And as a result, she had taken her own life.

And he had found her and raised her dying body and run with her over his shoulder, bundling her into the taxi Appleby had hailed on the Brompton Road.

There were things he needed to say to her that he would never be able to now. He began to wish for her presence after all, with an intense, regretful pang. He longed for the liquid gaze of her pewter-grey eyes, at first gently reproachful, but melting into forgiveness.

Of course, it was safe – as well as dishonest – to think like this now.

In the event, the person who burst out into the hallway from the parlour was the one member of the household who was probably as eager to avoid him as he was everyone else. This was Mary, Mrs Ibbott's daughter. He had no doubt that she was uncomfortable in his presence. But he could not for the life of him say what he had done to cause this, other than exist.

On reflection, he believed that it was probably nothing to do with sex. He was so old, in her eyes, as to be beyond consideration as an eligible bachelor. And therefore he was incapable of arousing any of the awkward feelings that might be associated with such negotiations. No, it was surely more that she saw him as a faintly sad figure for whom she had no use. Mary Ibbott did not want sadness in her life. She wanted laughter and gaiety and fun.

One glance at Quinn was enough to tell her that he was never going to be the source of such things. If he had managed to present himself as a kind of jovial uncle figure, always ready with a joke and a wink, then she might have been able to tolerate him. But he was invariably tongue-tied in her presence, which not only seemed to disgust but also frighten her. The irony was that it was not on her account that he was so ridiculously embarrassed. It was because she reminded him of another landlady's daughter, over whom, many years ago, he had made an absolute fool of himself.

Why must landladies insist on having daughters?

'Good evening, Miss Ibbott.' He was capable at least of being polite. But in such a way that made him wince at his stiffness.

To his surprise, she responded to him without her usual constraint. The excitement that had impelled her from the parlour animated her words. She was refreshingly free of any formality. 'They're here!'

'Who are?'

'The new lodgers! Mr and Mrs Hargreaves. They're taking Miss Dillard's old room.' Now it was Mary Ibbott's turn to wince. She closed her eyes tightly and bit her lip. 'I'm sorry. I know you were . . .'

'No, no, no! Not at all.' He must nip this in the bud.

'Mummy told me. How you . . . what you did for Miss Dillard. What you tried to do. I think it was very noble of you.'

'No,' he insisted. 'It was not that.'

His firmness seemed to take her aback, as if she had never considered him capable of any kind of resolute behaviour. He had the definite sense that he was being reassessed by everyone in the house. 'It's a proper tragedy. Did you love her very much?'

The question flustered him. 'I–I–I . . . At any rate, I am pleased your mother has been able to let the room. Hopefully now there will be no more difficulties over the rent.'

Mary's expression clouded. 'How can you say that? Are you saying that Mummy wanted Miss Dillard dead?'

'No, that wasn't what I meant. Of course not. Look, I'm sorry to disabuse you, but I didn't love Miss Dillard. Not at all. There was never any question of anything like that between us.'

'But she loved you.' Mary was insistent on this point.

'I don't know anything about that.'

'That's why she killed herself.'

'We don't know that. There was no note.'

'There are some things that don't need to be spelled out in a note.'

With that, she ran up the stairs to knock on the door of the new lodgers' room. The door opened and she was admitted to a chorus of easy rapport. Under normal circumstances, Quinn would have found that painful to listen to. But he was still reeling from the extraordinariness of his encounter with Mary Ibbott. He had not exchanged as many words with the girl in the whole of his time in the house. The death of Miss Dillard had clearly served as some kind of watershed.

Quinn looked up the stairs towards the door that had now closed behind Mary. He could hear muted laughter coming from inside. It was not a sound that had been associated with the room when it belonged to Miss Dillard.

He could not help feeling a stab of resentment on her behalf. Then he imagined her pewter-grey eyes gently chiding him. 'They don't mean any harm. Let them be.'

He was under no doubt that his own mind had generated the words. But for some reason it had chosen to present them to him in Miss Dillard's voice.

He felt a prickling in the hairs on the back of his neck. He even turned to look behind him. The late afternoon sun flared in the stained-glass panes of the door, before dimming. As the light changed, the gloom that draped the edges of the hallway stirred like curtains lifted in a breeze.

There was no one there, of course.

But his heart was beating faster. And the shifting shadows seemed to be charged with a familiar pewter gleam.

SIX

I t was in the nature of their work in the Special Crimes Department that there would be periods of intense activity, followed by long stretches when nothing much seemed to happen at all. The bursts of activity might last an hour or less, but they would be filled with a lifetime's worth of incident and drama. It takes less than a second, after all, for a bullet to fly from the barrel of a gun into a man's heart and kill him.

It might be argued that any subsequent lulls were necessary to allow the officers of the SCD time to recover from the more stressful moments. But Inchball, Macadam and Quinn were not such men as to relish sitting around on their backsides. If anything, they found the longueurs in their routine more stressful than the calls to action. Especially Inchball, who became jumpy and bad-tempered if he did not have criminals to chase down and preferably wrestle to the ground.

Macadam was quite capable of occupying himself with some book or journal that would furnish a gobbet of knowledge that might prove useful in a future investigation. That said, he was currently busy compiling the dossier on known pacifists, which he did mainly by scouring the newspapers for any accounts of recent pacifist meetings, making a note of the names of all those attending.

It was largely to allay his sergeants' restlessness that Quinn had set them to their various tasks.

Given his somewhat vague brief, Sergeant Inchball was rather more at a loss as to how to proceed. Last night he had spent a couple of unsatisfactory hours lurking outside a notorious Fenian pub in Holloway before finally, and unadvisedly, venturing inside. His attempt to order a pint of Guinness in an Irish accent was still more ill-advised, and had drawn the attention of a number of large, threatening gentlemen whose accents were rather more convincing.

One fella had got his face right in Inchball's, his massy beard specked with the froth from his stout. 'Are you a copper?'

'A copper, I? I not be a copper. Oh, to be sure, to be sure, not. I not be that. A copper, that not I be.'

'You look like a copper. You sound like a copper. And you smell like a copper.'

Inchball's accent entirely abandoned him at that point. 'I, ee, arrr, I, oh . . .'

It was not in his nature to run from a fight. But he saw little point in getting himself killed for the sake of one of the guv'nor's whims. Because yes, that was what this whole 'watch the Irish' thing was, he knew. And so he had made a dash for the door. Fortunately, there was no one blocking his way. It seemed the regulars of the Horse and Groom had no more desire for trouble than he had. He heard their raucous laughter as the door slammed behind him. Soon after, a fiddle started up in a lively rendition of 'The Minstrel Boy'.

Invited to give a progress report of his investigation, Inchball related an abridged version of the previous night's adventure. He left out the bit about his bad Irish accent, only saying that the Micks had rumbled him. 'Well, I can't show my face there again, can I?' he complained. It was typical of Inchball that he managed to make it sound as if his misfortune was someone else's fault. He cast a particularly recriminatory glance in Quinn's direction.

Quinn sighed but offered no comment.

'We need a real Mick to go undercover for us. They'll see right through me if I try that again.'

'I have a cousin who is Irish,' volunteered Macadam. 'Several, in fact.'

'You and your bleedin' cousins,' muttered Inchball. 'Let's say you have. Can he be trusted?'

'He's an Ulsterman. Of the Protestant sect. He hates the Fenians with a passion.'

'But could be pass for one?'

Quinn cut the discussion short. 'We will not involve any amateurs in our operations. It's too risky.'

'When war comes, everyone's involved,' observed Macadam darkly. 'Amateur or not.'

'We're not at war yet.'

'If you don't mind me saying, guv, this whole thing is a waste of our time. You mean to tell me that the Secret Service ain't already got its spies embedded in Fenian cells? There's a real danger I could go blundering into one of their undercover ops and blow the whole thing wide open. They won't thank us for that. If you ask me, we're better off leaving all these political shenanigans to the experts.'

Quinn decided to overlook the fact that he had *not* asked Inchball. 'I don't need to remind you, Sergeant Inchball, that the strategic direction of the department is not decided by you. Nor, indeed, by me. But by our superiors.'

'Henry told you to do this, did he?' Sir Edward Henry was the commissioner of the Police of the Metropolis. It was he who had set up the Special Crimes Department; Silas Quinn reported directly to him.

Inchball's tone was sceptical. Quinn's response, evasive. 'He gave me a broad directive, which I am interpreting.'

'What was it, this broad directive?'

Quinn answered the question with a distracted frown, and a glance towards the window, as if he had heard a noise he could not identify coming from outside. He trusted Inchball knew enough not to press him any further.

There were times when Inchball's characteristic bluntness came close to insubordination. But Quinn knew he meant no disrespect by it. If called upon, Inchball would lay down his life for the man he called guv. When it came to it, there would be no more questioning, no more grumbles. He would blindly, unhesitatingly put himself in peril at Quinn's command. Quinn knew this, because Inchball frequently had.

His loyalty was absolute.

It was just that he was in one of those moods. Quinn put it down to frustration, and the loss of face he had suffered the night before.

They needed a case, something tangible to work on.

'Well, now, here's a queer thing. A decidedly queer thing.'

Both Quinn and Inchball turned their heads eagerly towards their colleague. Quinn realized that Sergeant Macadam – unconsciously or not – quite often slipped into the role of mediator between himself and Inchball, diffusing tension and providing a way through any impasse by distracting them from their own positions.

Macadam's voice was brimming with promise.

'You remember that fellow I was telling you about? The one who got mauled to death by the polar bear. Well, there's been another one.'

'I'd say London Zoo need to sort out visitor safety arrangements for those new bear terraces, and pronto!' commented Inchball. 'But I still don't see . . .'

'No, no. This wasn't at the zoo.'

'There's a polar bear on the loose?'

'It wasn't a polar bear.'

'What kind of bear was it? A grizzly?'

'It wasn't a bear. It wasn't any kind of animal. This one threw himself off Suicide Bridge in Archway.'

'What the hell are you blathering on about, man? First off, what possible connection could there be between a man throwing himself off Suicide Bridge and a mauling at the zoo? Second off, what possible interest could either be to us? A man kills himself at Suicide Bridge. It's hardly an unusual incident. The clue is in the name. Suicide Bridge. They called it that for a reason.'

'There are certain details linking them. Both men were naked, having just discarded their clothes.'

'That doesn't mean—' But Inchball broke off. Perhaps it did mean something after all. 'Well, so what? They were obviously both lunatics.'

'But the curious thing, the really curious thing, is that the clothes that were discarded were, as far as I am able to ascertain from newspaper reports, identical. Before they disrobed and killed themselves, both men were apparently wearing brown corduroy suits and grey shirts.'

Quinn heard a strange strangled noise, halfway between a groan and a cry of protest, and only realized that it was he himself who had made it when both of his sergeants turned towards him at the same time.

SEVEN

T he first of the bodies, that of the man mauled by the bear at Regent's Park Zoo, was held at the mortuary of the Bloomsbury Coroner's Court near High Holborn. This was a purpose-built brick construction on an acute corner, the effect of which the architect had sought to soften by truncating the angle with an extra face. Presumably he did not want the building's plan to resemble too much the blade of a scalpel.

The court was located close to a council school. Quinn could hear the echoing cries of children at their play. The teacher's bell calling them back to their lessons began to toll as he entered the building.

He had declined Macadam's offer to drive him here. He did not want either of his sergeants with him when he confronted his suspicions.

Quinn recognized the court official who greeted him, a man whose face was contorted into a permanent wince, revealing wide gums and poor teeth. Quinn remembered him as being something of a stickler for procedure and so showed his warrant card.

The official hiked up his wince, when Quinn had explained the purpose of his visit. 'He's not a pretty sight.'

'I don't want to look at him. Particularly.' Quinn never ruled out entirely the prospect of viewing a corpse. 'I wish to see his effects.'

'Ah, yes.'

The official led him upstairs to a landing with three doors. One bore the sign: MORTUARY. The next: POST-MORTEM ROOM. The third, more prosaically: STOREROOM. It was this last that they entered.

It had the air of a lost property office where nothing would ever be reclaimed. The cubby holes were here and there veiled with cobwebs.

An elderly attendant in a brown overcoat sat behind a mahogany counter reading the latest Sexton Blake serial in the *Union Jack*.

'The bear attack, Pardew. Inspector Quinn wishes to examine the deceased's effects.'

A moment later, Pardew returned from the back of the room with a cardboard box, which he placed on the counter. Quinn felt his mouth go dry. His heart began to hammer. He was unsure whether he would be able to lift his hands to open the box.

'Has anyone come forward to identify him?' Quinn heard the tremulous quiver in his own voice.

'No,' said the official.

'And there was nothing found on him to indicate his identity?'

'Nothing was found on him at all. He was completely naked.'

'I meant, nothing was found in his clothes?'

'Everything is in the box. There were some papers. But the coroner was not able to draw from them any definite conclusions as to the deceased's identity. His face, as you will see if you examine the body, was partially eaten away. And so it was impossible for us to release a photograph, or to compare his features to any known missing persons. None of the witnesses to the event were able to offer any reliable confirmation of identity. The transcript of the inquest is available for you to read should you so wish.'

'I will take it with me if I may.' Quinn noticed resistance in the official's demeanour. 'I'll sign a receipt for it. Now if Mr Pardew could open the box for me, I would like to have a look inside.'

The cloth of the suit was visible immediately. Quinn recognized the shade of brown, the coarse corduroy ridges.

He closed his eyes and felt his body sway.

'Inspector Quinn? Is everything all right?'

'Please, Mr Pardew, could you take the items out for me?' For the moment, nothing could induce Quinn to handle that suit himself.

The jacket, waistcoat and trousers were laid out on the counter, together with a shirt of grey calico as Macadam had said, and as Quinn knew it would be. The undergarments were as he remembered them too.

'It's hardly a bespoke suit,' said the official. 'Quite crudely made, in fact. Almost homemade in appearance.'

'It's not homemade,' said Quinn.

'There are no labels in any of the garments. No sign of commercial manufacture. The coroner was rather flummoxed by that. It would have constituted what I believe you police detectives call a lead.'

'You mentioned some papers?'

'Pardew?'

The papers were kept in a separate file, together with the inquiry transcript, post-mortem report and various photographs of the Mappin Terraces and the corpse.

Quinn picked up a folded pamphlet printed on flimsy yellow paper.

RESIST THE EVIL OF WAR!

Do not be deceived by corrupt Imperialist warmongers! War will benefit no one, except for armament manufacturers and the rapacious despoilers of the Earth.

The headlong rush to conflict must be resisted!

It is every Christian's duty to refuse war. It is every worker's demand to resist war. It is every mother's prayer to reject war.

THEIR CAUSE IS NOT YOUR CAUSE!

A war in Europe will bring death and misery to millions. It will be on a scale that has never before been witnessed. Untold horrors will be unleashed.

Do not allow the greed and militarism of the governing classes to drag you into a war you do not want, to which you have not consented, and in which you may likely die. Their cause is not your cause. They do not deserve your sacrifice.

STAND TOGETHER FOR PEACE!

Already, by secret agreements and understandings of which the democracies of the civilized world know only by rumour, steps are being taken which may fling us all into the fray. We therefore call upon all citizens to stand together for peace. Combine and conquer the militarist enemy and the self-seeking Imperialists to-day once and for all.

There is no justice in the wholesale destruction upon

*which the enemies of mankind are bent. War is Hell. War
is Madness. War is Death.*

JOIN US!

*We are an open brotherhood – and sisterhood! – of
peace. We proclaim that for us the days of butchery and plunder
have gone by. We protest against the greed and intrigue of
militarists and armament-mongers. We are the Fellowship
of the Gracchi. Join us to-day!*

'This Fellowship of the Gracchi . . . did the coroner's inquest
look into it?'

'It's not a secret organization. Its leaders are well-known.
Some are even respected members of the upper classes, and,
uh, celebrated literary gentlemen. A number were called upon
to give testimony. It has long expounded principles of a
pacifist bent, which may be lamentable but is not illegal. These
pamphlets are handed out freely every Sunday morning at
Speaker's Corner. The fact that the deceased had one in his
possession was thought not to signify. There was also found a
music hall advertisement. Similarly, there is nothing to say that
he attended the music hall in question or that, if he did, his
attendance there is at all associated with his death.'

Quinn found the handbill in question. It advertised a show at the
Camden Empire, the acts listed in type of diminishing size:

MISS BELLE SWANSON
MISS ANNETTE TINKLEY
LITTLE JIMMY AND LITTLER JOHN
THE FABULOUS FLYING FORTESCUES
PROFESSOR PANDAEMONIUM
DON CLIFFORD AND HIS DOGS
THE LEGS-ELEVEN DANCING TROUPE
CROSS-EYED AL

The official winced emphatically. 'The only item that can with
any certainty be connected to his death is his ticket of admission
to the zoo.'

Quinn found the zoo ticket. He turned it over several times
before surrendering it dejectedly.

'The coroner's verdict was death by misadventure. Nothing found in his pockets contradicts that.'

'Not even this?' Quinn now held up a card depicting a crudely printed illustration of a red hand. It was the size of a cigarette card, but there was no indication of any brand or maker. On the reverse of the card was written 'F.J.S.U.' in black ink. Beneath that, the number seven.

'You will have to read the coroner's report yourself. I am sure he addresses the card in that.'

Quinn nodded. 'I will. I would like to take the whole file away with me, along with the box of his . . . effects.'

'Very well. Will that be all?'

'While I am here . . .' Quinn cocked his head in the direction of the mortuary.

EIGHT

For Quinn, there was always a moment of theatre before a body was uncovered on a mortuary table. He had never been present at the unveiling of a work of art, but he imagined that the sense of anticipation must be similar. Except that there was nothing artificial about this tableau. It was the truth to which all art aspired.

He had to admit, he had seen worse: corpses that were even more badly mangled. This was still recognizably a man's body. It held its shape. All its limbs and extremities were still attached.

At the same time, it was also recognizably the remnants of a meal.

The hair was seemingly untouched, when viewed from the front at least. Close cropped and the colour of iron filings, it was that thick, superabundant type of hair that held its own in any situation.

The face, as the court official had said, was completely eaten away. The skin was missing, except for shredded tatters on the forehead. The nose and cheekbones were crushed to splinters in a dark pulpy mince, giving Quinn some inkling of the size and power of the animal's jaws. One bite, he suspected, was enough to create this carnage.

It was strange, perhaps, that the bear had chosen to feast here, when, considered as prey, the body must have offered more rewarding morsels elsewhere. But it was unlikely that the biting was done for the purposes of feeding. The animal was presumably well fed. And there was something desultory about the wound. Quinn imagined that the man must have been screaming as he faced up to the bear. He imagined the bear's confusion, and the gradual stoking of that into rage.

The face was not the only part of the body that had been savaged. The throat was a scooped-out glistening hole. Much of the torso was flayed. Strips of skin hung off, ribboned by the beast's claws. The stomach was ripped open, as if the bear had gone rooting for jam sandwiches there. One forearm was gnawed.

Other less severe wounds appear to have been sustained in the animal's casual discarding of a thing it had tired of: abrasions picked up as the man's body skimmed and bounced along the rough concrete of the Mappin Terraces.

Quinn asked the mortuary attendant to turn the body. There were more of these secondary, more superficial wounds visible on his back. Still raw patches of exposed sinew where the skin had been scraped away. The hair at the crown was slick with blood. The wounds of the dead do not heal.

With that thought in mind, Quinn leant down to peer closely at an area of the man's skin that was still in place. It was cross-hatched with a series of scabbed weals that appeared to have been caused by something serrated being drawn, or whipped, across his naked flesh. It was like trying to decipher the original text of a palimpsest.

'What did the medical examiner have to say about these scars, do you recall?'

The attendant's gaze followed the direction of Quinn's pointing finger.

'They are evidently old wounds,' he observed condescendingly. 'Therefore of no relevance to the inquiry.'

'But they may help us in identifying the deceased.'

'You'll have to take that up with the coroner.'

Quinn continued his close reading of the man's wounds, scanning down his body until he spotted something that pulled him up short.

'What of these marks here?' Quinn pointed to two dark circles, one on each of the man's thighs. They were the size and colour of copper pennies.

'Ah, yes. We noticed those.'

'And?'

'They looked to Dr Richard like burns. Electrical burns, he rather thought. Dr Richard once conducted the post-mortem examination of a girl who was struck by lightning. These marks, he told me, resembled the burn he found on the top of the child's head, where the electricity entered her.'

'How interesting. Did Dr Richard have any theories as to how these marks came to be on the back of this gentleman's thighs?'

The mortuary attendant stifled a grin. 'He did not think the bear was responsible for them.'

'And so, no doubt, he did not consider them relevant to the inquiry?'

'Oh, he mentioned them in his report. He thought they were rather interesting.'

'I am glad he found something to interest him.'

'Have you seen enough?' The attendant's tone suggested that he had certainly seen enough of Quinn.

But Quinn's gaze lingered over the lacerated body, like a lover who could not tear his eyes away from his loved one.

Quinn took a motor taxi to the Hackney Mortuary, with the box of the man's belongings on the seat beside him. He scanned the coroner's file en route. It contained a number of statements from witnesses, all alike in their essential details. Everyone was intent on watching Aguta the polar bear as he sat eating fish and inspecting his toes. At first no one noticed the strange behaviour of the man in the brown suit, or the man *not* in the brown suit, as he was soon to become.

It was a married lady who first raised the alarm. She discreetly nudged her husband to draw his attention to the unfolding scandal. He was initially amused rather than concerned by the man's undressing. It was only when his wife pointed out the presence of children and unmarried young women in the crowd that he realized the seriousness of the situation.

But by then it was too late. The man was already naked. The crowd could only look on as an even greater horror unfolded.

Some of the men claimed to have called out to deter him. But they attested that he was deaf to their cries and protests, as if in a world of his own. Some said it all happened too quickly for them to intervene. Others said that it was as if time had slowed down, like in a dream. They found that they were rooted to the spot by the unexpectedness of the spectacle. It seemed they could not quite believe it was really happening. Perhaps it was some stunt organized by the zoo?

Quinn suspected there was something else going on. The desire to see a unique event through to the end. Of course, no one would own up to that, however human the impulse might be. In retrospect, one always feels bad for failing to prevent an atrocity.

None of the witnesses were able to give a useful description of the man. They disagreed on the colour of his hair, his height, the regularity or otherwise of his features . . . No doubt his nudity, and the subsequent attack, distracted them from remarking such trivial details.

Dr Richard expounded at length on the nature of each separate area of attack, describing the depth, extent and angle of every wound in some detail, and giving his considered opinion as to whether it was caused by the teeth or the claws of the animal. It was the accumulation of so many wounds that killed him, although the fracture to the skull sustained when his head struck the concrete may have proved critical. But a naked man in a fight with a bear is always going to die, one way or another.

The old scars that Quinn had noticed on the man's back were dismissed, along with the copper-coloured marks, as 'historic and no doubt self-inflicted given the deceased's evident propensity to self-destruction.'

No doubt!

Dr Richard noted in passing that the deceased's tonsils had been recently removed, possibly at the same time as the teeth from his lower jaw had been extracted. It was impossible to tell whether the teeth from the upper jaw were also in place or not, as that part of the face was missing entirely.

Quinn returned the file to the box as the taxi turned into the churchyard of St John-at-Hackney. In his time as a detective, he had visited a fair number of public mortuaries. The one at Hackney, which served the north London police area, was one of his favourites. The setting was peaceful, set back as it was from the main road and surrounded by trees and grass. The area had the feel of a village green.

Made from tawny London bricks, the mortuary building itself looked like it might be someone's house, the kind of place anyone might want to settle down in. It presented a welcoming, cheery face, double-fronted with twin gables and large windows. One side of the ground floor was taken up by a wide red gate, through which the hearses passed into the yard.

There are always some places at which a man is known, at least by face, if not by name. For Quinn, it was mortuaries. The clerk here greeted him with a nod of recognition. There was no need to produce the warrant card this time, which was just as well given that both his hands were occupied carrying the box.

'You had a body come in here. The suicide off the Hornsey Lane Bridge.'

'The naked fellow?' As if there was someone else who had jumped off fully clothed. Perhaps there was.

'That's right.'

'Do you want to see him?'

'First I'd like to take a look at his effects. Were his clothes found?'

'Yes.'

'You have them?'

'Yes.'

'I'd like to see them. And any items that were found in the pockets. And the medical examiner's report, if the post-mortem examination has taken place.'

'It has. It appears to be a straightforward case of suicide. The coroner has not conducted his inquest yet, but I am sure that will be the verdict.'

The clerk's expression clouded with the unspoken question: *So why the interest?*

Quinn did not feel the need to explain himself. This man was not one of his officers.

A similar box containing an identical corduroy suit, together with a grey calico shirt and familiar items of underwear, was produced from a back room. The sense of urgency that possessed Quinn now was enough to overcome any squeamishness. He sorted through the garments while the clerk went for the file.

The touch of that material ought to have been repulsive, painful even. But somehow he was able to dislocate himself – his present self – from the part of him that would have crumpled and wept to handle the clothes in the box.

He gave it up as soon as the clerk returned. 'There was nothing of any real interest found in his pockets. Nothing that enabled an identification to be made.' It was a discouraging observation.

Quinn frowned dubiously. 'There wasn't found, by any chance, a sort of cigarette card?'

'It's all in the file.'

There wasn't much to sift through. Quinn paused over the photographs of the body. In particular, he was interested in a close-up of the back of the man's thighs. Two small dark discs, one on each leg, were clearly visible. Referring to the medical examiner's report, no theory was proposed as to the cause of the marks. Their presence was merely noted, as was the presence of scabbed striations across the back. Quinn read that the deceased's tonsils had been recently removed, together with all his teeth.

However, he found no cigarette card. Quinn could not suppress his disappointment. 'The card I mentioned, could it have fallen out? Or been removed?'

The clerk took obvious umbrage at Quinn's suggestions. 'I assure you that is not possible. If there is no such card in the file, no such card was found.'

There was no pacifist leaflet or music hall playbill either. In fact, apart from a small amount of loose change which had been sealed in a brown envelope, the only items the second deceased man had had in his possession were a till receipt from a Lyons teashop, and a dog-eared postcard bearing a Salvation Army tract: *Whosoever believeth in the name of the Lord Jesus Christ as the Messiah will be saved.*

Underneath, someone – presumably the dead man – had scrawled in pencil: AND WHAT IF YOU CANNOT BELIEVE? The words were deeply scored into the card, in a stilted, irregular hand, and were underlined three times. The postcard had been folded into quarters and was almost falling apart at its creases. There was nothing written on the reverse.

The jarring clamour of the mortuary telephone's bells disturbed Quinn's thoughts before he had the chance to form them. The clerk listened to a wasp-like buzzing in the earpiece before holding it out towards Quinn. 'A Sergeant Macadam for you.'

Macadam's voice came to him from the other side of the universe, infinitely small, fragile and trembling. 'Sir . . .'

There was a long, crackling pause. Quinn thought he had lost him. Then it came: 'There's been another one.'

Quinn's voice sounded calmer than he felt. 'I see. Where?'

'Bankside. The power station there. A man, naked, of course. His clothes were found nearby.'

'A brown suit?'

'A brown suit,' said Macadam over the question.

'Corduroy?'

'Yes.'

'How did he die?'

'That's the thing, sir. This one's not dead. They've taken him to Guy's Hospital.'

'I'm on my way.'

'We'll meet you there, sir. Inchball and I.'

Quinn did not demur.

NINE

D arkness is all around him.

He feels himself moving through the darkness. His body, tightly bound. He cannot say how he is moving. His arms, bound to his sides. His legs, trussed together. He is bound by the darkness. It is an immense weight pushing in on him from above and below. From every side at the same time.

He has the sense of his body being suddenly too small for him. As if it has contracted to the size of a taut, bursting pea.

He knows that the darkness contains something terrible and malign. Something intent on destroying him.

The darkness is filled with teeth. Sharp, vicious teeth biting at every part of him, tearing him apart.

The darkness is filled with pain.

He is drifting through it on an inky black river of pain. He has been tightly swaddled and laid in a canoe and cast adrift. From time to time, the conviction grips him that the canoe is on fire, but that can't be. He can see no flames. Only blackness. But it feels as though he is on fire. Then the answer comes to him: these are black flames that consume him. He can hear their crackling as he drifts.

A far-off light flickers in the darkness. In the instant of illumination he sees what the darkness contains and it is worse than he imagined.

It is filled not with teeth, but with millions of fat black buzzing bees. It is the bees he can hear, not flames.

The flicker of light dies. But his panic stays with him.

All he can do is stay as still and silent as possible so that he doesn't attract the attention of the swarming bees.

An even more frightening thought occurs to him. He is drifting not on a river, but on a stream of bees.

His father's voice comes to him. 'It will soon be over.'

At first he finds the words consoling. But then he remembers that the man was not his father after all. So how can he believe anything he says?

Another voice speaks. A man's voice again, but one he does not recognize. 'Soon we will be together.'

This time he chooses to believe in the consolation he is offered. He knows, somehow, that this is his true father speaking to him.

TEN

Quinn ran out on to Lower Clapton Road. The faces of the living that he now confronted were sullen and bewildered. They shied away from him as the dead never did. A running man, a man out of breath, a man exerting himself in the commission of some urgent act, was no doubt an object of suspicion in these parts, if not fear. Either he was a villain running from a crime or a policeman in hot pursuit. Both were equally to be shunned.

The traffic was thin. A horse-drawn collier's cart on its rounds headed away from him into Mare Street. A delivery van passed it moving in the opposite direction. Its engine strained noisily against unseen forces intent on holding it back. There was something plucky about its determined progress, which seemed against all the odds somehow. Quinn was hypnotized by its approach. It was only when it had passed him that he thought perhaps he should have flagged it down and requisitioned it. The next vehicle he saw, he would.

But now the road was empty. He regretted not keeping the taxi waiting on its meter. But even though it was not his money that he would be spending, he baulked at the extravagance of it.

The Georgian facades of the houses around Clapton Square enticed him with their air of village England. If only one could live in a house like that, on good terms with one's neighbours, terms of understanding and tact, where nothing was said because nothing needed to be said. Quinn felt a pang of nostalgia for a life he had never lived. A life of pipes and slippers and well-set fires. Where the hardest puzzle he had to solve was *The Times* crossword. And the greatest drama was someone's leaving the lid off the butter dish. He might indulge his fancy by imagining himself a wife! How about that! A wife for Quinn! He couldn't picture her face. Conveniently for his poor imagination she was in the next room, busy with . . . whatever it was that wives did. Her perfume wafted to him, chorused by her contented trilling.

She had a good singing voice, it seems – that was an unexpected delight. And although he couldn't see her, he knew she was pretty without being threateningly so, and comfortably proportioned.

Most of all, she put up with him.

There might even be a couple of children, one boy, one girl, though the girl was rather tomboyish, which he approved of enormously. They were both pestering him to put down his pipe and paper, to exchange his slippers for shoes, and take them out into the square to sail their model yacht on the pond. But Quinn could see that in reality there was no pond in Clapton Square. So wherever this fantasy life was located, it was not here.

The steady rumble of a motor drew his gaze, again in the Mare Street direction. A long black vehicle was speeding towards him. It was larger than a car, but not as big as a van. Quinn ran out into the road and stood facing it with his arms raised above his head. He crossed and uncrossed his arms slowly several times. For a long time, it seemed the driver hadn't seen him, because he showed no sign of slowing down. Then, eventually, he gave several angry honks on the horn. At the last moment, when he was less than twenty yards from Quinn, he slammed on the brakes and skidded to a halt, spinning the vehicle forty degrees.

The driver leapt out, his face ashen.

'Are you mad?'

Quinn produced his warrant card. 'I am Detective Inspector Quinn of the Special Crimes Department. I need you to drive me to Guy's Hospital. If you refuse to do so, I am empowered to arrest you for obstructing the course of justice.'

The driver held up two black-gloved hands in a placatory manner. 'All right, all right. There's no need for that. It's just I've got to get her back to the shop for a bit of a polish. I've got another funeral at twelve.'

It was only now that Quinn took in that the vehicle was a motorized hearse. He also appreciated the driver's formal mourning attire, though his black swallow-tail jacket was oddly set off by a tweed flat cap. Another man sat in the passenger seat with two black top hats dressed with black crepe ribbon on his lap.

'It won't take long. Guy's isn't far from here and the traffic is light.'

Quinn went round to the passenger side. The other undertaker glowered back at him resentfully.

'He'll have to get out.'

In the event, the other man lay down in the back of the hearse, in the space reserved for the coffin. It was left to Quinn to sit with the toppers on his lap.

The driver seemed to relish the licence to speed that Quinn's presence legitimized. He no doubt chafed at the necessity to drive at a funereal pace for at least half of every journey. The man in the back slid from side to side as they took the corners. He grumbled 'Have a care!' every time he collided with the interior, and 'Have a blinkin' care' whenever he was made to bump over one of the brackets designed for holding the coffin in place.

Quinn touched the mahogany detailing on the dashboard. 'I haven't seen many of these. Motor hearses.'

'We still have the horse-drawn variety. Naturally, some of our clients prefer those.'

Quinn wondered how a dead man could prefer anything.

'But this is the future,' added the driver.

'The future?'

'Of the industry.'

Quinn had never thought of undertaking as an industry before.

The hearse bumped violently over a deep pothole and landed with an axle-bending thud.

'Oh, do have a blinkin' care!' came from behind.

They sped through the wrought-iron gates of the St Thomas Street entrance. It was the sharpest corner the driver had yet taken. The rear end of the hearse swung wildly. There were no grumbles from the man in the back though. His eyes were closed and his mouth was clamped tightly shut. From a quick glance over his shoulder, Quinn had the impression he was either praying or trying not to vomit.

Quinn placed the two top hats on the passenger seat and nodded tersely to the driver. He was not inclined to offer anything more by way of thanks.

He ran into the hospital and asked the first nurse he saw for the Emergency Ward. He assumed that was where the man would have been taken.

He met Inchball and Macadam in the corridor outside the ward.

'Who is he?'

'We don't know that yet, sir.' Macadam winced, sensitive to Quinn's disappointment. 'He's alive but unconscious.'

'So what happened?'

Macadam provided what details they had. 'Somehow he got himself inside the power station at Bankside. He may have stowed away on one of the barges bringing in coal, or he was just lucky. Timed his entry when there was a rush of activity, so he slipped in unnoticed. It seems he was trying to pass as one of the workmen.'

Inchball pulled a face. 'Come on! Face it. We haven't got a clue what was going through his head.'

Macadam carried on, undeterred. 'One of the men at Bankside thinks he might have seen a fellow in a brown suit hanging around looking suspicious. Likely the bargemen thought he was a power station employee and the CLEL Company men thought he was with the barge. Next time our witness looked, he was gone.'

'Did he not think to raise the alarm?'

'It don't look like it,' said Inchball, shaking his head in contempt.

'This sighting took place at five o'clock yesterday,' Macadam continued. 'We don't know where he went or what he did between then and half past midnight when the accident occurred.'

'Accident? It weren't no accident.'

'What exactly occurred?'

'He entered a building to the west of the boiler rooms. This is where the generators are housed that produce the electricity for Fleet Street's printing presses.'

'Is that significant?'

'We don't know as yet what is or isn't significant, sir.'

'We don't know nothing,' added Inchball gloomily.

'Go on, Macadam.'

'He must have climbed to the top of one of the gantries in the engine room. His clothes were found discarded there. The brown corduroy suit, the grey shirt, et cetera. From the gantry he evidently threw himself on to a thousand kilowatt Allis Chalmers direct current dynamo, which was in motion at the time of contact. His body came in contact with a part of the machinery that was live and he was thrown into the air by the violence of the shock. He then, as ill luck would have it, landed on another generator, again touching live metal and being thrown from that on to the ground. The power supply to Fleet Street was disrupted as a result of the incident. The presses ground to a halt, which was not a happy outcome for the Company or its clients.'

'Not a happy outcome for the poor fucker in there either,' said Inchball, hitching his thumb towards the ward.

'His right arm caught fire and he has sustained second to third degree burns over fifty percent of his body. He's in a bad way.'

'But he's alive.'

'For the time being.'

'What's happened to the suit?'

'It's being held at Southwark police station. I have instructed the local bobbies not to do anything with it until we have had a chance to examine it. I told them it was a SCD matter now. Did you discover anything of interest at the mortuaries, sir?'

Quinn ignored the question. 'Very well. Shall we go in and see him?'

'What are you men doing in here?' A ward sister in a starched cap and a pinafore as sharp as a blade rushed towards them. Her crisp skirts crackled angrily. Her arms were brawny from hefting the incapacitated. She came to a stop in front of them, blocking their way, balled fists resting on her hips. If it came to a fight, you would not have fancied the three SCD men's chances.

Quinn flashed his warrant card. 'We've come to see the man you admitted from Bankside power station in the early hours. The electrocution victim.'

'What on earth for? He's unconscious. You'll not get anything out of him.'

'Nevertheless,' began Quinn. It seemed a little prurient to admit that they just wanted to look at him. 'He may be known to us. There's a chance he's someone we have encountered in the course of our investigations. So far as I believe, his identity has not yet been ascertained. Somewhere there may well be family members, a mother, a wife perhaps, who are desperate for news of their missing loved one. Perhaps children.' Quinn was discovering that he had quite a talent for inventing families.

The ward sister frowned dubiously. 'If he should come round . . .'

'Is there a chance that he may?'

'One never knows. But if he should, you must not excite him. No questions. Indeed, you may not speak to him at all. You may only, briefly, look at him.'

She led him to a bed that was surrounded by a screening curtain. As the ward sister pulled aside the curtain, a faint smell of bleach came up from the bed.

His arms, legs and much of his trunk were wrapped in dressings. His face, however, was exposed, apparently undamaged by the massive electrical charges he had sustained. He lay with his eyes closed. There were some abrasions to his forehead, but nothing that would have prevented anyone who knew him from identifying him.

Macadam, ever sensitive to his chief's moods, must have noticed the change that came over Quinn.

'What is it, sir? Do you know him?'

Quinn's heart pounded so heavily that, for a moment, he could hear nothing else. 'I believe . . . that is to say . . . I think . . . he is my brother.'

'Brother?' said Macadam. 'I did not know you had a brother.'

'Gor*blimey!*' added Inchball, with feeling.

Quinn turned to the ward sister, who was now regarding him with a mixture of wonder and sympathy. 'He will . . . I mean to say . . . he will be all right, won't he?'

'One never knows.' She said it almost brightly. But perhaps she felt that had offered too much hope, so she repeated it with an ominous finality. 'One never knows.'

And in her refusal to meet his eyes, he knew he had his true answer.

ELEVEN

Macadam drove, staring fixedly ahead. He was paying attention to the road with more than his usual concentration. Inchball fidgeted next to him. Quinn could tell he was itching to ask questions, but a stern glance from Macadam earlier had warned him off. Still, discretion did not come easily to Inchball. The only way he knew to show his feelings was to bark bullish questions until he reached some kind of understanding.

Quinn sat in silence in the back, slumped into a corner, as if he wanted to merge with the interior of the car.

In truth, he did not know how he felt to discover that the man in the hospital bed was Malcolm Grant-Sissons, whom he had recently been told was his half-brother, the fruit of a secret affair that his father had once had. His face felt numb. His hands, cold. His feet, sore. And his heart – his heart felt number, colder, sorer than any other part of him.

The two of them had met only once, just a few months ago, and had barely spoken a word to each other at the time. A man called Hugh Grant-Sissons claimed to know Quinn's father. He claimed that they had both loved the same woman, Grant-Sissons' wife, Louisa. Malcolm's mother. It was Hugh Grant-Sissons who had told Quinn that his father had killed himself because of the guilt he bore over Louisa's death.

As he told him all this, Hugh Grant-Sissons lay dying. Virtually the last words that the man had said to him were: 'Look out for Malcolm . . . Keep an eye on him, for me. A brotherly eye . . .'

But Quinn had walked away and not given Malcolm Grant-Sissons a second thought. There was no proof that they were brothers. The idea seemed to be as unwelcome to Malcolm as it was to Quinn.

There was a squeak of brakes. The car rocked on its suspension. Macadam ratcheted on the handbrake but kept the engine running.

Quinn looked out. They were outside a police station.

He saw Macadam nod to Inchball, who nodded back and got out of the car.

'Where's he going?'

'It's Southwark police station, sir. He's going to get . . . uh . . . your brother's things.'

'We don't know that he is my brother. It's what I was told but . . . I have seen no proof of it.'

'If you don't mind me saying, sir, once you mentioned that he could be related, I couldn't help looking at him, you know, to see if there was any family resemblance, and you know, well . . .'

'What?'

'I wouldn't have said it before, but once you mentioned it . . .'

'What?'

'He's the spit of you, sir.'

'Nonsense.'

And yet Quinn felt a kind of easing of tension throughout him. He recognized the truth of what his sergeant said, though he had not acknowledged it when he first met Malcolm. But now he accepted that he had seen it and known it from the first.

'Not the spit.'

'Very well. Not the spit. Perhaps he takes more after his mother in some respects. Did you know the lady?'

'No I did not!'

'I beg your pardon, sir. I meant no offence.'

The rear door across from Quinn opened and Inchball deposited a cardboard box on the seat.

'Did you look inside?' asked Quinn.

'I thought I would leave that for you, guv. Seeing as how you have eyeballed the other geezers' clobber.' He slammed the door and got in the front.

Quinn lifted the flaps of the box, revealing the brown corduroy material of the suit.

'Same?' Inchball grunted over his shoulder.

Quinn nodded silently.

'What do you think it means, guv? Some kind of uniform?'

Quinn said nothing. It was his practice when he did not know the answer to a question.

'The last time you saw your brother,' began Macadam. 'Back

in April, wasn't it? When we were looking into all that business
with the moving picture people. Was he wearing this suit then?'

'Stop calling him my brother,' said Quinn. 'But no. I don't believe
he was. And I think I would have noticed if he had been.'

'You wouldn't necessarily, sir. I mean to say, you wouldn't
have appreciated the significance of a brown corduroy suit at
that time.'

Quinn was on the verge of pointing out that he most certainly
would have, but let it go.

'Back to HQ?'

'We need to call in at Hackney Mortuary first. The effects of
the other two are there, together with the case files. I didn't take
them with me to the hospital.'

Macadam released the handbrake and pulled the car out. 'Funny
isn't it, sir. If only you'd let me drive you, as I'd suggested . . .'
He gave a little chuckle to himself and shook his head.

Quinn felt a surge of feeling rise in him. It wasn't irritation. Nor
was it grief. It was a sickening and oppressive anxiety, the sense
that things were closing in on him, and an almost overpowering
desire to leap from the moving car and run.

Back in the attic room of the Special Crimes Department, Quinn
had the three cardboard boxes placed side by side on his desk.
He opened the one containing Malcolm Grant-Sissons' clothes,
and looked down at the rectangle of brown corduroy revealed.

Inchball was standing at his shoulder. Quinn moved half a step
away from his sergeant as he felt himself begin to tremble.

'Ain't ya going to take it out?' Inchball peered down into
the box.

Macadam joined them. 'It can't be called a coincidence,' he
said brightly. 'Not now that we have three men wearing the
same suit. Or rather not wearing it. What about brand labels?
Were any found in the suits, to indicate where they were made
or bought?'

'No.' Quinn said the word as if it gave him satisfaction.

'Does it appear that such labels have been removed? Or were
they never there?'

'I do not feel that the suits, the provenance of the suits . . .'
Quinn felt his two sergeants watching him anxiously. 'It need

not concern us.' He did not add the reason why he said this. Because he knew full well where the suits came from and what they signified.

Quinn stood for a long moment, swaying slightly on his feet, as he had done once before that morning. And then, without warning, he plunged his hands down into the box and drew up the jacket.

The texture of the cloth was both shocking and familiar. For a moment he was transported back to a place and a time that he had long ago expunged from his memory. The echoes of screams and other sounds, doors slamming, keys turning, the snores and whimpers of a dormitory night, came to him down an infinitely long corridor. The smells of that place – dominated by the stench of human waste – filled his nostrils once more. Quinn gagged.

He let the jacket drop back into the box.

'Guv?'

'What's wrong, sir? You look like you've seen a ghost.'

'Look *like* a ghost, more like.'

What tormented him, he realized, was not just the memory of being in that place, but also the idea of Malcolm being there. It was not out of any great sympathy for a man he hardly knew. But because it seemed to prove their kinship. They were related by madness, it seemed, which proved their blood relation. They had inherited their madness from the same suicidal father.

Malcolm's sojourn in Colney Hatch must have been brief. Presumably it had been brought on by Hugh Grant-Sissons' death, and the discovery that the man he had thought was his father was not.

'Macadam, will you look through the pockets of this suit, please?'

'Of course, sir. Do you want to sit down?'

'I think I will, thank you.'

'A glass of water? Or perhaps Inchball would be kind enough to fetch you a cup of tea from the canteen?'

Inchball did not even bristle at Macadam volunteering him for the errand.

'No, that won't be necessary.' But Quinn's throat was all at once unbearably parched. 'Although perhaps a glass of water, after all.'

A brief nod passed between the sergeants before Inchball dashed off.

Macadam busied himself searching the pockets of the suit. The first item to come to light was an envelope, which had already been opened. Macadam showed Quinn the address: M. Grant-Sissons Esq., of 3, St John's Passage, Clerkenwell.

'This is your brother?'

'Yes. Malcolm. Malcolm Grant-Sissons.'

'Yes, I remember now. We went to St John's Passage together. You went in alone. You didn't tell us . . .'

'I had other things on my mind. We were in the middle of an investigation. It was not relevant.' Why did Quinn suddenly feel that his sergeant was interrogating him? His answer sounded suspect, even to his own ears. 'Is there a letter?'

Macadam took out a brief typewritten note from Finsbury Public Library concerning an overdue library book, *A Furious Energy* by W.G. Portman. There was a fine of two shillings and threepence to pay. 'He must be a slow reader,' observed Macadam.

'Or perhaps he was unable to return the book due to . . .' But Quinn broke off his speculation, uneasy about where it led.

Macadam studied the letter. 'I'm sure I've read something by this Portman fellow. Can't remember the title. I don't think it was this one. He writes rather fantastical adventures. The one I read was about a space voyage to Mars. A race of fearsome red-devil type creatures was found to inhabit the interior of the planet, while peace-loving beings of a more human appearance dwelt on the surface. The red devils, who are actually more like giant ants or cockroaches, I think . . . They have these horrid twitching antennae. They demand daily sacrifices from the surface dwellers otherwise they will wipe them out in a wholesale planetary massacre.'

Inchball came back into the room and handed Quinn a glass of water. He stood watching Macadam with a look of open-mouthed stupefaction.

'The surface dwellers are innately unable to fight, you see. They're pacifists! So the space voyagers live happily among the surface creatures. One of them even mates with a female. It's all very idyllic and wonderful. Until the devil cockroaches take this fellow's mate. And, uh, well you know . . . eat her. As is their way. First they dissolve her in this acidic slime that they secrete. Not very pleasant at all. And her space voyager lover witnesses all this, you see. So then, well, you can probably tell where this is going . . .'

Inchball shook his head vigorously.

'The space voyagers tell the surface dwellers that they really shouldn't stand for this sort of thing and fire them up to fight against the . . . the . . . now what were they called? The red-devil insect creatures? They had a name. The Zarians! That was it. The Zarians . . . How do they think of this stuff? That's what I wonder. So anyhow, the space voyagers, led by Captain Thomas, persuade the surface dwellers. They were the . . . uh . . . the . . . oh, it will come to me . . . They were the Tsangi! That's it! With a T. Tsangi. They were sort of African, if you ask me. Like an African tribe, very noble and primitive. But utterly, utterly incapable of warfare. They don't even have a word for "weapon" in their language. And their skin's red, not brown.'

'What the buggeration is he going on about?'

Quinn held up a hand to silence Inchball. He nodded for Macadam to go on.

'So, urged on by the space voyagers, the Tsangi go to war with the Zarians. Captain Thomas and his men teach them about warfare and show them how to manufacture spears and bows and arrows. And all that sort of thing. And they also have these guns that fire sonic waves which they brought with them on their space ship. But there aren't enough of those to go around, obviously.'

'And? What happens?' demanded Inchball belligerently.

'Oh, the Tsangi are wiped out. Completely wiped out. They can't fight, you see. It was hopeless right from the start. The planet is stained red with their blood. That was it! That was the title. *The Blood Planet*! I knew it would come to me.'

'So it is an argument against pacifism?' wondered Quinn.

'Well, not quite, you see. Because the thing is, once they had wiped out the Tsangi, the Zarians began to die off too. By utterly destroying their enemies, they destroyed themselves. It was not so much that they needed the Tsangi to feed on, rather that their enemies gave their lives purpose and meaning. The daily sacrifices were a symbol of their power over the Tsangi. But once the Tsangi were gone, their lives were empty.'

'And so they just died out?'

'Not quite. They began to devour each other. They formed factions, each demanding sacrifices from the others. Acidic slime secretions all over the place. Until all life on the Blood Planet was wiped out. In fact, there's one last Zarian surviving, and he's the creature who had eaten the space voyager's female. And as it happens, the very same space voyager – the lover of the Tsangi female – is the only one of the human visitors left alive and in the big finale he encounters the last Zarian in a cave and blasts him with his sonic gun. After which, he returns to Earth, alone. It's through his account that we know the history.'

'What a load of tosh,' commented Inchball.

But Quinn was not so quick to dismiss the story. 'The book that Malcolm Grant-Sissons had out from the library, do you think it is a similar kind of story?'

'Probably. From what I can gather, W.G. Portman seems to specialize in this sort of thing.'

Quinn had a mental image of Malcolm eagerly lapping up such adventure stories. It did not – yet – help him understand why he had thrown himself naked on to an industrial dynamo, but it did make him feel that he knew his half-brother a little better.

Macadam returned to searching the crudely stitched on patches that formed the pockets of the jacket. 'Something here.' He fished out a card, the size of a cigarette card, and held it up. It bore a crude illustration of a red hand, identical to the one Quinn had seen earlier.

'Does it say anything on the back?'

Macadam turned the card over. 'F.J.S.U. Seven.'

Quinn raised himself from his seat and retrieved the other card from the coroner's file. 'This was found in the clothes of the man who died at London Zoo.'

'It's the same,' observed Macadam.

'A clue!' cried Inchball.

'Although no such card was found belonging to the second man.'

'Still, two out of three,' insisted Inchball. 'We've got the suits. The undressing. And the cards.'

'There is something else. The first two men had small burns on their thighs. As well as indications of old scars. In the case of Malcolm Grant-Sissons, we do not know yet whether such marks exist.'

'So,' began Macadam. 'All three men are linked by brown corduroy suits and undressing. First man and third man are linked by red hand cards. First man and second man are linked by burns and scars.'

'The suits are the only thing linking all three of 'em,' said Inchball.

Macadam put down the card and tipped out a handful of change from one of the trouser pockets. From the other he retrieved a ring with two keys on it. One appeared to be a house key; the other was smaller and perhaps opened a drawer or a box of some kind.

'There were no keys found on the other two men,' Quinn pointed out. 'Or rather, in their possession. Which may suggest that they were vagrants.'

'Maybe they were on the run from somewhere?' suggested Inchball.

'Why do you say that?' asked Quinn sharply.

'The uniform?'

'Perhaps they belonged to some sort of irregular group?' suggested Macadam. He picked up the card again and studied the image of the red hand closely. 'The cousin I was telling you about, the Irish one. He belongs to a voluntary regiment in Belfast. All the men in it agree to wear the same style of pinstripe suit. Perhaps this is a similar thing?' Macadam turned the card over and tapped at the reverse with the nail of his forefinger. 'These letters. Perhaps they stand for the name of the unit. Indeed, U could be unit. Or Ulster. F could be federation. J – J is a tricky one. Judgement, perhaps. Or juvenile. They were all quite young, these men.'

'But not juveniles,' said Quinn.

'Jokers?' Inchball's suggestion was met with silence.

'What about jumpers?' said Macadam. 'They all jumped. The first into the bear enclosure. The second off Suicide Bridge. The third . . . I mean to say, your brother, sir, he jumped from the gantry on to the generator, did he not?'

Quinn shook his head discouragingly.

But Macadam was not to be deterred. 'The S could be for secret. That gives us Secret Unit, at the end. Or perhaps special. Special Unit. Or society. Society of Ulstermen. The Something Something Society of Ulstermen.'

Inchball was having none of it. 'Fat and jovial? The Fat and Jovial Society of Ulstermen.'

Quinn decided that the best way to neutralize Inchball's joke was to take it seriously. 'None of them were fat, and the fact that they took their own lives, or attempted to, suggests that they were not jovial.'

Inchball frowned and shook his head. 'It may as well mean that as anything Mac has said. I mean, it's all guesswork. It gets us nowhere.'

'F could be Fenian,' persisted Macadam.

'Malcolm Grant-Sissons isn't Irish,' objected Quinn.

'First? Foremost? Flying?' Macadam was clutching at straws.

Inchball kept up his mockery: 'Friendly?'

'Free!' cried Macadam triumphantly. 'Or freedom. All these armies claim to fight for freedom's sake.'

'Very well, but what about the J?' said Quinn. 'You still don't have anything plausible for J.'

'Jew?' blurted Inchball. 'Is it some kind of secret Jewish army?'

'Is . . . could . . .' Macadam was having difficulty overcoming his tact. 'Is it possible that Malcolm Grant-Sissons is Jewish?'

'Not on his father's side,' said Quinn.

'Do we have to keep an eye out for the Jews now?' said Inchball glumly.

'It could be a German word?' said Macadam, a little more brightly. 'Lots of German words begin with J, do they not? What about Junkers? Junkers means something, doesn't it? Isn't it some kind of officer or nobleman?'

Inchball shook his head. 'No, no, no, we're barking up the wrong tree here. Even if it is some kind of special unit, or secret political grouping, the question is why? What purpose is served by all these young men topping themselves in such weird and wonderful ways?'

'It draws the public's attention,' answered Macadam. 'In the same way that a bomb blast might, but without the associated loss of innocent life. They are sacrificing themselves to make a political point. Perhaps they are militant pacifists? There was that leaflet found on the first of them, remember. The Fellowship of the Gracchi, wasn't it? Perhaps they were all members of that group? If we can get a list of members, we can find out whether Malcolm Grant-Sissons was on it. And we can check the names on the list to find out if any of the members are missing.'

'Sounds like a lot of work,' grumbled Inchball. 'For a wild goose chase.'

Inchball looked like he was about to offer an alternative theory but Quinn cut him short: 'It is an interesting theory, Macadam. We will work with it for now.'

What Quinn didn't tell his sergeants was that the reason he liked the theory was not because he believed it to be true, but because it drew them away from a line of enquiry that he was far from eager to pursue. From Inchball's frown of dissatisfaction, it seemed he had more than an inkling of what that might be.

TWELVE

Wilfred George Portman stood on the balustraded balcony of the Grahame-White watch tower, looking out over the airfield at Hendon Aerodrome. His aviator's goggles were pushed up on to his forehead. His leather helmet sat loosely on his head, the chinstraps as yet unfastened. For something that was designated a tower, the building was modestly low. For the most part it was a solid two-storey brick construction, from the centre of which the observation tower itself projected. The tower's pyramid-shaped roof gave the whole thing the appearance of a modern ziggurat, tiered and upward yearning. A staging post to the heavens.

It was a fine, clear day. The uninterrupted sky beckoned. Portman sniffed the air, and breathed in the scent of the future, heavy with machine oil and churned mud. The guttural thrum of an aircraft engine somewhere overhead was the sound of the future.

The future was everything for Portman. It was not simply the days not yet reached in the calendar, or that part of the countryside concealed around the next bend in the road. Nor was it just the direction in which the arrow of time was flying. It was something real and concrete. It was a dynamic force, an energy that was capable of converting the present into a new reality. It was that which a man forged out of the raw material of the present.

As for the past, he had no time for it. He experienced it as a desolate, sterile wasteland. Nostalgia, the allure of the past, was hateful to him. Whenever he felt its weighted hooks pulling at him, he suffered the most fearful depression.

He refused to forget. But he would not seek to remember. He would live only with one foot in the present, and the other striding out towards the future.

He sometimes wondered if it was to escape the tyranny of the past that he had turned to aviation.

He heard his name called. 'Billy.' And turned to see a young woman dressed in pale diaphanous layers draped over an ankle-length skirt. One hand held a silk parasol, open behind her head, the handle resting on her shoulder. She held her other hand out towards him, as she executed a smile of half-rebuke and half-enticement. 'There you are. I might have known.'

'Reg, old girl.'

He saw her wince at his familiar shortening of her name. He was the only one who called her that now. She had been Reg at school, but her parents – well, her mother at least – had always preferred Gina. To her father, these days especially, she remained steadfastly Regina.

His smile was designed to win her over, and there was every sign it succeeded. She allowed herself to be pulled towards him and kissed.

A moment ago, he had been thinking only of the flight he was about to make in the Type XV. But that thought was in the past now. Now Reg was here with him, her body coming out to meet his, her softness a cushion for his sudden tension, her lips parting to allow the questing of his tongue, her scent rushing through his veins. A new future had been made. A future of sensuality and pleasure. And it was towards that that his being hurtled now.

The parasol clattered to the floor. Both her hands were on him now, pulling him even closer, as if merely touching were not enough, would never be enough.

But then she pulled away from him and tilted back her head, gulping in a deep draft of air. 'Darling! Someone might see.'

'What do we care?'

She looked nervously behind her, into the observation lounge. Portman suspected that although she affected otherwise, she cared really quite a lot. At heart, she was nothing more than a petite bourgeoise – for all her radical sentiments, which she claimed to have inherited from her firebrand father.

Portman wondered if he had tired of her in that very moment. Was it possible that one could attribute to such minuscule, seemingly trivial incidents, the catastrophic swings of the pendulum of human emotion?

She turned from him to retrieve her parasol. He studied her stooped form with a detachment that almost chilled him.

Certainly he believed he had gained an insight into something at that moment. He saw clearly that a political position – he was thinking of a left-leaning one – may easily be nothing more than sentimental posturing. Was it all fake then, the whole cause? And what of her father, Oscar Villiers, one of the founders of the movement? The aristocrat who had given up his title for the sake of his socialist principles. Was all that just a pose too? After all, Villiers disapproved heartily of his daughter's affair with Portman. When it came to sexual morality, Oscar Villiers was as conservative as any of the stolid shopkeepers who had sat on the district council with Portman's father, the town pharmacist.

And was it some kind of joke that the great republican socialist had given his daughter the most regal of names? Or was that how he saw himself, as the father of a future Queen? Perhaps he didn't object to the institution of monarchy at all, merely to the accident of birth that had precluded him from being King.

Reg turned back to face Portman with a conciliatory smile. A promise of delights to come. Her eyes sparkled. *Tonight!*

Could he wait that long? He wanted the future, whatever future it was, now.

Theirs was an affair across the class divide. He wondered if that was the only attraction in Reg Villiers for him. And if he offered a similar but opposite attraction to her. He was a social-climber in the bedroom. She was a posh girl slumming it.

The thought made him grin at her. And she inevitably misinterpreted his grin.

He was her bit of rough. Oh, a well-educated, prodigiously clever, really quite famous bit of rough. But with his Black Country accent and chippy swagger, he still was and always would be a bit of rough to her.

Or maybe it was even worse than that. It was all about her father, the great Oscar Villiers. Somehow they were both testing the old man. With their affair they were saying to him: do you really believe in that socialist rot? Very well, how do you like it when your daughter takes a grammar school upstart to her bed?

The truth was, he didn't like it one bit.

Reg sealed her promise with a peck on the cheek. With it, she reminded him of her scent. And with the press of her body against him, of her softest flesh. Oh, what did it matter? What did any of it matter?

Was the only valid stance utter selfishness? Sometimes Portman believed he could swing to the political polar opposite without compunction. He felt himself to be a pendulum in everything. Perhaps that was because he feared his true nature, which he suspected to be that of an unconscionable cad, or worse, an uppity shopkeeper's son.

But again, what did it matter? What did any of it matter? All that mattered was the ineluctable flight into the future.

The door to the balcony opened again and Gus from the flying school poked his head out. 'Mr Portman, the Type XV is ready for you.'

'I'm on my way.'

Behind his head, the Gnome eighty horsepower rotary engine snarled and rattled as it shredded the air. It was a 'pusher' engine, placed to push the craft ahead of it, rather than draw it in its wake. It was like having a tethered beast squatting at your back, one that was capable of far more savagery than any creature of nature.

The Grahame-White Type XV aircraft resembled an oversized box-kite in appearance, or perhaps several box-kites tacked together. It shivered and bobbed on the spot, as if the energy of the engine would shake it apart before there was any chance to become airborne.

The Type XV was a two-seater. Portman occupied the front seat of the open nacelle. Claude Grahame-White himself – by his own account, the greatest aviator of his age – was in the instructor's seat behind. The great man eschewed aviator's helmet and goggles, preferring to fly in his trademark cloth flat cap, broad as a plate.

The din of the engine made any verbal communication between the two men practically impossible. Portman felt Grahame-White's hand on his shoulder, his signal to open the throttle and start the takeoff run.

It was always a thrilling moment. More than thrilling. There was dread and power and elation, and a nameless sense of being on the cusp of something. His heart would fall into exact synch with the revolutions of the rotary engine. And his bones would vibrate at the frequency of dissolution.

Even stationary, the craft had within it the potential for flight. It looked so flimsy and light that you felt the lightest gust would lift it off the ground. Add forward motion, and you immediately felt the uplift whip into the wings as the crisscross of wires between the stanchions snapped taut.

There was no going back. No room for prevarication. Something bigger, stronger than mere human will had gripped the craft. It was out of Portman's hands. Not that he wanted to back out. Not that he wanted anything other than this headlong lurch into the future.

The craft bounced and rocked as it traversed the ground. He felt every bump and rut of the runway. Then, for a split second, the course was unbelievably smooth, as the aircraft skipped excitedly, skittishly, but prematurely. It felt like the whole world was holding its breath. Before the shuddering thump of coming back down to earth.

He kept up the acceleration. The engine's snarl was angry and impatient now.

Soon, soon now . . .

And there it was. The leap. The leap that stretched into ascent. The very sky took hold of him and pulled him to it.

His goggles protected his eyes from the raw whip of the wind, which he felt across his cheeks and in his quivering moustaches. Even so, his eyes filled with tears.

It was a paradox he could not fathom. At the very moment that he rose to meet the future, the past he sought so desperately to escape came grabbing at him, like a surge of gravity threatening to nosedive the aircraft.

He was thinking of the boy. He would have been seventeen now. He had kept track of every birthday. He was thinking how splendid it would be to take the boy up in an aircraft. If only he had lived.

And now he was thankful for the relentless clatter of the Gnome engine, drowning out the sobs that he howled into the oncoming blast.

The engine had settled into a deep, contented thrum, the tethered beast grown companionable. The wires were in full voice now, singing their eerie high-pitched hymn to flight. The unruly emotion that had wracked Portman at takeoff had receded. He settled back into that sense of untethered freedom known only to aviators and possibly birds. His heart still raced a little. He could never be entirely calm piloting an aircraft.

He was in his element.

Portman held a steady course at around 5,000 feet. Having turned after making his ascent, he was flying east now. A mild southerly wind blew across him. He felt it as a contrary will driving the aircraft in its own direction. But Portman, like any human aviator, was cleverer than the wind, even if he wasn't stronger. He knew how to trick it into blowing him exactly where he wanted to be.

He had leisure now to look down at the countryside below. The way the fields locked together looked to him like the scales of a monstrous reptile. Clusters of dots twitched and teemed like parasites over them, sheep moving in their placid, mindless career of gorging.

He despised nostalgia, that sense of merry England that certain writers of his generation seemed to espouse. If the human race was to survive, the future had to be organized along entirely different lines, rational, unsentimental, efficient. There must be a move away from the pastoral to the industrial. The patterns of land-holding of the past were no longer relevant. He did not know with what they would be replaced; he was not an agricultural scientist. But if it was with vast, scientifically regulated factory farms, run by technicians and land economists, then so be it. It was to such men that they must look for a vision of the future countryside. Not to the poets and painters of bygone ages. And certainly not to the gentlemen farmers.

And yet, at the same time: the way the sunlight burnished the land, turning each blade of grass into a tiny green flame, the silent stealthy spread of incandescence across field after field, as effortless and wondrous as a miracle; all this caught at his heart and dared him not to celebrate. Even with the detachment afforded by elevation, from which he looked down on the realm of the earth-bound with godlike omniscience, he could not but be moved.

It would be a hard comfort to give up, the rural idyll, and it would need eloquent men like him to persuade the lawmakers of the future of its necessity. As well as to soothe a sluggish, sentimental populace into compliance.

They were over Hendon golf course now. Tweed-clad insects paused in their pursuit of an invisible goal to look up at the clattering sky. Portman smiled at their puny bewilderment.

The landscape to the east of the golf course grew markedly more built-up, as the outskirts of north London made their presence felt. Rows of houses sprouted like a crop of unnaturally cuboid mushrooms. A network of straight new roads set at right angles to one another imposed an artificial rigour, infecting the land with shape and purpose.

Then, as quickly as it had appeared, Finchley was behind them. The buildings thinned out, replaced by a hotchpotch of allotments.

The wind was adding a northerly curve to their trajectory east. But Portman knew full well where they were tending.

He checked the gauges, and made a few small adjustments to the altitude and course. Then glanced out over the starboard side of the nacelle.

There it was. A palace set in parkland.

Colney Hatch Lunatic Asylum.

And although it was, in one sense, a symbol of the past, and he, W.G. Portman, was very much the angel of the future, still he never tired of looking down at it. It was a paradox, perhaps. But he lived in an age of paradox. And he was the foremost prophet of that age.

THIRTEEN

The room looked much the same as the last time Quinn had been there, except that now there was no dying man propped up on the camp bed.

A sour and complex smell permeated everything: of unwashed bodies, of seeping wounds and discarded medical dressings, of pill bottles and off milk, of old mite-eaten journals, their pages yellowed and brittle, of stale air and dead houseplants, of mouse droppings and rat poison and rotting vermin.

The camp bed itself was still in evidence. It looked like it had been slept in recently. The impress of a head showed in the lank, sweat-stained pillow. A coarse grey blanket hung limply over one side, the leg of a pair of grubby flannel pyjama trousers peeped out, like a hostage looking to be rescued.

In truth, it was hard to imagine anyone actually sleeping on that narrow, rickety bed. Least of all Malcolm Grant-Sissons. He can't have enjoyed very many good nights' sleep on the bed in which his father – or the man he called his father – had died.

But Quinn guessed this was where he was living. 3, St. John's Passage, Clerkenwell. Quinn had used the house key that Macadam had found among Malcolm's belongings to let himself in.

He did not know for sure that Hugh Grant-Sissons was dead. He had not read any obituary, or seen a death notice in *The Times*. But the man was close enough to death the last time he had seen him to assume the worst.

Nor did he know for certain that he had died in that bed. But it looked like a bed a man had died in. And if that were the case, then what a miserable, stark and comfortless death it must have been.

He had died surrounded by the accumulated junk and clutter of his failed life. Grant-Sissons senior had been an inventor. But he had become convinced that the design of his greatest invention – a shutter mechanism for a moving picture projector

– had been stolen from him, along with all the profits that were
rightfully his.

The idea had come to obsess him. He wallowed in his sense of
grievance for decades, fixating on the success of his enemies,
which came to include the entire motion picture industry. They
were all against him. And they were all to blame.

What he should have done was confound his imagined enemies
by inventing other, even greater contraptions. Instead, he devoted
his energies to a hopeless case. So long as the public had moving
pictures to enjoy, they little cared who had invented what in the
machine that brought those flickering dreams to life. And he was
up against some powerful vested interests. Those who had stolen
his idea had grown rich off it. They could afford the very best
legal representation. Grant-Sissons had been forced to represent
himself. He may have understood the mechanics of motion picture
projection, but he failed to grasp the basics of patent law.

His bitterness poisoned and ultimately destroyed what was left
of his life. It was almost as if the cancer that was racing through
him at the end was the incarnation of that bitterness.

At least, Quinn conjectured, he had not died alone. Malcolm
had surely been there with him. But that was perhaps not as
much a comfort as it ought to have been. The son who was not
a son. The truth of their relationship no longer concealed from
either of them.

All manner of detritus littered the floor, filmed in a thick layer
of grease and dust. There were no curtains at the window; instead,
an old corrugated cardboard box had been splayed and tacked
up. Half-assembled – or half-disassembled – machines lay about
like gutted automata. Smashed bulbs crunched under Quinn's
feet, together with discarded lenses, that must have cost a fortune
to commission. An oilcan sprawled on its side, leaking inconti-
nently from its hummingbird snout. Torn and crumpled sheets
of newspaper, oily rags and scraps of paper on which calculations
and sketches had been furiously jotted down, bore testament to
the anguished disorder of an obsessed mind. Overturned jars
spilled out nuts and bolts and screws and cogs, to be trodden
into the obscurity of an unseen rug, among the desiccated insect
husks and food scraps.

The room resembled nothing so much as a clock that an

inquisitive boy had taken apart without knowing how to put it back together.

But the debris and despondency concealed a truth about the elder Grant-Sissons. His life had been defined by love as much as failure. He had known all along that Malcolm was not his son. And yet he had brought the boy up as his own.

If Louisa had lived, perhaps he might have been able to put his disappointment behind him. Even if she had left him for Quinn's father. Knowing human nature as he did, Quinn had to admit that was unlikely. But who could say what a devastating effect his wife's awful death had had on him, believing as he did that he was at least partially responsible?

She too had died from cancer, which she had contracted as a result of the experiments in X-ray photography to which Quinn's father and Hugh Grant-Sissons had naively subjected her, a willing volunteer.

That knowledge had, it seemed, driven Quinn's own father to kill himself.

As Quinn surveyed the scene, he tried to remember what he was doing there. He felt in his pocket for the second, smaller key that Macadam had found. He scanned the floor, looking for a tin box perhaps, or a small trunk, that it might open.

He moved over to the window and pulled the cardboard down, allowing the full force of the day to stream in. The sudden action stirred a thick cloud of motes and filled Quinn's nostrils with a musty smell that set him sneezing. He felt like he was vandalizing a shrine, or breaking into a sealed tomb beneath a pyramid.

In the sudden light, the full despondency of the room was revealed. This was the wake of something. The wake of a life, slowly collapsing in on itself, into nothing. Other lives would come to claim this space, and one day all trace of it would be gone.

Quinn glanced around, his gaze desperate to latch on to something that would make sense of the various tragedies that had culminated in the disorder before him. He saw a row of photographs on the mantelpiece, neatly arranged, the only bit of order there was. He picked his way over to look at them.

His eye was drawn to a recent studio portrait of Malcolm, in a dark three-piece suit (not the corduroy of Colney Hatch), his hair neatly parted. The young man looked surprised more than anything, as if he could not imagine any possible reason why he should be photographed. But his gaze was shy, too, not quite meeting the viewer in the eye.

Quinn wondered what the occasion had been. Perhaps a birthday. Other photographs showed a baby and various versions of the same boy, growing gradually older in each portrait. As well as the simple changes wrought by ageing, there was something else visible in the progression of images. Something seemed to go out of the boy as he grew older. A light in his eyes died. And Quinn realized that the quality he had thought was shyness in the first photograph was more likely to be unhappiness. Was it something to do with his mother's death, or perhaps with his learning the truth about the horror of it?

There was no photograph of Hugh Grant-Sissons on display, as if his enmity with the moving picture industry had led him to boycott having his image recorded in any form whatsoever. But there was one picture of a young woman. She was strikingly beautiful. Dark haired and pale skinned, and delicately featured. He felt he understood his father's infidelity a little more now. Not just because of her physical beauty. But because there was something complex, challenging and restless in her eyes. Something you wanted to get to the bottom of.

She was smiling. But her smile was wistful, as if she had an inkling of the unhappiness she would cause, and the pain that she would suffer. He had the feeling that her affair with Quinn's father had already begun when the photograph was taken.

He picked up the photograph and unfastened the frame, taking out the print and pocketing it. Then he did the same with the most recent photograph of Malcolm.

Next he went over to the camp bed and knelt down. After years in the force, he had learnt never to rule out the obvious. He was looking for anything valuable or important to Malcolm. It was likely that he would keep such an item close to him when he slept.

The first thing he saw was a book, partially pushed underneath the bed. He pulled it out. It was the overdue library book, *A Furious Energy* by W.G. Portman. It was bound in a green cloth cover with gold lettering and a debossed illustration of two stylized lightning bolts, one gold, one black. That is to say, one the shadow of the other. Quinn held it for a moment, as if he could know his half-brother better simply by feeling the heft of the last book he was reading. He turned the book over to examine the back cover. The double lightning bolt was repeated as a decorative motif in the corners and centre.

He opened the book to the frontispiece, which showed an engraving of the author, gazing with a visionary gleam into the distance. If the illustration was anything to go by, he was a handsome enough individual, something of a ladies' man no doubt, especially with those profusely masculine moustaches. There was a confidence to his expression, an urgency of purpose, but also a kind of haunted humanity. It was an attractive combination, Quinn didn't doubt.

He turned the page to a list of W.G. Portman's other titles:
THE DISTANT MOONS
THE LAST MORTAL
A GODLIKE NOTION
MR HARTLE'S DOPPELGÄNGER
WORLDS WITHIN WORLDS
INFINITY'S PLAYTHING
AGENTS OF PARADOX
THE VISITORS
THE BLOOD PLANET

As a youth, Quinn had enjoyed the stories of Jules Verne. He understood the appeal of fantastical adventures in imaginary worlds. When the difficulties of the real world threaten to overwhelm you, such fiction offers a welcome escape. But what had he been trying to escape from back then? Naturally, he had known nothing about his father's affair with Louisa Grant-Sissons. But he had been aware of his father's long absences. And he had grown sensitive to his mother's moods, her cold, silent anger, and her nurtured bitterness. All the reproaches that she should have cast at her husband, she converted into a constant griping dissatisfaction with her son. Nothing he did could ever please her, so he gave up trying.

So was this taste for astounding tales – which Quinn had not indulged for a long time, not since his father's death – something that he shared with Malcolm?

Quinn settled back on to his haunches and began to read the book.

CHAPTER 1. SOMETHING IN THE AIR.

Peter Pilling could still remember the day that electricity came to Godalming. He was only three years old at the time. But even at that tender age, he knew that the world would never be the same again.

He was allowed to stay up late to see the Great Switching On. One by one the lamps on the High Street buzzed and flickered into life, to a chorus of gasps and rapturous applause from the watching crowds. Little Peter and his older brother Michael slipped away from their distracted parents to chase one another up and down the street, weaving between the lamps and shouting, 'Trick, trick, electric trick!' at the top of their lungs.

Their mother, as soon as she noticed them missing, was filled with alarm, especially when she realized their game. She feared that, if they ventured too close to the streetlights, sparks of the mysterious new power would leap out and electrify them, possibly to death. And so with one hand on her bonnet, and the other hitching up her skirts, she gave pursuit.

Picturing the scene many years later in his imagination (for that is what memory is, the recasting of a tale we are told into something we imagine actually happened), Peter came to see it as epitomizing a moment in history. For his Victorian mother, the new source of energy was a thing of danger and fear. For Peter and his brother, who were children of the future, it was a thing of joy, a cause for celebration and dancing. Despite the wording of their chant, they did not consider it a trick. That was purely a childish jingle, prompted by simple verbal coincidence. No, to them, this was magic, pure magic.

And indisputably a force for good.

Why the Fates had picked Godalming to be the first place in the world to receive a public electricity supply, Peter Pilling could not say. But as a resident of Godalming, he was grateful to those antic sisters for the signal honour they conferred upon his home town . . .

Quinn gave a deep sigh of regret as he closed the book and laid it to one side.

He cleared a space and stretched out, trusting to his ulster to act as a protective layer between his person and the indeterminate seediness of the floor. The smells that he had noticed when he first came in grew stronger the closer he got to the boards, as if the misery of Hugh Grant-Sissons' life, and death, had sunk and settled at the lowest point of the room.

His hand reached out and touched something metallic. A moment later he retrieved a cashier's box from under the camp bed.

The key fitted. The lid sprang open.

The box contained a bundle of letters wrapped in a pale blue ribbon.

He did not need to take them out to know who they were from, and to whom they were addressed.

Quinn sat up and covered his face with his hands.

In the same instant he felt his palms grow wet as a surge of emotion shook him.

FOURTEEN

As a copper, Macadam had interviewed all sorts. Toffs and low-lifes, artist types and stockbrokers, hard-working labourers and bone-idle drunkards, penniless writers and millionaire businessmen. But he'd never interviewed anyone like these socialists.

Adam Manley Adams lived with his wife and sister in a four-storey house in Fitzroy Square. Macadam supposed there was a bob or two to be made in this socialist lark. He was admitted by a maid. His professional glance took in the quality and expense of the furnishings and decorations. The oil paintings on the walls would not have been out of place at the National Gallery, if he was any judge.

Manley Adams' name came up repeatedly in all the articles he had read about the Fellowship of the Gracchi. He was one of the co-founders, along with Oscar Villiers. Both men had inherited fortunes, and in the case of Villiers, a title too. Until ten years ago, Villiers had been the Fourth Viscount Penryn.

Macadam had to admit that the aristocratic name and origins of the other man, even if he had given up his title, had put him off talking to him. Once a nob always a nob, was his view. And he knew how these upper-class types liked to look down their noses at a chap.

On the other hand, Manley Adams sounded like the sort of fellow you could get a straight answer from.

Macadam was shown into a drawing room and invited to wait for the Master who would be along presently.

Before too long, the door opened and a woman of middle years came in. She possessed that confidence that came from being born into money. She radiated command. It was her birth-right. And yet Macadam felt that she would find it very interesting – because it would be novel – to have anyone stand up to her. It seemed likely that she had once been beautiful but that this had never mattered to her. Perhaps she had not even noticed.

So, he thought. *This is a socialist.*

'Are you the policeman?'

'That's right, ma'am. And you are . . .?'

'That need not concern you.'

'Oh, but I am very much afraid that it does concern me. I like to know to whom I am speaking, you see.'

'How very extraordinary. Have you come to arrest my brother?'

'Is your brother Mr Manley Adams?'

'Of course.'

Then that would make her Cordelia Manley Adams, Macadam knew from his research. 'Is there some reason why I should?'

'He is the most frightful pacifist.'

'I see. It is on account of that that I have come to speak to him. But I know of no reason why I should arrest him.'

'Is it not against the law to be a pacifist?'

'There is no specific offence of pacifism. But if one's pacifism causes one to break the law, for example to obstruct the course of justice, or vandalize the Houses of Parliament, then one may well find oneself on the wrong side of a cell door.'

'I like you.'

Macadam bowed.

At that moment, a dark-haired man with an equally dark beard entered. Behind his silver wire-framed spectacles, his expression appeared preoccupied to the point of distraction. When he saw Cordelia already there, he rolled his eyes.

'Don't pay any attention to my sister. She's mad.' The man held out his hand to Macadam. 'Adam Manley Adams, what's this all about?'

A much younger woman with fine fair hair tied up at the back and a wistful expression followed him into the room. She flashed a shy look at Cordelia and blushed.

'Oh,' said Manley Adams, becoming distracted again. 'This is my wife, Bella.'

'No, no, she's my wife,' corrected Cordelia. 'We're all adults here, there's no need for all this pretending.'

'She can't be your wife!' Manley Adams' voice rose to a near scream. 'You're a woman! She's a woman and you're a woman! And besides, she's married to me! You were at the ceremony, I believe.' Turning to Macadam, he added: 'I told you she was mad.'

'I'll tell you what's mad!' Now it was Cordelia's turn to scream. 'Mad is printing leaflets calling on this country to abandon its national defences and surrender abjectly to a foreign power!'

Macadam thought that perhaps this was his moment. 'Ah, yes. It's about those leaflets that I wished to speak to you.' He produced the piece of paper that was found in the clothes of the first suicide. 'Is this one of yours?'

'I knew it!' cried Cordelia delightedly. 'They're going to take you away!' She turned to the other woman. 'We can be together at last, Bella.'

'But I don't want him to go to jail!' cried Bella.

'What do you want?' demanded Manley Adams, ignoring the leaflet Macadam had given him. Perhaps sensing that he was upsetting his wife, he softened his tone. 'That's what you need to decide, Bella dearest. At the moment, it seems that you want . . .' He threw up his hands in exasperation. 'Well, I don't know what you want!'

'I want both of you,' said Bella simply. And the way that she said it, even Macadam had to admit it sounded quite reasonable.

'May I suggest,' Macadam interjected, 'that you settle this issue at some other time?'

All three of them turned to him with a look of surprise, as if they had forgotten he was there.

A pensive frown settled across Manley Adams' brows, defining itself into a look of cunning. 'Is it legal? What they do?'

'I don't know what they do. And I don't want to know. It's not about that that I have come.'

'Despicable!' cried Cordelia. 'You would have your own sister and wife arrested!'

'Not her. She's innocent in this. You've corrupted her.'

'Oh, you fool. No one has corrupted anyone. What we have done is express our love for each other. It's a beautiful, natural, physical expression of love!'

'There's nothing natural about it at all. You're my sister. She's my wife. It makes my skin crawl.'

'Then go, leave. Absent yourself, far from this ménage.'

'This is my house!'

'Daddy left it to both of us.'

Macadam cleared his throat. 'If I may. The leaflet, sir. Do you recognize it as one of yours, that is to say, is it one you have caused to have printed and distributed?'

'Yes, of course. What of it?'

'It was found in the pockets of a gentleman who died at London Zoo. You may have read about it in the newspapers. He was mauled by a bear. A polar bear,' added Macadam to clarify, as if men were getting mauled by all sorts of bears all the time.

'The naked one?'

'That's right.'

'But I don't see what that has to do with us. Anyone might get hold of one of these leaflets. We give them out all the time, all over the place.'

'So far, we have not been able to identify the gentleman. We are looking into any lead whatsoever. We thought he might be a member of your organization. The Fellowship of the Gracchi, I believe it's called.'

'It's possible, I suppose. Our membership runs to several thousands and includes people from all walks of life.'

'It would help us greatly if you could provide me with a list of members.'

'Out of the question. I cannot aid the forces of oppression in the persecution of our members.'

'It is simply that we wish to inform his next of kin. No one has come forward. It is a terrible tragedy.'

'I see what's going on here. This is a fig leaf for oppression. There's nothing to link this naked man to us at all. How do I even know you found this leaflet on him? Where did he put it? Up his anus?'

Macadam thought there was no need for that. 'His clothes were found near the scene of his demise.'

'Demise!' cried Cordelia appreciatively. 'Did you hear that? So like a policeman.'

'Well, I don't care. You're not having our members. That would be a betrayal of the first order. Good day.'

Macadam produced a monochrome photograph of one the cards printed with the red hand. 'Have you ever seen a card like this before? The hand on the original card is printed in red.'

'No.'

The two women also shook their heads.

'Does the symbol of the red hand mean anything to you?'

'No. It's not our kind of thing. A bloody hand? Hardly appropriate for a pacifist organization.'

Macadam showed them a second photograph, of the reverse of the card. 'And what of these letters? F.J.S.U?'

'Haven't got a clue, old bean.' It seemed to satisfy Manley Adams that he was unable to help.

'One last thing,' said Macadam, pocketing the photographs. 'And then I'll be on my way. Do you have among your members a gentleman by the name of Malcolm Grant-Sissons?'

'What do you take me for, some kind of fool? I wouldn't tell you if we did!'

'But if you *didn't* . . . perhaps you could see your way to telling me that?'

Manley Adams thought about it for a moment and sighed. 'Well, if it will get rid of you. No, I've never heard that name before. What was it you said? Malcolm?'

'Grant-Sissons.'

'No. He's not one of our members. Now, will that be all?'

Macadam placed one of his cards on a table. 'If anything should come to mind, I'll just leave this here.'

He gave Cordelia Manley Adams a sympathetic smile on the way out.

Macadam drove the Model T over to Bedford Square, where Oscar Villiers lived, in an even grander house than the Manley Adams'.

An ageing butler informed him that his Lordship was not at home. Either he had never been informed of his master's abdication of his title, or simply refused to accept it.

Macadam wondered if Adam Manley Adams had telephoned ahead to warn Villiers. He wouldn't put it past these socialists to use telephones. After this morning's shenanigans, he wouldn't put anything past them.

FIFTEEN

As the motor taxi approached Bankside, the air grew progressively murkier, thick with the filthy smog that the power station's eighteen massive chimneys spewed out. Quinn could taste the grit in each breath.

The taxi pulled up in the vast shadow of a long shed-like building, black with its own grime. Every brick and detail of the structure was swallowed up in a layer of obscurity. It seemed that if a man stood still for long enough in this neighbourhood, he would turn into a pillar of soot. It was a factory for generating darkness as well as electricity.

As Quinn stepped out, he felt the ground vibrate. He was aware of an increase in pressure between his ears, and he sensed rather than heard a low humming all around him. It seemed to be borne in the smog that filled the air. He looked up, in the hope of seeing at least a patch of the clear blue sky that he knew was up there. A flat grey cloud filled the space between the power station roof and the adjacent buildings.

Quinn had put the Portman novel inside the cashier's box with his father's letters to Louisa Grant-Sissons. He felt the weight of this burden in his hand as he mounted the steps to the entrance. The vibrations that he had noticed a moment before intensified with each step he took.

A man in a company uniform sat behind a counter inside the bland, marble-tiled foyer. Quinn showed his warrant card, which the man took his time examining.

'How may I help you?'

'It's concerning the accident that took place last night. I'd like to see where it happened.'

'We've had the police here already.'

'I'm sure you have. But I am different police.'

'I'll have to check with my guv'nor.'

'You do that.'

The counter was equipped with a telephone. The man kept his eyes fixed on Quinn as he made the necessary call.

'Mr Kibblewhite will be along presently.'

'I really don't want to trouble anyone. If you just point me in the right direction.'

'We can't allow that. Especially not after what happened to that . . . person.'

'I'm hardly likely to throw myself at a dynamo.'

The man's expression seemed to suggest that he wouldn't be so sure about that.

'At any rate,' began Quinn innocuously, 'it's good to see that you're being more careful now.'

'I beg your pardon?'

'Though it does strike me a little as closing the stable door after the horse has bolted.'

The Company man was affronted by Quinn's insinuation. 'He *snuck* in!'

'Or to look at it another way, someone negligently allowed a potentially dangerous intruder on to Company premises. It's perhaps fortunate that the poor wretch was only, as it seems, bent on his own destruction, and was not a saboteur intending to wreak more wide-scale havoc. I dare say what happened was inconvenient enough, but a bomb blast would have been catastrophic.'

'No one could foresee . . .'

'Of course, should he die, there may be criminal charges brought. Culpable negligence. Manslaughter.' Quinn's needling of the man was to a large degree instinctive. It was a basic inter-rogation technique, to hang the threat of prosecution over a witness so that you could withdraw it in return for cooperation. But Quinn had to admit that there was very little pertinent to the investigation that he could hope to get from this man.

'I wasn't here last night!'

The truth was, it made him feel better. It helped him focus all the obscure emotions that had troubled him ever since he saw that it was Malcolm Grant-Sissons in the hospital bed. They came together into a simple anger. It surprised him now to learn how deeply felt and genuine it was. And it reached a climax when he expressed the possibility of Malcolm dying.

Quinn suddenly knew that he was a hair's breadth away from screaming at the man.

Fortunately, at that point, another man appeared through a door behind the reception counter. This one was wearing a swallow-tailed suit and tortoiseshell glasses, with precision-parted hair but an unruly black beard. He looked like a curious combination of a maître d' and a theoretical physicist.

He approached Quinn with hand held out and fluttering eyelids, as if he was trying to bat away any suggestion of scandal. Quinn had the impression that he had been standing behind that door for some time, trying to soothe his features into this expression of rehearsed insouciance.

'I am Kibblewhite. General Manager of the City of London Electric Lighting Company Limited Bankside Alternate and Direct Current Generating Station.' It was as if he was bolstering himself up with terminology, stoking his importance with every word he could add to the description of his realm. It was a warning, as well as a buttress. 'I hear you wish to see the site where the unfortunate gentleman met with his accident?'

Kibblewhite stopped blinking but he did not meet Quinn's gaze. Quinn couldn't blame him. He must be feeling the heat. There could be no worse customers to let down than the printing presses of Fleet Street.

Quinn nodded and allowed Kibblewhite to lead the way, back through the door from which he had emerged.

The room he entered was a vast hall, which appeared to extend to the full height, and almost the full length, of the building. Particles of coal dust swirled in the air, shrouding the scene in a shifting black veil. Open carts tipped coal into massive bunkers, from which men with shovels fed the banks of furnaces that lined the hall. Such was the heat that some of the workmen had removed their jackets and worked in shirt sleeves and waistcoats, though they kept their bowler hats on, together with their collars and ties.

Above the furnaces, the boiler cylinders bulged, like monstrous bellies that could never be sated.

Gargantuan pipes, some as wide as three feet in diameter, veined the walls, with lesser pipes threaded in between. A maze of ladders and platforms giving access to the red-painted wheel valves gave the impression of a giant game of snakes and ladders.

The hum that Quinn had sensed earlier was now distinctly audible. It was overlaid with the general clatter and thrum of industry. He had to shout to make his voice carry to Kibblewhite. 'Do you have many accidents here?'

Kibblewhite smiled blandly and shook his head. If he resented the question, he was determined not to show it. 'Our safety record is second to none!'

'No accidents then, until last night?'

'Very few. The men are well trained.'

'But he was not one of your men. He was an outsider.'

'That's true.'

'I am surprised he was able to gain access to the plant.'

'We are looking into what happened.'

'So nothing like this has ever happened before?'

'No. Nothing like this. Once . . .' But the resounding clang of an emptied coal cart gave Kibblewhite pause. He thought better of whatever he was about to say.

Quinn could feel the ever-present vibration of the floor in his calves and in the muscles of his face. 'Doesn't it get on your nerves?'

'What?'

'The vibrating.'

'You get used to it. In fact, it is more that you miss it when you leave the station. It's like a sailor's sea legs.'

Quinn nodded. 'You were going to say? Once? Another accident?'

'It was nothing like this. But once a boy fell into the river and was drawn into one of our suction pipes. He ended up in a sealed vacuum chamber, not before being pulled a hundred and fifty feet through a double bend.'

'Good God.'

'The miracle is, he survived.'

'Do you think the man who did this will survive?'

'He is not dead yet?'

'No.'

Kibblewhite raised his eyebrows. 'I am surprised. But glad.'

Kibblewhite led Quinn through another door, into a smaller

room, which was filled with rows of engine-like machines spinning and shaking at tremendous speed. Here, the hum was an intense, almost unbearable throbbing din. The vibrations spread throughout his whole body, which felt as if it was about to be shaken apart.

Kibblewhite indicated a metal gantry against one wall. 'He climbed up there,' he shouted.

Quinn pointed upwards questioningly, and Kibblewhite nodded consent. 'Don't take the chain off,' he warned.

'Chain?'

'Across the top.'

'Was it on last night?'

Kibblewhite nodded. 'Always. Unless one of the engineers is working up there.'

Quinn gripped the handrail and stepped on to the ladder of the gantry. He had found the source of the hum. He felt it transmitted through the bones of his arms and legs, taking him over entirely, like a possessing demon.

As he reached the platform of the gantry, his legs turned to jelly. Perhaps Malcolm hadn't intended to jump. He had simply lost his balance and fallen. But as Quinn looked down at the wrought-iron lattice beneath his feet, he remembered that Malcolm had taken off his clothes. Quinn saw the protective chain stretched across the yawning gap at the front of the platform. If what Kibblewhite had said was true, Malcolm must have unhitched the chain, which indicated intent.

Quinn peered down over the edge of the gantry platform. Directly below he could see sparks fly from the moving parts of the spinning dynamo.

It was a strangely enticing vision. There was something so enviably perfect about the smooth, relentless motion of the dynamo. The evanescent beauty of the sparks both teased and comforted. It was like a dance of fairies.

A shout of 'No! Stop!' broke the enchantment. He looked down in annoyance at Kibblewhite. Then saw his own hand on the chain and snatched it away, as if the links had grown suddenly white hot.

SIXTEEN

Sunlight filled the Special Crimes Department. The weather had been changeable these last few days. One day, cold and wet; the next, like an oven in the attic room. Today was an oven day. As well as the sun beating down on them through the roof, they were warmed from below by the heat rising from the rest of the building.

Inchball pulled at his collar. He was a big man and it didn't take much for his body to overheat. He hated being cooped up behind a desk at the best of times, but today he felt like a lobster in a slowly boiling pot. He had tried opening the windows, but a high breeze had played havoc with their papers. 'Where is he then?'

Macadam looked up quizzically from the brown corduroy jacket he had spread out on his desk.

'The guv'nor,' said Inchball.

Macadam shrugged.

'What's his game?'

'He's pursuing a line of enquiry.'

'What line of enquiry?'

'Something to do with his brother, I think.'

'That's fishy, ain't it? This one being his brother. What do you make of that?'

'It's . . .' But it seemed Macadam was unable to say what he made of it.

'I tell you what I make of it. It's fishy. That's what I make of it.'

'So you said.'

'You don't think so?'

'These things happen.'

'These things happen! Three geezers stripping off and killing themselves – or trying to. I ain't seen nothing like this happen before.'

'I meant connections between investigating officers and those involved in cases. And besides, it's not as if Inspector Quinn is particularly close to his brother. He did not even know he existed until recently, or so I believe.'

'Yeah, so we believe. I mean, we only have his word on that, don't we?'

'I see no reason to doubt him.'

'I do.'

'You do?'

'I do.'

'What reason?'

'It's right in front of your nose.'

Macadam looked down. 'This jacket?'

'The suits, yes. The three identical suits. Which he says is nothing that need concern us.'

'I must admit, it is a little peculiar. He did seem to be most interested in the suits, and then suddenly he decided they were no longer pertinent.'

'And when did he change his mind, do you remember?'

Macadam answered Inchball's question only with a confirm-atory nod.

'That's right, after he clapped eyes on that Grant-Sissons fellow in the hospital. After he realized that one of the men mixed up in this was a relative of his.'

'You think the suits are important then, after all.'

'Of course they blinkin' are! It's obvious, ain't it?'

'Well, yes, we agreed that, I think. They could be the uniform of an irregular paramilitary unit.'

'That don't make no sense.'

'You don't think so?'

'Nah! What kind of army has its soldiers strip off before they top themselves? Nah, there's only one type of person who goes in for that kind of applesauce.'

'And that is?'

'Loonies!'

'Loonies?'

'That's right. Certifiable lunatics. That's what we're dealing with here.'

'And the suits?'

'You ever been in a loony bin?'

'No, I can't say that I have.'

'Well, I have. When I was a PC. There was this fella. Went completely doolally, he did. His family were at their wits' end. He was terrorizing the whole neighbourhood. In the end, they had no choice. They had to have him certified. I was the accompanying officer at his admission. Took him to Hanwell we did. And the loonies there, the ones I saw at any rate, the men all wore brown suits.'

'Like these? Why didn't you say so?'

'Keep your hair on! They weren't exactly the same. The ones I saw were tweed. Not corduroy. But it's the same principle.'

Macadam fell into a thoughtful reverie.

Inchball couldn't resist a joke. 'You're in a brown study!'

Macadam gave no indication of having heard it. 'But still, why did you not say something before?'

'I was waiting for the guv'nor to say something.'

'How would he know if he hasn't been inside an asylum, as you have?'

'Well, maybe he has. There are plenty of coppers as have. It seemed to me he had a pretty good idea what the suits signified. Only . . . he didn't want to say as much.'

'Why would he not?'

'Well, his brother!'

'Half-brother,' corrected Macadam.

'It's all the same, ain't it? Same father. Same blood. Same mad blood.'

'Inchball!'

'I'm not saying that. But I reckon that was what he was thinking.'

Macadam fell silent again. After a long, pensive moment, he wondered: 'What do we do?'

'What do we do? We do what we always do. We do what we're told. We're good boys, ain't we?' But he gave a wink that went some way to belying his claim.

Before they could discuss the matter further, the door to the office opened and Inspector Quinn came in. He was carrying in one hand a tin cashier's box, which he placed on his desk before taking off his ulster and bowler hat, which he persisted in wearing despite the warm weather. Inchball couldn't help noticing that the overcoat seemed even grubbier than the last time he had seen it.

'What you got there?' Inchball nodded at the box.

'I found it at Malcolm Grant-Sissons' residence.'

'Ah, so that's where you were,' said Inchball pointedly.

'I'm sure I told you that was where I was going.'

Both sergeants shook their heads.

'Anything interesting in it?' demanded Inchball.

Quinn thought for a moment before replying. 'Yes. The overdue library book.'

Macadam sat up excitedly. 'Ooh, the latest W.G. Portman novel? Splendid! I'll read it for you if you like.'

'No, thank you. I can read it myself.'

Inchball waited for Macadam's disconsolate face to turn towards him, before treating him to a provocative leer.

'Sir, may I at least see it?'

Inspector Quinn unlocked the box with the small key that Macadam had found in Malcolm Grant-Sissons' pockets. He took out the book and held it over his desk.

'Do you think it's significant?' asked Macadam as he rose to take a closer look at the book. In his eagerness, he banged his head on the sloping ceiling.

'People read books. All kinds of books,' came Quinn's illuminating answer.

There's no doubt about it, thought Inchball. *The guv'nor's in one hell of a mood.*

Quinn thought about the story Kibblewhite had told him, of the boy sucked into the induction pipe at Bankside. He rose from his seat and crossed with stooped head to Macadam's desk. 'I hope you're not getting these suits muddled up.'

Macadam looked up from the Portman book. 'No, sir. Of course not. I am most meticulous.'

'Which are the second man's clothes? Suicide Bridge.'

Macadam put both hands on the side of the middle box in front of him. Quinn took it and carried it over to his own desk.

As he took out the jacket, he felt Inchball watching him closely. 'What is it?'

'So you think the suits are significant, after all?'

Quinn was not inclined to answer. Indeed, he could not think of an answer that would satisfy Inchball that he was prepared to give. At last, he said, 'We must look into everything very closely.'

True to his word, Quinn methodically probed every pocket with his fingers. He found what he was looking for in the inside breast pocket: a hole through to the lining. He held the jacket by the collar and shook it down, then felt along the bottom hem. There it was. A small rectangle of something resistant, about the size of a cigarette card.

He teased the shape up to the hole in the pocket and worked it out, brandishing by the edges a third card printed with a crude illustration of a red hand. Turning it over, he read F.J.S.U. Seven. 'It's time, I think, that we should have these cards examined for fingerprints.'

'I'll see to it, sir,' said Macadam, rising eagerly. He gave Inchball a pointed nod, the meaning of which Quinn could not decipher. But from the buoyancy of Macadam's step and the enthusiasm of his tone, Quinn guessed that the discovery of the card had gone some way to restoring him to the position he had formerly occupied in his sergeant's estimation.

He heard Inchball mumble something about needles and haystacks.

That evening Quinn chose to eat alone at the Lyons teashop on Parliament Street, the nearest one to the Yard. He was in no hurry to return to his lodgings, at least not until he could be sure of making it up to his room without encountering any of the other occupants. The couple who had taken over Miss Dillard's room unsettled him. He had not seen them yet, but he had heard their laughter.

Quinn had no hankering for the company of his colleagues either, which was why he was avoiding the canteen, and why he chose a teashop over any of the local public houses, where coppers were more likely to be found. Any police officers who came here were undoubtedly loners like him.

He liked the food at Lyons teashops. It wasn't imaginative, but it was consistent. And it tasted of what it needed to. The mutton pie was meaty and salty and solid and satisfying. So although he often went into the place with the intention of trying something new, he invariably reverted to mutton pie at the moment of ordering. Tonight, as a concession to the warmer weather that seemed to be on the way, he had also ordered a Russian salad and some lettuce hearts.

He welcomed the transience and anonymity of the place, although he suspected that the waitresses recognized him as a regular. Sometimes he had the sense that they had already written his order down before he had given it. But no matter how many times he ate here, he steadfastly refused to look them in the eye.

He had with him the tin cashier's box he had found at Malcolm's house.

Quinn sipped from his teacup and pretended to be staring dreamily into space. In truth, he was carefully scoping out the room. It was not inconceivable that he was being watched, whether by the idly curious, the professionally jealous or the covertly hostile. Maybe some newspaperman who was on the lookout for the next Quick-Fire Quinn story. Or one of those grey men of the shadows of dubious loyalty and obscure purpose who made it their business to know what the department was up to.

You could never be too careful.

The likeliest suspect would be the least likely looking. The blatantly theatrical gentleman in the silk coolie jacket poring over *The Stage*. The Norland nanny pouring tea for her two young charges. The elderly couple with nothing left to say to one another, chewing their teacakes like cattle chewing the cud.

Quinn had chosen a corner table at the back of the room. He sat with his back to the wall, with the whole of the floor in view.

He took out the small key and opened the tin, lifting the lid so that it partially obscured the contents from any onlooker.

A scent of something was released with the opening. Of dust, of paper brittled by age, of sadness and tears, and most faintly of all, of lavender, as if the letters had been kept for decades locked in a drawer next to the potpourri. Which in all likelihood they had.

Quinn sat for a long time staring down at the bundle of letters. It was as if he feared them, in the same way that another man might fear a scorpion. Instinctively, viscerally, for reasons of self-preservation.

Did he really dare to do it? To read the love letters that his father had written to another man's wife? It felt as though he would be breaking a fundamental taboo. And yet, of all the mysteries that he had been called upon to investigate in his career, his father remained the most unfathomable. Here at last before him on the pristine white table cloth was, possibly, the solution to that enigma.

He picked the bundle up by one end of the ribbon that tied it and teased it out of the tin.

Laying the bundle on the table before him, he pulled now at both ends of the ribbon. Released from their confinement, the pile of letters crackled gently as they expanded. Quinn even imagined he could hear them heave a sigh of relief.

At that moment the waitress brought him his dinner, and he was obliged to sweep the letters to one side. He might have expected to feel a jolt of electricity as he touched them. But in fact they felt exactly like what they were: a bunch of old letters.

First he would eat his dinner, slowly savouring each solid mouthful. He even asked for a helping of bread and butter to prolong his main course, and then ordered a rum baba.

The dessert came far too soon. And was eaten far too quickly.

He could delay reading them no longer.

My dearest, darling L,

You say I must not declare my love for you as to do so will only hurt us both. But how can I not declare it when to remain silent is torturing me? You say our love will hurt others who are blameless and good. What do I care about the blameless and good? I do not want to be blameless and good. I want only you. Do not misunderstand me, my dear, I do not desire to hurt anyone only for the sake of causing pain. I am not a sadist. I will not cause pain needlessly. But our love is not needless. Our love trumps everything else. Any sacrifice that our love demands must be made, however painful. It will pain me never to see my son again but it will pain me more to be separated from you. But this is more than a question of balancing pains and losses, or rights and wrongs. We have a duty, dearest. It is not to those good and blameless others. It is not even to ourselves.

It is to love. The highest duty that we owe is to love. We are not sinners, we are lovers, and in loving we cannot sin. Whatever we do in love, for love, and because of love, is necessarily good. Whatever love asks of us, we must obey its command. Love demands first and foremost that we declare it. Therefore my dear I will declare it now and I will declare it forever and I will never tire of declaring it: I love you. I love you passionately and fiercely and dangerously and tenderly. I love you with all my heart and soul and body. With every sinew of my muscles, every fibre of my bones, every cell of my flesh. You are everything to me, Louisa, and I would give up everything for one moment in your arms. Without regret.

I am yours,
Only yours,
Q.

SEVENTEEN

I t was dark when he got back to the lodging house.

He had sat in the tearoom reading his father's letters, long after the other diners had left.

The letters told the complete story of his father's love affair with Louisa Grant-Sissons, from the first dawnings of their mutual feelings, through the physical consummation of the affair, to Louisa's pregnancy, the birth of their son, Louisa's sickness and rapid decline. There were no dates on any of the letters, though the events they referred to clearly took place over several years. It also appeared that Hugh Grant-Sissons knew about the affair and turned a blind eye to it. He seemed to have been a man driven by other passions. From his own experience of Grant-Sissons, Quinn would have described him as a monomaniac. Possibly he considered his wife's amour with his business partner as a blessing in disguise, relieving him as it did of the tedious responsibility of attending to her happiness himself.

Perhaps he had even encouraged it.

Quinn had found one letter unopened, and it remained unopened even now. It was one thing to tip letters out of already cut envelopes. Quite another to breach a virgin envelope himself. It seemed an intrusion too far, almost a violation.

But there was more to it than that.

His father's suicide all those years ago had precipitated a mental breakdown in Quinn. He had reacted to it the only way he knew at the time. He suppressed his emotions and allowed the rational part of his mind to take over.

In short, he saw it as a puzzle that needed solving, through the exercise of logic. But that logic soon became distorted. His *a priori* assumption was that it was inconceivable that his father had taken his own life. Logic demanded that he posit certain dark forces, malign agents and byzantine plots to explain what had happened. His father had been murdered, and his murder had been made to look like suicide. This was the only explanation that Quinn could accept.

All he had to do was prove it. He had to prove it to redeem his father, not only in his own eyes, but to the world; most of all to his mother. Her tight-lipped coldness in the face of her husband's death had been inexplicable to Quinn at the time.

He had set out to prove the unprovable. And, as seemed likely now, the patently untrue. No one had murdered his father. He had taken his own life.

The attempt to prove otherwise had cost Quinn his sanity.

Quinn now believed that this one last unread letter held the secret of his father's death. He speculated that it had been sent to Louisa after her death, which was the reason it remained unopened. There was a very real possibility that it was his father's suicide note.

Reading the details of his father's love-making had inspired a particular species of queasy horror. He could not now get out of his mind those descriptions of his father's tongue flicking Louisa's nipple into playful pertness, his lyrical appreciations of his lover's pubic hair, and worst of all his raptures at feeling his stalwart manhood buried deep within her warm enfolding flesh, and the joyous explosion of his love as she gasped her simultaneous ecstasy and clawed his back with her fingernails.

But to read his father's justification for taking his own life would be a different level of horror again. Especially as it had been written to a woman who was already dead, and who had died in the most horrible circumstances – one of those hands with the very nails that had clawed his father's back having been amputated to stop the spread of a ravenous cancer.

Quinn held the tin box tucked under his arm. He felt that its weight came entirely from that single letter that he had yet to read. It had its own morbid gravity. He felt it pulling at his heart.

It was strange, he reflected, how Hugh Grant-Sissons had respected his wife's privacy in not opening this last letter. He couldn't help wondering if he had read the other letters, and what he had made of the more explicit passages.

And why had he kept the letters at all? Perhaps out of some perverse, masochistic wallowing in his own humiliation. Or perhaps he enjoyed a different kind of perversion, that of voyeurism. Maybe the letters gave him a vicarious thrill, as he read about the physical satisfaction that his wife had enjoyed with another man?

There was another possible explanation. He had kept the letters because he really did love his wife after all. In his own flawed, failed way, but truly and honestly. The letters must have caused him pain. As Louisa herself had caused him pain. But they were hers – a record, in fact, of her happiness – and he clung on to them and treasured them as he clung on to and treasured everything that reminded him of her.

Quinn must have been distracted by his thoughts of the letters, because he did not exercise his usual caution in closing the front door behind him. He told himself that he had got into the habit of stealth out of consideration for the other residents. As a police officer, he was required to be on duty at all hours. So his comings and goings were hardly regular. There was a certain dishonesty in this explanation, because he contrived to be as quiet when he came home at six o'clock in the evening as he was at three in the morning.

But tonight he merely pushed the door to behind him. There must have been another door open at the rear of the house, because a through draft took hold of the front door and slammed it into its frame.

There was an excited shriek from the drawing room, and a moment later Mrs Ibbott came running out. 'Ah, Inspector Quinn! It's you! I did not think it would be you because you are usually so quiet.'

Quinn did not wholeheartedly welcome his glamorous elevation from plain old Mr Quinn to Inspector Quinn. 'Forgive me, Mrs Ibbott. I did not mean to make such a racket.'

'No, no, it's quite all right. It's very good to see you, in fact. We see too little of you. Oh, I know you work long hours, and your work is very important. But it's important to have a home life too, you know, Inspector Quinn.'

She seemed to be making all together too much of the Inspector title. He gave a bland smile and nodded.

'You're always creeping upstairs without saying hello.'

'I don't want to disturb anyone.'

'You're not! Of course you're not! Now, tell me, have you met our new guests, Mr and Mrs Hargreaves?'

'No, I . . .'

'Splendid! Then you must come in and meet them now.'

'I'm afraid I . . .' Quinn lamely tapped the cashier's box under his arm.

'Nonsense. I won't hear it. Whatever is in there can wait, I'm sure. What is it, some murderer's confession? You can come in and tell us all about it. Perhaps we can help you crack the case?'

'No, I . . . that wouldn't . . .'

'I know, I know. I'm teasing you, Inspector.'

'Please, there's no need to . . .'

'So that's settled then. You'll come in and say hello.'

The door to the drawing room was held open for him. There was no way to extricate himself. Indeed, Mrs Ibbott as good as pushed him into the room.

He came in at the climax of a lively exchange, to which Messrs Timberley and Appleby were loudly contributing, in their usual vying way. Quinn could understand their excitement. With them in the hot over-furnished room was a young woman, whose physical presence exercised an immediate and disconcerting effect on Quinn. He supposed she was beautiful, but in all honesty he found it difficult to look at her.

Her eyes glistened with a lively, sympathetic interest. Her smile was ready and warm, and revealed two rows of the most perfect teeth, small, white and evenly spaced. He was no aficionado of fashion, but to his eye at least her dress appeared perfectly judged. It was not showy, but it was elegant.

Mrs Ibbott had followed him in. She waited for the hilarity to die down before introducing him. 'Well look who I found! Our very own police detective. The celebrated Inspector Quinn of the Yard!'

Quinn held up his free hand in demurral. He felt *her* gaze on him. Curious, interested, even perhaps a little in awe. He sensed her lean forward in the winged armchair in which she had been sitting back, as if his entrance had enlivened her, and drawn her out.

Mrs Ibbott continued the introduction. 'This is Mrs Hargreaves. And Mr Hargreaves, of course.'

Ah yes, of course. Though it was only now that his attention was directed to the other man in the room that Quinn noticed him. They seemed a spectacularly mismatched couple. Hargreaves had a rather shifty, ferret-like look about him. He acknowledged Quinn with the merest upward tilt of his head. It was an arrogant, sneering gesture, to which his unprepossessing physicality did not entitle him.

Naturally, despite his antipathy to the man, Quinn held out his hand. Hargreaves did not rise from his seat to take it, but reached up in a lackadaisical manner which struck Quinn as bad form.

'Very nice to meet you. Both,' he added with a bow to Mrs Hargreaves. 'I do trust you are settling in?'

'Oh, yes!' she said with a bright smile. 'Everyone has been so welcoming. And now that we have met you . . . well, we have heard so much about you.'

'You have?' Quinn was rather alarmed by this.

'All good, believe me. We heard how you . . .' But Mrs Hargreaves caught a swift shake of the head from Mrs Ibbott which seemed to throw her off her stride. 'How you . . . how kind you were . . . to the lady who . . .'

'Steady on, Cissy,' warned her husband.

Quinn felt his face flush with ridiculous hot embarrassment. So, they had been talking about him and Miss Dillard. 'If you will forgive me, I must go upstairs now. I still have some work to do this evening.' He fled the room.

He did not blame her. How could he? Indeed, the fact that she had brought it up attested to her goodness and candour. He blamed Appleby and Timberley, to whom everything, even Miss Dillard's death, was one great joke.

He bounded up the stairs. On the landing outside Miss Dillard's old room, he paused and closed his eyes.

He was trying to conjure up the image of Miss Dillard's pewter-coloured irises.

But the image of a tongue teasing a nipple into playful pertness was all that came to mind. He opened his eyes in horror. It was himself and Mrs Hargreaves he had been thinking of.

Like father, like son.

The thought came to him as he sat in his room with the final letter in his hand. He was in the armchair next to the bed. His head was heavy with weariness.

The letter was still in its sealed envelope. Perhaps he would never read it. Perhaps he didn't need to. Or perhaps it would be better if he didn't.

The curtains were open, and light came in from the street lamps outside. He had not switched on a light in his room. He could take out the letter and still not be able to read it. But he baulked at doing even that.

It wasn't always necessary to know the truth. Nor desirable.

That seemed a strange thing for a police detective to admit. It went against all his instincts and training. He lived his life in the belief that he had a duty to uncover the truth. Whomever it hurt.

But he found that that duty was not so easy to perform when the person hurt was himself.

Without absolute evidence for a given hypothesis, it was always possible to entertain an element of doubt towards it. It was looking increasingly likely that his father had committed suicide. But part of him could still cling on to the old consolation that he had been murdered. It couldn't be definitively ruled out.

Not until he opened that letter.

Quinn's hand relaxed and the letter dropped on to his lap.

He let his head fall back and sank swiftly into a welcome oblivion.

The next day was wet again.

Quinn's ulster was speckled with dark spots as he hung it on the hatstand in the attic room.

Even though he had his back to Macadam, he could sense his sergeant's excitement. Instead of turning directly to face him, he flashed an ironic questioning glance at Inchball, who merely shrugged in return.

'Well?' Quinn finally asked as he looked up from behind his desk.

'We've had the results in, sir. Of the fingerprint analysis of the three cards.'

Quinn nodded for him to go on.

'It's messy, and not conclusive. But it seems that none of *their* fingerprints was found.'

'What do you mean?'

'I mean none of the men who had the cards touched them. Which makes it seem like someone slipped the cards into their pockets, perhaps without them knowing.'

'I see. Anything else?'

'Yes, as it happens. A few rogue prints have been ruled out as belonging to coppers. Yours included, sir.'

'I was most careful to handle the cards by the edges.'

'I'm sure you were, sir. Which is why yours were ruled out.'

'Please get to the point, Macadam.'

'Oh, he loves to drag it out, don't he!'

'The point, sir, is that one set of prints – excluding yours – was found on all the cards. The same thumbprint, quite clearly and decisively identifiable.'

'I see.'

'The same person put the cards into the clothes of these three men.'

'Yes, I gathered that, Macadam.'

'That is a breakthrough, is it not, sir?'

'Do we know to whom this thumbprint belongs?'

'Well, no. Not yet, sir.'

'Then I fear it is too early to talk of breakthroughs.'

Macadam said nothing. He merely bowed his head slightly in acknowledgement of Quinn's judgement.

EIGHTEEN

The ticking of the office clock sounded like a tiny hammer driving fine nails into an infinite coffin.

It was the most frustrating investigation that Inchball could ever remember being involved in. He was not even sure it was an investigation.

Even Macadam's announcement of a definitive thumbprint did little to convince him that they were not wasting their time. 'It's a needle in a bloody haystack!' It was his favourite analogy whenever discussing fingerprint evidence.

The rain didn't help. A fine, cold, needling rain that seemed not so much to fall through as fill the air. It was hard to believe that only the day before they had been baking away in stifling heat.

But even with the rain, he would rather be outside pounding the streets, knocking on doors, dragging suspects in than . . . well, than whatever it was he was supposed to be doing here.

'What am I supposed to be doing again?' he even asked at one point.

Quinn offered him no answer to that question, but just stared at him with an outraged expression. Was it Inchball's imagination or was there also a glint of fear in the guv'nor's eyes?

He began to wonder if his boss wasn't losing the plot.

When Quinn left the room, Inchball vented his frustration on Macadam. 'What's the matter with you, man? You've got a face like a smacked arse.'

'Not at all.'

'So you're happy then? Happy with the way his nibs is handling this?'

'It's not my place to question Inspector Quinn's methodology. Nor yours neither.'

'Don't make me laugh!'

'What would you have us do?'

'We need to follow up the suits.'

'We have the fingerprint lead. The suits may turn out to be irrelevant.'

'You are assuming that the fingerprint belongs to a known criminal. And that we can identify him.'

'That's true but . . .'

'It could turn out to be a wild goose chase.'

'Well, yes, but I don't see what else . . .'

'What else? The suits, I tell you!'

'What about the suits?' It was Quinn, returned from wherever he had been. He stood in the doorway like the spectre at the feast.

Inchball exchanged a glance with Macadam and swallowed once. 'You ever been in a loony bin, guv?'

'What do you mean?'

'Well, once I had to take this fella into Hanwell. You know, the big asylum. I got an eyeful of all the loonies there. They all wore the same suits. Which as it happens were brown tweed. They looked a lot like these ones. Only these are corduroy. But apart from that, they was the same. So, me and Mac, we was wondering, whether these three fellas might have come out of a loony bin? Maybe we should look into that, guv?'

Inchball watched Quinn closely. He was sure of his ground. But there was something going on with the guv'nor and no mistake. He had a theory of his own, most likely. Sometimes even the best coppers could have blind spots. But Inchball was determined to put his case firmly and not give ground until the guv'nor gave him an answer one way or the other. It was time to have it out.

He knew what they thought of him. He was the muscle. Brawn not brain. Handy for putting the fear of God up a suspect, but not the sharpest tool in the toolbox. Not to be trusted with all that deduction business. Leave that to them. That's what they thought. But he knew what he knew. And he knew that, for once at least, Mac agreed with him.

Quinn could deny it all he liked, but the suits were a lead.

Quinn's face was suddenly drained of colour, his lips clenched. A hand came up to conceal his eyes. Inchball saw a spasm of distress shake the detective's entire body. Both his hands reached out to steady himself in the frame of the open door.

He lurched over to his desk and slumped down heavily behind it, pretending to busy himself with some papers.

It started as a barely perceptible tremor but grew into a convulsion that shook both arms, rattling the desk. Quinn gave a high-pitched whimper as the piece of paper in his hands ripped apart. He shook the fragments of paper away from him and placed one hand over his eyes again. This time when he removed it, Inchball saw the moisture pooling.

'I'll not go back there.' Quinn spoke so quietly and intently that at first Inchball couldn't be sure he had heard him right. He cast a questioning glance at Macadam, whose minute shake of the head cautioned restraint.

Quinn let out a deep sigh. His body was still quaking. The extended murmur he was now emitting sounded much like sobbing. It wasn't long before it became the real thing. And it was appalling to witness. Fragmented jags of sound gurgled in his throat. His chest heaved. Tears flooded his face.

Then came the snot, streaming and bubbling out of both nostrils, without any decency or self-control.

That was the worst of it, for Inchball watching. Not the distress itself, though that was bad enough. But Quinn's total surrender to it. He was beyond himself. Heedless of his own degradation. Shameless, because shame no longer meant anything to him.

Inchball wanted it to stop, more than anything. He wished to God that he had never seen it. At the same time, he could not tear his eyes away.

He was too horrified, too alienated by what he was seeing, to have sympathy.

Quinn's teeth began to chatter. Inchball realized he was trying to speak.

Quinn began to strike his forehead with the heel of his hand. Then he struck his head with startling force down on the desk.

When he raised his head, his eyes were pink, and the flesh around them puffy.

But he was calmer.

'It's not Hanwell,' he said. 'The suits don't come from Hanwell. They come from Colney Hatch.'

A red mark on Quinn's forehead mushroomed into a lump before their very eyes.

'It was all a long time ago.' Quinn wiped his face with a large white handkerchief. He studied the inside of the handkerchief for a moment as if he expected to find the solution to a mystery there.

'Sir, you don't have to . . .' Macadam broke off.

Quinn frowned at him, not in anger or confusion, but almost in regret. He knew that he owed his sergeants an explanation. 'There can be no excuse for the outburst to which I have just yielded. It is beyond reprehensible. I would not blame you, men, if you decided to take the matter above my head to Sir Edward Henry himself. I would not blame you if you called for my replacement.'

'No,' said Inchball decisively. 'They'll put some blithering idiot in charge of us like they did last time.'

'Coddington?' Quinn shook his head ruefully. 'You have a right to be led by a senior officer worthy of you. A man who has earned your respect.'

'You have, sir. You have our respect,' insisted Macadam.

'No. There can be no question of that. After . . . after what I have just subjected you to.'

'We all . . .' But Macadam, who had begun so brightly, couldn't complete his thought.

'No, Macadam, we have not all, we have never all.'

'We all have our moments, sir. That's all I was going to say.'

'You're very good, Macadam. Too good. But the fact is, you need to know that you can rely on me. It's a question of trust, and I do not feel that you can trust me any more.'

'Begging your pardon, guv,' said Inchball. 'But that ain't for you to decide.'

'Do you think I would allow either of you men to remain in this department if you had just indulged in such behaviour? For your own good, for your own safety, for the safety of the department, I would insist on . . .'

'But it ain't us, it's you. And you ain't going anywhere. We ain't having that Coddington again.'

'Not Coddington, no. I agree with you there. But someone. There are other men. Better men.'

'No one better than you,' said Inchball quickly.

'You saw how my hands shook! Imagine if I had been holding a weapon, covering one of you men as you were about some perilous business. Imagine my finger had squeezed the trigger by accident!'

'It didn't happen,' said Macadam.

'It ain't gonna happen,' said Inchball.

'It could,' insisted Quinn.

'There ain't nobody like you with a gun in his hand.'

'Oh, Inchball! Inchball, Inchball,' murmured Quinn, with his eyes closed.

'Let's put it to the test.'

Quinn's eyes opened in surprise. He looked at Inchball to see if he was joking. He didn't seem to be.

'What do you mean?'

'Hold out your right hand. Your gun hand.'

'Inchball!' objected Macadam. 'You can't . . .'

But Quinn was already doing as Inchball had directed. His hand shook wildly.

Inchball opened the drawer to his desk and took out his Webley service revolver. He broke the revolver open and checked the cylinder, before snapping it together again and rising from his desk.

The trembling in Quinn's hand intensified. 'Is it loaded?'

Inchball nodded grimly.

'It doesn't need to be loaded,' objected Macadam.

'If we're going to do this, we do it properly,' said Inchball.

Quinn did not comment.

Inchball strode decisively around his own desk and across to Quinn. He gripped the gun by the barrel and held the butt out for Quinn to take. The closer the gun got, the worse Quinn's shakes became.

'Take it. And point it at me.'

'Point it at you?'

'That's the idea, guv.'

'But I don't know whether it's a *good* idea, Inchball.'

'It's all right, guv. I won't hold it against you if you shoot me.'

'But this is ridiculous!' objected Macadam.

'I want to prove to him that he's all right,' explained Inchball, with patient emphasis.

Macadam was having none of it. 'Madness. Sheer madness.'

Quinn's hand flew up and snatched the gun. At the same moment, Inchball withdrew his hand and stepped back.

The effect on Quinn's trembling was startling. His hand steadied instantly. He held the gun up in front of him and took aim at Inchball's head.

'There! See!' cried Inchball triumphantly. 'Steady as a statue.'

Quinn had to admit, it felt good to have the gun in his hand.

He stood up, keeping the gun held out at the end of a rigidly locked arm. He moved out from his desk and stalked the room, taking aim at imaginary targets with crisp, decisive movements. At one point, he looked down the sights at Macadam, who held up his hands in mock surrender. Then Quinn swivelled his arm towards the window and pointed the barrel at the bleary sky.

After a moment, he turned to Inchball. His gun arm relaxed and he threw the gun across the room.

There was a shriek of panic from Macadam. But Inchball caught the spinning weapon by the butt, without much trouble.

'Don't worry,' said Quinn. 'It wasn't loaded. I could tell by the weight.'

'He's right,' admitted Inchball delightedly. 'He's only bloody right!'

Quinn looked down at both his hands, fingers splayed as if to grasp the air.

'So . . . guv?'

Quinn met Inchball's question with a blank stare. His sergeant was looking directly at the middle of his forehead. It felt like his gaze was drilling into his head with a beam of throbbing pain. Quinn's fingers probed the spot Inchball was looking at and was surprised to discover that his head came out to meet his fingertips more eagerly than he expected.

'The suits?'

'Look into it.'

As he uttered the three simple words, Quinn experienced a welling of emotion that once again threatened to overwhelm him. A moment before, it had been the fear of discovery; now it was a sense of release brought on by the very thing he had feared.

'You want me to go there? To Colney Hatch?'

Quinn nodded once, so tersely that it might not have been a

signal of assent at all, but just an involuntary twitch. 'Talk to Pottinger. Dr Pottinger. He is the superintendent and chief psychiatrist there.' Quinn didn't add that Pottinger had treated him when he had been a patient there. He sensed Inchball watching him with a questioning look. 'Start with Malcolm Grant-Sissons. Find out if he has been an inmate there. Then, well . . . you don't need me to tell you your job.'

'Shall I telephone ahead?'

'I often find the element of surprise pays dividends on these occasions, don't you?'

Inchball gave a satisfied nod and rose from his desk. By now, the shower had passed and sunlight was beginning to warm up the room. A smile flickered across the sergeant's face as he retrieved his bowler from the hatstand. 'I'll keep my eyes open. And my wits about me.'

NINETEEN

S team from the departing GNR locomotive billowed around him. As it cleared, Inchball found himself alone on the platform. The sign read New Southgate for Colney Hatch, making explicit the connection between the station and the asylum. It served visitors and staff and presumably also patients, although their journeys were necessarily infrequent. For many, a one-way ticket was all they needed.

He stood for a moment to get his bearings. The clamour of birdsong struck his ear as discordant and angry.

Facing him across the track was a high, blank railway embankment, encroached by nettles at the base, fringed at the top by a screen of trees.

The recent rain was a memory now, a trace scent in the air. The sun was in his eyes. It shone through the trees, turning their foliage black. He caught a glimpse of a building, a high corner where the jutting brickwork met a gleaming panel of sky.

Inchball was fond of saying that he was a simple man. There was a lot he didn't hold with, and more he wasn't given to. Sentimentality fell into both categories. But even he, at that first vision of innocuous masonry, felt some deep stirring of foreboding.

A secure door was set in the high wall that skirted the grounds. He rang a bell and was admitted by an attendant, who did not seem particularly interested in checking his warrant card. It struck Inchball that getting into Colney Hatch was easier than he had expected. Certainly easier than getting out, for some of those who came here. He thought about turning that into a joke, but something about the man's humourless expression deterred him.

Inchball asked for directions to Dr Pottinger's office. The man pointed abruptly to his left. 'Stick to the path.' This seemed to be a warning as much as a direction.

He now had his first clear sighting of the main building, but it was so immense that it could only reveal itself to him in pieces. First the shoulder of one wing. Then, as he rounded the corner, the face of a high block that projected forwards. Banks of windows were turned to mirrors by the sun's rays. Some of the windows were partially opened. All were barred.

The scale of the place did not surprise him. He knew how big these asylums were, how big they had to be. Vast repositories built to house the ever-increasing numbers of the mad. Yes, he felt sorry for them. But his sympathy only went so far. They were a bloody nuisance. Some of them were worse than that, a danger to themselves and others. You had to put them somewhere, he supposed.

And yet . . .

He must be getting soft in his old age. But he had to admit, it was a terrible thing to happen to anyone.

And here they were, now, all around him. Men in brown corduroy suits, heads cropped, though they were most of them bearded. He supposed the less contact they had with razors, the better.

The women disturbed him more, in their black and white checked dresses. They seemed so defeated, lost, as they shuffled listlessly and purposelessly about.

Some of the men had been trusted with garden tools. Others were occupied in exercise. At his approach, they stopped whatever they were doing and followed him with their gaze, their poses frozen as if they were figures in a photograph.

He felt their gaze burn into the back of his neck. He imagined them rushing at him with their spades and forks. He braced himself for the first blow. But when he glanced back, they hadn't moved, except to turn their heads to track his progress. It seemed they were waiting until he was safely on his way before they resumed their activities. They were more afraid of him than he was of them.

Vast lawns dotted with buttercups and daisies sloped gently upwards away from the long sprawl of the asylum building. The lawns were interspersed with well-established trees of all varieties. A magnificent weeping willow particularly caught his eye, as did another tree he could not identify whose thick limbs were twisted and contorted as if in the throes of a fit.

*   *   *

'Who are you?' A female nurse in a starched cap and white pinafore dress belted at the waist regarded him with watchful and suspicious eyes, a reflex aggression in her voice. Her face was pinched and exhausted.

Inchball showed his warrant card again. 'I've come to see Dr Pottinger.'

'Is he expecting you?'

'Unless he's clairvoyant, no.'

The nurse led him under the grand portico of the main entrance, which gave this part of the building the appearance of a temple.

The first thing he noticed when he stepped inside was the smell. Either they had a problem with sewer gas, or this was what you got when you confined thousands of distressed and barely functioning human beings, many of whom, he presumed, had a difficult relationship with the waste their bodies produced.

The entrance foyer itself was in good array. The floor had been recently polished, and the waxy smell overlaid the faecal ground notes without obliterating them.

He was prepared for all this. He'd been inside Hanwell, which was on a similar scale. He was prepared too for the muted screams, the sounds of blatant distress which came to him from distant rooms. But even though he was prepared, they still shocked him.

The nurse bade him wait while she knocked on a door which bore the sign SUPERINTENDENT. A negotiation took place around the narrowly opened door – she seemed to be at pains to shield whatever was inside from the view of the uninitiated – before he was shown in.

Dr Pottinger did not rise to greet him from behind his substantial desk. He didn't even look up from the papers he was studying. He was no doubt keen to give the impression of a busy man, burdened by weighty responsibilities. *I'll talk to you*, he seemed to be saying, *but make it quick. I have other more important matters to attend to.*

At last, he laid the papers down and threw a perfunctory nod in Inchball's direction.

'Please sit down.'

As it happened, Inchball preferred to remain standing. You

could say it was a rule of his: to ignore the commands of those who had no authority over him but thought they did.

It got Pottinger's attention. 'What is this about?'

'It's about two dead men and one nearly dead.'

'I don't understand.'

'Name Malcolm Grant-Sissons mean anything to you?'

'Should it?'

'We have reason to believe he was a patient here.'

'My good man, do you have any conception how many patients we have at Colney Hatch at any one time? Over two thousand. I cannot be expected to recall the names of them all.'

'Young fella. Must have been let out recently. Only stayed for a short time.'

'Ah yes, now that you mention it. Malcolm, of course. One of our successes. He came to us as the result of a nervous breakdown following the death of his father. In a state of extreme nervous excitement. My colleague Dr Leaming was able to achieve a quite remarkable and rapid improvement. Malcolm isn't dead, is he?'

'He ought to be. Threw himself on to a high voltage dynamo at Bankside power station.'

'That was Malcolm? I read about it in the news. There was no name given of the poor unfortunate man.'

'We've had two others do similar things. Top themselves in the buff. One climbed into the bear pit at London Zoo. The other threw himself off Suicide Bridge. We think they were all here.'

'But why do you think that? Not all suicides have passed through our doors, you know.'

'We found their suits. Just like the ones them geezers outside are wearing.'

'I see.'

'Now that you have confirmed that Grant-Sissons was here, it makes it more likely that the other two were an' all. Could you provide me with a list of all male inmates who have been recently released – those aged, say, between nineteen and thirty years of age?'

'Of course.'

'In particular, I would be interested in any inmates who had the same treatment as Grant-Sissons. Any who were treated by this colleague of yours, Dr Leaming, was it?'

'Anything else?'

'Have you lost any patients recently?'

'Lost?'

'Had any escape.'

'This is not a prison. However, our patients are kept securely enclosed for their own protection. By virtue of the mental disarrangement that has brought them here in the first place, they are unable to function in the world outside our perimeter. Indeed, it is not until we professionally adjudge them to be capable of that adjustment that we release them.'

'Is that a yes or a no?'

'No. No one has escaped from here.'

'Ever?'

'Recently.'

'Maybe one or two could slip away without anyone noticing?'

'We would know. Now then, if you would be so good as to provide me with an address, I shall see to it that the information you require is sent to you.'

'Not so quick. I ain't finished with you yet.' Inchball produced his wallet and took out a photograph of one of the cards found in the men's suits. 'Ever seen anything like this before?'

Pottinger was quick with his answer. 'No.'

'Sure about that?'

'Yes.'

'How about these letters? F.J.S.U?'

This time he was more hesitant. But the denial was just as emphatic when it came. 'No.'

Inchball pocketed the photographs. 'What exactly is it your Dr Leaming did to Malcolm Grant-Sissons?'

'He helped him. He cured him. Malcolm came in here a wreck. Quaking, weeping, flailing . . . He could not speak, could hardly stand up. Couldn't walk. Had to be stretchered in. A kind of paralysis had gripped him, which had no physiological basis. In an extraordinarily short space of time, after little more than two weeks of treatment, Dr Leaming was able to restore him not only to his former self, but to a stronger, braver, more confident

Malcolm than he had ever been. He left here at the beginning of June, smiling, shaking hands with the staff, embracing Dr Leaming in gratitude for his help.'

'And then, a few days later, he strips off and tries to top himself.'

'In our profession, we must accept that there will be setbacks as well as breakthroughs.'

'What was it he did, exactly?'

'The therapy is complex but effective.' It was Pottinger's way of saying Inchball wouldn't understand.

'Does it involve whipping out their tonsils?'

'That isn't part of Dr Leaming's treatment.'

'But it's something you like to do?'

'It is a pioneering treatment based on the latest ideas. It is now understood that all mental illness has a single underlying cause – a toxin caused by a germ infection that enters the brain from certain other parts of the body, including the colon, stomach, sinuses, teeth and tonsils. In an ideal world, we would remove all these offending body parts. But we find that we can achieve moderate results simply by extracting the tonsils and teeth.'

'Why do you still have loonies in here, then? If you know the cure?'

Pottinger gave Inchball a long, silent look that suggested that he would like to remove more than his tonsils. 'We can't operate on everyone. We don't have the resources.' At last he looked away and the interview was over.

Inchball hurried back along the path towards the station.

The place was beginning to give him the cold creeps. If he was honest, it was the staff he was worried about more than the patients, most of whom seemed harmlessly wrapped up in their own worlds of misery and confusion.

The nurses and attendants, on the other hand, had a cold watchfulness about them that was one provocation away from sadistic. Inchball himself had used techniques that some might consider brutal, but always against villains who would do far worse to him given half the chance. The same could not be said for the listless, cowering wretches he saw around him now.

The sight of them brought to mind the guv'nor's recent unfortunate episode. So, old Quinn had been a patient here. Poor fucker.

Well, at least it showed there was hope for some of them. The guv'nor was a model citizen these days.

The thought was pleasantly diverting. Inchball chuckled silently to himself.

'Something funny?'

It was one of the loonies, hoeing a flowerbed. He looked at Inchball with a bold, challenging stare, so unlike the shrinking evasiveness of his fellows. Inchball had the definite feeling that he had met this man before. 'Do I know you?'

'If you have opened your heart to the Lord, then verily, you know me. For I am your God.'

'Timon Medway!'

'I do not acknowledge that nomenclature. You may address me as the Lord God Our Saviour, the One God, the True God, the Only God. Though I will also answer to Jesus of Nazareth or Sir Isaac Newton, as these were the identities I assumed in my most notable earthly incarnations.'

'Still keeping up the act, are you? You never fooled me, Medway. I know you're not mad. You're just fucking evil.'

'*In nomine Patris et Filii at Spiritus sancti.* That is to say, in my name, for I am the Father, the Son and the Holy Spirit.'

'Bollocks.'

'I forgive you that blasphemy, for I am the God of forgiveness.'

'Fuck you.' Inchball waved a hand dismissively and walked on, shaking his head.

'Give my regards to Silas Quinn,' shouted Medway after him. 'I hope to see him soon.'

Inchball continued walking. He was aware of his heart beating forcefully and fast. His fists were clenched tightly. It was the response that genuine danger always provoked in him.

TWENTY

Malcolm had been in hospital for just over a week now. He had still not regained consciousness. His surgeon seemed dubious that he ever would. 'Frankly, I don't understand how he's still alive.'

'He's my brother.'

The surgeon's expression softened. 'I'm sorry. I thought you were here on police duty.'

Quinn kept up a vigil at Malcolm's bedside. He brought with him the library book, *A Furious Energy*. Macadam had been reluctant to hand it back, but when Quinn explained why he needed it, he relented.

Quinn let the book fall open where the page was turned over. He began to read aloud, in a low, hoarse, even tone. Only occasionally did his voice crack, for no reason that he could understand.

Peter Pilling placed both hands on the glowing orb. It felt as solid as any table: it was impossible for him to push his hands into it, although he knew that its solidity was temporary, if not illusory. The orb was a mass of floating electrical particles generated by the Elektronikon. As soon as he switched the giant humming machine off, the orb would disappear.

Contrary to Professor Kureshi's warnings, he received no electrical shock from the orb. This was as he had calculated. The Elektronikon converted electrical current into a field of energy that simulated matter. Indeed, Pilling had dubbed the machine's product 'Simu-matter'.

He removed one hand from the orb and gestured to Professor Kureshi. 'It's perfectly safe,' he assured him.

Kureshi put down his pipe and approached the orb; his face lit up eerily from below as he peered at it. He spread out one hand and held it about three inches above the orb.

Pilling placed his own hand on top of his old mentor's

*hand and gently guided it down until the palm made contact
with the incandescent surface. Kureshi winced, in expectation of pain. When he felt none, he opened his eyes wide in
wonder.*

*'Allah be praised, Peter! You have done it! You have
created solid matter from electricity!'*

*'Not quite, Professor. The object has no independent
existence as yet.'*

*'There is no electrical sensation whatsoever. Only the
impression of touching a solid object.'*

*Pilling removed his hands from the orb. 'Impression?
It's more than an impression.' He crossed to a workbench
on the other side of his laboratory, from where he took a
claw hammer.*

'Stand back, Prof!'

*Kureshi did as he was directed. Peter Pilling brought the
hammer down on the orb from high above his head, holding
nothing back from the force with which he wielded it. The
hammer head struck the orb with a heavy clank and was
thrown violently back up into the air.*

*'Impression, you say?' Pilling's laughter was charged
with a manic, almost hysterical animation. At the same time,
he seemed to be on the verge of collapse. He was simultaneously exhausted and energized.*

*'Let's switch it off, shall we?' advised Professor Kureshi,
noticing his friend's peculiar excitement. 'Then we can talk.'*

*Since the death of Peter's parents in the explosion,
Professor Ali Kureshi had been like a father to the young
scientist. It was a relationship that they had both fallen into
naturally, without questioning. Kureshi had no family of his
own. He had devoted his life to science. And Peter, orphaned
through his own actions . . . More than orphaned, the explosion in his laboratory had killed his brother too . . .*

Quinn looked across at Malcolm. His eyes were closed, but
he was far from tranquil. Every breath was a struggle. His hair
was drenched in sweat. His face glistened and rippled with agonies
that Quinn could only guess at.

Quinn had seen men die before. He knew that sometimes, even

when the injuries were as catastrophic as Malcolm's, it could take a long time for the end to come. A space would open up into which hope could be poured. Surely, if they could survive this long, they would make it through?

But Malcolm seemed to be physically shrinking before Quinn's eyes. At the same time, the strange animation of his face suggested that there was something trying to burst out from within. Intolerable pressures were at work on his organism from all directions.

Darkness.

A glimmering speck forms, barely visible, sensed rather than seen.

The speck settles and grows.

It is revealed to be a distant light, a beacon perhaps, or light at the end of a tunnel.

Is he in a tunnel then?

The light's apparent growth is the effect of his approaching it. Or is the light coming towards him?

It makes no difference. Wherever he is, that distinction does not exist.

A voice is speaking, though he cannot make out what is being said. It is a constant low murmur, like a prayer. A prayer that's being said for him.

He feels the indistinct words of the prayer floating beneath him, bearing him up, bearing him along. A river of goodwill.

A river flowing through a tunnel? But there is no river and there is no tunnel.

The black bees are gone now. Their buzzing ceased as soon as the words began. If the words stop, will the bees return? He feels this is so, and fearing the bees' return, he hopes that the prayer will last forever.

Whether the light is moving towards him or he towards it, the progress is infinitely slow. As if there is all the time in the world for this to happen.

The movement is so slow that he has no sense of it. Except that the light continues to grow, in infinitesimally small increments.

It is now a circle of light. Or rather a sphere. He can detect its three-dimensionality.

Not the light at the end of a tunnel then.

A ball of light rolling towards him.

As it approaches the words of the prayer become more distinct.

. . . floating . . . disappear . . . received . . . assured . . . approached . . . above . . . gently . . . guided . . . wonder . . . be praised . . . from high . . . laughter . . . energized . . . father . . . brother . . .

All the time, the extent of the sphere continues to grow until its light is all there is. It has edged the darkness out.

He is at the surface of the light now. He sees that it is formed from an infinite number of particles. From a distance, the light appeared white. Now he can see that it pulsates with swimming colours, some of breathtaking delicacy, others unbelievably vibrant. They shift and merge so quickly that it is almost as if they are creating new colours, ones that he has never seen or even imagined before.

And then it happens. He passes through the colours and the colours pass through him. And as they pass through him, they dissolve him. It is a soft and infinitely slow explosion.

The particles of his being swim and shimmer with the shifting colours.

Until there is nothing.

Malcolm's eyes opened. His eyeballs swivelled in their sockets before staring straight ahead in an expression that may have been amazement or terror, softening into something more resigned. His breathing quickened into sharp, desperate drags and then stopped.

He fell back and seemed to shrink one last time as if something had collapsed inside him.

TWENTY-ONE

Quinn hesitated at the door to the department, watching his sergeants in silence. They were engrossed in their work and unaware of his presence as yet. It seemed that it would be an easy thing to turn round, walk away and never come back. They gave the impression that they did not need him.

At last, Macadam looked up and saw him. 'There you are, sir.'

Quinn placed the copy of *A Furious Energy* on Macadam's desk without a word. Then turned to hang up his ulster and hat. He could sense them watching him closely.

'So,' he said, facing them again. 'Malcolm Grant-Sissons is dead. He died last night. I was with him.'

There were noises of condolence from Macadam and Inchball.

Quinn batted them away. 'I hardly knew him.'

Macadam touched the book with his fingertips. It was almost a caress. 'It didn't work then, sir?'

'You can't save a man's life by reading to him, Macadam. So, Inchball, how did you get on at the asylum?'

'Your brother . . .'

'Grant-Sissons. Call him Grant-Sissons. That is more professional, I think.'

'Grant-Sissons was indeed an inmate there. According to the superintendent there, Dr Pottinger, he underwent some kind of miracle cure, by the sounds of it. Came in a blithering wreck, and left after a couple of weeks sane as you or me. Well . . . I mean . . . you know . . . completely sane.'

Quinn nodded. 'Remarkable.'

'Mind you, I have to say, there's something fishy about that Pottinger fella. I wouldn't trust him as far as I could throw him.'

'What do you mean?'

'Well, first off, he's never heard of Grant-Sissons. Couldn't possibly know the names of every loony who gets admitted there.

That sort of thing. Then it suddenly comes back to him. How Grant-Sissons is some kind of marvellous success story.'

'I see. And what about any other patients who may have left there recently?'

'Nothing came to him, off the top of his head. He said he'd look into it and get back to me. Stalling for time, if you ask me.'

'Very likely. Keep on him. If we don't get those details soon, we'll go back and take them.' The terms under which the Special Crimes Department was established allowed wide-ranging powers of search and seizure, without the necessity of specific judicial warrants.

Inchball nodded approvingly. 'One thing he did confirm. It is their practice now to remove the tonsils and teeth from some patients. Summink to do with the germs what cause madness. Didn't make no sense to me. They ain't got round to doing everyone yet. But didn't them first two geezers have their teeth and tonsils removed?'

'So, further proof they were at Colney Hatch.'

'As if we were in any doubt. And here's another thing. As I was leaving, you'll never guess who I bumped into.'

Quinn shook his head.

'Only Timon fucking Medway.'

'Timon Medway?'

'That's right.'

'Yes, of course. We know he was allowed to stay there after . . . well, after the jury accepted his barrister's plea of insanity.'

'He's no more mad than—' Inchball broke off, no doubt remembering his earlier embarrassment around the same question. 'It's all an act.'

Quinn thought back to the Medway investigation. It must have been ten years ago, or possibly more. Four children were murdered and mutilated, their body parts left at various locations around London. In fact, Timon Medway was admitted to Colney Hatch on the very day that Quinn had gone to arrest him. If his insanity was a pretence, as Inchball claimed, he had played it very cleverly indeed, establishing the evidence of his madness before his identity as the murderer had come out.

And perhaps Medway actually was mad. The fact that he had killed those children ought to be enough to establish that. His claims to be God – or the Son of God – and a whole gamut of other people was merely window dressing.

'Do you think that Timon Medway has something to do with the deaths of these young men?' wondered Quinn.

'It did seem like he was expecting me.'

'How do you mean?'

Inchball's expression clouded. Quinn had the impression that there was something he wasn't saying. 'Very well. Dig out the Medway file, will you?'

'I'll sort it,' said Inchball, rising from his seat.

On his way out, Inchball crossed paths with one of the boys from the post room, a podgy youth of about sixteen years. Out of breath after his climb to the Special Crimes Department, his face was red and resentful, with sweat trickling from his temples.

'Which one of you is Macadam?'

Macadam identified himself and the boy threw a large manilla envelope across the room to him.

'Have a care!' objected Macadam, but the youth was already gone.

Macadam opened the envelope carefully with a paperknife. He took out several sheets of foolscap folio, stapled together. 'Well I never!' he exclaimed, after briefly examining the first page. He turned the pages excitedly.

'What is it?' asked Quinn, approaching Macadam's desk. Macadam handed the document up to him.

The pages bore the letterhead of THE FELLOWSHIP OF THE GRACCHI. On the first page, there was the heading CURRENT MEMBERSHIP. Beneath was a list of names and addresses, which continued on the next pages.

'Who is it from?' Quinn asked.

Macadam tipped the envelope up. Nothing came out.

Macadam smiled to himself. 'The old girl came through for me. I'll give her that.'

The names were organized alphabetically according to surname. Quinn turned to the second page and found the Gs. 'He's not here. Grant-Sissons wasn't a member of the Gracchi.'

'So, Manley Adams wasn't lying about that.'

Quinn turned over several pages. 'But look at this. Portman, W.G. And according to his listing, he is the secretary.'

'There is a connection then?'

'It seems so.'

'Do you think Portman had some contact with your brother
. . . with Grant-Sissons?'

'I don't know. Not everyone who reads a book has had dealings
with the author. Perhaps we are in danger of finding connections
that are not there, simply because we go looking for them.'

'Like seeing pictures in the clouds?'

Quinn frowned at Macadam's fanciful analogy.

'Perhaps Grant-Sissons did not join under his own name,'
wondered Macadam.

'Why should he not?'

Macadam shrugged. 'Manley Adams was certainly cagey about
handing the names over. Some of the members might not want
it to get out.'

Quinn shook his head dubiously. 'I don't see why Grant-
Sissons would want to keep his membership secret if he was a
member. His father, I mean Hugh Grant-Sissons, was well known
as a troublemaker.'

'Even so, you might look for his address, sir. I mean to say,
I am the member of a number of societies. They all send out
newsletters and communications of various kinds. One may use
a false name, but the address has to be genuine, otherwise there
is little point in being a member.'

'Good thinking, Macadam.'

'And might I suggest you look first at the Qs?'

'The Qs?'

Macadam hesitated tactfully before explaining: 'If he joined
recently, he might have chosen your father's name, sir. That is
to say, his father's.'

Quinn flicked to the last page. 'No. There is no Quinn listed.'
He handed the sheets to Macadam. 'You'll have to go through
them all.'

'That's quite all right, sir. It won't take long. St John's Passage,
wasn't it?'

Quinn nodded and crossed to his own desk.

A moment later, Inchball returned with the Medway file. Quinn
took it off him without a word. As he opened the file, he noticed
that his hands were shaking once again.

*   *   *

Quinn turned over the crime-scene photographs quickly. He did not need to be reminded of the viciousness of Medway's crimes.

Timon Medway was a gifted mathematician. He had been the Senior Wrangler of his year at Cambridge, graduating with the highest-scoring first-class degree, a full twelve per cent above the Second Wrangler. In fact, his marks were near perfect. It was typical of him that he saw the few points that he did drop as indicating the stupidity of his examiners, rather than his own failings.

He had surprised many by turning his back on an academic career, instead entering the insurance profession as an actuary. It seems he found the work lucrative but undemanding, leaving him free to pursue other interests.

Among these other interests was murder.

For Medway, murder was never a distinct pursuit from mathematics. In his own twisted mind, nothing he did was distinct from mathematics. For him, mathematics was the glue that held the universe together. As the foremost mathematician since Sir Isaac Newton (by his own assessment), he saw himself as being in a unique position not only to understand the universe, but to control it. Which he did through mathematics. And murder. The mathematics of murder, you might say.

He came to believe that he was a reincarnation of Isaac Newton, who in turn had toyed with the idea that he was a reincarnation of Jesus Christ. And so, Timon Medway was able to combine in his own person arguably the greatest human intellect there had ever been with the human incarnation of divinity. He was encouraged in this belief by the fact that he shared a birthday with both his avatars. Medway was born on 25 December, 1878.

Mathematicians look for patterns. In that sense, Quinn mused, they are like detectives. Both are at risk of mistaking random coincidence for significance, noise for meaning.

All this would have been enough to have him certified insane. Even before he started murdering and dismembering children.

His justifications for his crimes were incomprehensible to a lay person. And when Quinn had shown them to various professors of mathematics, they proved to be equally incomprehensible to the experts. He reduced child murder to a set of formulae, in which the age of the child, and various other factors and functions, were used to calculate the time, place and means of that child's death, as well as the number of pieces into which their corpses should be cut.

Medway acknowledged no peers. And in fact he believed that the field of mathematics as traditionally understood and studied was now defunct. It was time for a 'New Mathematics'.

The principles of his New Mathematics, together with his justifications for murder, were contained in a treatise extending over a thousand densely handwritten pages of calculations and exegesis. According to the professionals Quinn consulted, there was nothing very new contained in it at all. Medway showed a sound understanding of some of the more outlandish theories currently in fashion, although his claims to be their discoverer – and to have had his ideas stolen by his enemies – were generally thought to be without foundation.

In fact, Medway's Philosophiae Naturalis Principia Mathematica Nova turned out to be an incoherent mishmash of second-hand ideas, mediaeval numerology and nonsense. There could, in all honesty, be little doubt that its author was mad.

The four children Medway had murdered had all been aged seven. He had located them through his access to insurance files. The first was Gladys Bailey, the daughter of a solicitor and his wife. The second, Emmanuel Peters, a vicar's son. Next came Dorothea Chapman, whose father was a colonel in the Coldstream Guards.

So far, Quinn remembered, there seemed to be a pattern in the choice of victims. The families were all stolidly respectable and middle class. They represented three pillars of the establishment: the Law, the Church, the Armed Forces. But then the fourth victim, Wilfred Thomas, was the son of an unmarried mother of decidedly bohemian habits. Elena Thomas was an actress, Quinn remembered, a star of the West End stage. It seemed her immorality had not hindered her in her chosen career.

He remembered breaking the news to her, that they had found another body, or rather more body parts. And that they believed them to be those of her missing son.

Her grief was the most shocking and dramatic display of emotion that Quinn had ever witnessed. He found it hard to imagine her ever recovering from it. And he had no doubt that she was not acting at that moment.

How many more children Medway would have gone on to murder if they had not caught up with him was difficult to say. His voluntary admission to Colney Hatch Asylum had possibly curtailed his killing spree. Perhaps he had done enough to prove whatever insane theorem he was pursuing. Or perhaps he merely intended to lie low until the investigation was suspended and it was safe to resume his activities. If he had been allowed to continue, the pattern that the first three victims suggested would either have been confirmed or unravelled completely.

Like many of the most prolific killers that Quinn had encountered, Medway seemed to flirt with the idea of his own capture. A part of it was the desire to be recognized as the author of the terrible deeds that had shaken society. This class of criminal would often deliberately leave clues taunting the police, confident that their adversaries were too stupid to solve them.

In Medway's case, the clues were mathematical. Or, as it turned out, New Mathematical, which is to say nonsensical. He had written to the London Mathematical Society revealing details about the crimes that were known only to the police and the murderer. The letters contained some of the calculations from Principia Mathematica Nova and were signed Jeova Sanctus Unus, which Quinn subsequently learnt had been Isaac Newton's alchemical pseudonym.

The writer of the letters demanded that they be published in the society's journal, otherwise there would be more murders. The London Mathematical Society had passed the letters on to Quinn, who had advised them to publish the mathematical parts of the letters, leaving out anything connected to the murders. He also encouraged the head of the society to manufacture a specious academic dispute with the writer of the pseudonymous letters, not only pointing out supposed mistakes in the calculations, but also attacking their theoretical basis and questioning the author's mathematical competence in no uncertain terms. An important part of this attack was the assertion that no serious mathematician could be found who would give the theories outlined any credence whatsoever.

This was enough to draw Timon Medway out. He wrote in his own name, giving his credentials as Senior Wrangler and indeed as a prominent fellow of the society, defending the mathematical calculations submitted. Although Medway's letter was typewritten and the Jeova Sanctus Unus letters were handwritten, there were enough stylistic similarities between them to arouse suspicion. Besides, Quinn had also ensured that crucial mathematical details were omitted when the letter was published. Medway could not help revealing his knowledge of these omissions in his refutation and accusing the editor of butchering the elegance of the original calculations. It seemed certain that Jeova Sanctus Unus and Timon Medway were one and the same person.

Medway had assumed that countless other members would flood the society with letters of support. There were none forthcoming but his own.

Perhaps he realized his mistake as soon as the letter was sent, because he soon after made sure of his admission to Colney Hatch, laying the ground for a plea of insanity.

'Well, here's something,' said Macadam, with that self-conscious restraint that heralded great excitement.

'He's listed?'

'Not Grant-Sissons, as far as I can tell. There is no one listed as residing at St John's Passage. However, one member gives his address as The Asylum, Friern Barnet Road, Colney Hatch.'

'Indeed?'

'Yes. And he gives his name as Unus, J.S.'

'Jeova Sanctus Unus. Timon Medway.'

'It must be.'

Quinn felt the pieces falling into place. 'The cards. The letters on the back of the cards. F.J.S.U. We have, I think, the J, the S, and the U. And seven. The number seven was of great significance to Medway, I seem to remember. It was the age of all his victims. And . . .' Quinn broke off to leaf through the Medway file. 'There was something else. Mumbo jumbo. Nonsense. But it seemed to mean a lot to Medway. The way he used to add things up to arrive at a number. Here it is. The numbers of his date of birth, twenty-five plus twelve plus one thousand eight hundred and seventy-eight. Add them together and you get one thousand nine hundred and fifteen. One plus nine plus one plus five is sixteen. One plus six is seven. It was the same with the letters of his name. There is a way of giving them numbers. If you do it, it adds up to seven. Same with Jeova Sanctus Unus, which was an anagram of Isaac Newton's name in Latin. It's all nonsense, as I say. But Medway believed in it. As far as he was concerned, the number seven had magical significance. I wouldn't be surprised if we discover that the thumbprint on the cards belongs to Timon Medway. Inchball . . .'

'I took the liberty of calling in at the forensic lab on my way to the records archive. I told them to look into it.'

'We will await the result of the fingerprint analysis. In the meantime, I suggest we pay a visit on the secretary of the Fellowship of the Gracchi. I have one or two questions I would like to put to him.' Quinn rose from his seat decisively. 'Macadam, will you drive us?'

TWENTY-TWO

Quinn felt the Model T's familiar vibrations throb comfortingly in his bones as he settled back in the seat beside Macadam.

It felt good to be driven by Macadam again.

Quinn knew that the responsibility for any distance that had grown between him and his men was entirely his. He had not trusted them with the truth about his past. He had deliberately kept them out of his confidence, allocating them spurious tasks to divert them from the real investigation.

If he were called to account for his conduct so far, he would be able to justify every decision. In any investigation, one can never know for sure what leads might arise and where they might take you. It paid to cast the net as wide as possible. Admittedly, with a core of three men, this meant that resources were inevitably spread thin.

All this might have fooled his superiors, but it did not fool him.

He had known where the investigation was heading as soon as he saw the first brown corduroy suit.

He had underestimated his men. And his decision to keep his knowledge of the suits to himself may even have hampered the investigation.

When Timon Medway's name came up, he had not been surprised. As soon as a link with Colney Hatch was established in his mind, he had thought of the notorious child murderer. Had he known all along that Medway was behind the deaths? If so, why had he kept quiet? Was it possible that he was being controlled remotely by Medway in the same way that the dead men had been?

It was impossible, absurd. It was over five years since he had seen Medway, who had been locked up in the asylum all that time. But Medway was highly manipulative. Perhaps he had agents who were at liberty and acting on his behalf. Could one of them have somehow influenced Quinn's behaviour without his knowing? He remembered the Blackley case. Benjamin Blackley had hired the services of a man called Yeovil in an attempt to manipulate and control the behaviour of his employees. Quinn had seen some evidence that Yeovil possessed the abilities he claimed.

The car moved inexorably along the London streets, weaving in and out of the traffic. Macadam was handy with the horn today. Every plodding dray cart, every dawdling omnibus or stalled motor had him reaching for the rubber bulb.

Quinn understood his sergeant's impatience, and he knew that in part it was for his benefit. Macadam was as eager to serve as ever. But there was a part of Quinn that didn't want the journey to end. It was taking him closer to the solution to the case. But it was also taking him closer to Timon Medway.

W.G. Portman lived on Westbourne Park Villas, in a modest house facing the railway tracks. There were four steps up to the front door, and a primitive pediment above it. Even so, it lacked the grandiose portico of some of its more pretentious neighbours.

The door was opened by a young woman in a loose-flowing dress. She was pretty and slim and at ease with herself. She arrived at the door still glowing with the excitement and hilarity of the conversation she had just come from. Her smile faded as she saw the three stern men before her, arranged awkwardly on receding steps. A look of mild curiosity quickly darkened at the sight of Quinn's warrant card.

'Mrs Portman?'

'No . . . not exactly.'

'This *is* the home of Mr W.G. Portman, is it not?'

'It is.'

'Is Mr Portman at home?'

A muffled voice cried out from the depths of the house, male, with a distinct Midlands accent. 'Who the Devil is it, Reg?'

She invited their indulgence with a colluding smile, which seemed to be at the expense of the shouting man. 'Would you care to come in? I'll take you through. We're in the garden. There's lemonade. It would be delightful if you could join us.'

It was typical of these people, thought Quinn, by which he meant people of her class, the way she took the initiative and turned the situation around to her advantage. It was no longer an unwelcome intrusion. It was an invitation graciously extended.

As if she would be personally offended if these three policemen did not come in and interrogate her lover.

She led them along a narrow corridor, into the kitchen, which was in a state of scandalous disarray. Several days' worth of dirty pots were spread over every surface, the plates littered with cheese rinds, orange peel and shrivelled grapes. There were ashtrays overflowing with cigarette butts, empty wine bottles and smeared glasses still containing the dregs of last night's binge. The air was sour and vinegary.

Their feet crunched over a layer of breadcrumbs strewn like sawdust on the floor.

'Forgive the mess. Willy won't have servants, even though he can afford it. He says it's against his socialist principles. And doing his housework for him is against mine. So . . .' Her smile distracted them from the sordidness of the surroundings. 'He says that in the future there will be machines to wash dishes. I suppose we'll just have to wait for that.'

A door from the kitchen led out into a small shaded garden.

Portman sat at a circular garden table in a collarless shirt, his sleeves rolled up. He wore a wide-brimmed straw hat, adorned with flowers. It was a woman's hat, or possibly the sort worn by donkeys once holes had been cut for the ears. Portman appeared utterly unabashed. He stared up at them with a look of bullish amusement, as if he were aware of his own absurdity but challenged them to make something of it.

'Hello, hello, hello. Who have we here?'

'It's the police,' announced Reg, raising her brows warningly.

'Yes, I sort of surmised that. Hence my . . . joke.'

Reg frowned uneasily. 'Shall I fetch some more glasses?' She answered her own question by disappearing back inside. Quinn could hear her sorting through the pots and debris of the kitchen.

'Were you expecting the police?' wondered Quinn.

'Not at all. It's just . . . you have that look about you.'

Suddenly Quinn had the sensation that he had met Portman before. It was always possible.

'You are W.G. Portman?'

'I confess!' Portman held out his arms with his wrists together. 'Cuff me. Lock me up. Throw away the key. I am indeed that dreadful sinner who goes by the name of Wilfred George Portman.'

'And you are the secretary of the Fellowship of the Gracchi?'

'Ah, so that's what this is all about? Old Manley Adams did warn me to watch out for a visit from the boys in blue. You think I'll tell you what he wouldn't?'

Quinn blinked away the question. 'Do you know a young man called Malcolm Grant-Sissons?' He took out the photograph of Malcolm that he had retrieved from Grant-Sissons' house.

Portman shook his head. 'Never seen the fellow.'

'He is not a member of the Gracchi, as far as we know. This has nothing to do with that. You will not be betraying any confidences. We believe he was an admirer of your books.'

'As am I, if I may say so,' put in Macadam, who immediately blushed and looked abashed.

'So I take it that in itself is not a crime? If a policeman admits to it.'

Quinn looked at the picture of Malcolm for a moment before returning it to his pocket. 'Malcolm died as the result of a terrible accident at Bankside Power Station. He was reading your novel, *A Furious Energy*, around the time of his death. The story, as you will know, is centred around the theme of electricity.'

Portman winced. 'Electricity is not the theme, Inspector.'

Quinn wondered how the author knew his rank. Perhaps they *had* met before, after all.

'Electricity is a metaphor. Power is the theme. Its uses and abuses. Did you read the book?'

'I haven't finished it yet.'

'I have,' said Macadam, eagerly.

'At any rate, I'm afraid I don't quite follow your drift. This fellow was reading my book. And then he had an accident. What of it? I am not on intimate terms with every single one of my readers.' Portman shuddered deliberately. 'Heaven forfend.'

'No, of course not. We must look into everything, you understand. Is it not the case that sometimes readers write letters of appreciation to authors they admire? Particularly young readers. Malcolm was a young man. And somewhat disturbed in his mind. If he did write to you, such a letter might help us to better understand his state of mind when he died.'

'You think he sent me his suicide note?'

'You know that he killed himself, I see.'

'I had read about the incident. It was of a piece with those other deaths. The men all remove their clothes before killing themselves. I can assure you that I received no letters from anyone concerning such matters.'

Just then, Reg returned with three smeared and mismatched glasses, which she set down on the garden table as quietly and unobtrusively as she could.

'Does the name Timon Medway mean anything to you?'

'Timon Medway?'

Quinn noticed the change in Portman's demeanour. Beneath the brim of his hat, his face was suddenly drained of colour. He noticed, too, a complex look pass between Portman and Reg. But as yet he did not have enough information to interpret its meaning.

'I read about that case too. It was in all the newspapers. As were you, Inspector Quinn.'

So that was it. His celebrity went before him. 'Are you aware that Timon Medway is a member of the Fellowship of the Gracchi? He goes by the name of Jeova Sanctus Unus and gives his address as the Colney Hatch asylum.'

'Yes. I knew it was he. Anyone who kept up the accounts of his trial will have known of his pseudonym.'

'It does not trouble you that such an individual is a member of your organization? Doesn't it rather undermine your pacifist ideals?'

'Because he is a murderer?'

'A man of violence, yes.'

'What is it that it says in the Bible? I am myself an atheist, you understand. Nonetheless, the Bible is a marvellous source of quotations. There is more rejoicing in Heaven over one sinner who repents . . . isn't that how it goes?'

'You think he has repented? From what I know of Timon Medway, that is highly unlikely.'

'I don't concern myself with his past. If he shares our political ideals now, that is good enough for me.'

'I wonder if the parents of his victims would say the same?'

'You will have to ask them that question.' There was a strange tension in Portman's face. His jaw was gripped in anger. Reg must have noticed it too, for she went over to him and laid a hand on his shoulder to relax him.

Portman sighed. 'It is hard, sometimes, I admit, having principles.

Sometimes, one principle comes in conflict with another. It's true, I'm not a Christian. But I do believe in forgiveness, perhaps more than any Christian since the man himself. Not to compare myself to the Son of God – I don't share that delusion with Timon.'

'Timon? You call him Timon?'

'Yes, I make no secret of it. I have corresponded with him. I have even visited him in Colney Hatch.'

'Why?' Quinn could not keep his horror out of his voice.

'I am a writer, Inspector. My stock in trade is character. Timon Medway is the most extraordinary character of our age. Is it not natural that I would want to study him up close?'

'He is a heartless murderer of children.'

'Oh, he has a heart. And it pumps blood around his body as any other man's does. And besides, he can't kill any children where he is now. There are none there. And he is watched ever so closely.'

'It is not for you to forgive him.'

'Very well, let us not use that word. Forgiveness. It is too fraught with scripture. But society must find a way to rehabilitate men like Timon Medway. No good is served by his continued incarceration.'

'Children are protected. Lives are saved. I would count that as a good.'

'But if we could find a way to excise from him the murderous impulse, as a surgeon excises a tumour! He is an extraordinarily talented man. One of the greatest intellects I have ever encountered. He has devised a whole new system of mathematics, you know? We are depriving the world of his talents while he festers in that place.'

'I will gladly forego such talents as his.'

'We must accept that he was sick when he did what he did to those children. Mad, not bad. The efforts of the psychiatric profession should be directed to curing him. It is not enough to simply contain him. That is a failure.'

'But how could we ever be sure that he is cured?'

'That is a challenge for greater minds than mine. For the doctors of the psyche. I am a simple storyteller, a dreamer. A visionary, perhaps. Some have called me that. I merely present my dreams to the world. It is for others, those of a more practical bent, to convert them into reality.'

'And what if he can never be cured?'

'Ah, Inspector, unlike you I am an optimist. That's to say, I believe in the future. The future has to be better than the past, does it not? Otherwise, what is the point of going forward into it?'

'That's all very well, but it doesn't take account of Timon Medway. It would have been better for all if he had been hanged on the gallows.'

'It will not surprise you to learn that I am an opponent of judicial murder. If we kill those who have killed, we render ourselves no better than they. And that is to say nothing of miscarriages of justice, innocent men hanged in error, or wilful oppression. In the wrong hands, the law becomes a political weapon, you know. And besides all this, I am a great believer in giving people a second chance. Capital punishment rather rules out the possibility of second chances, do you not think?'

Quinn felt something snap inside him. A surge of rage was released.

This man knew nothing, and yet acted as if he had the answers to all the world's most difficult problems. Just like Medway with his system of New Mathematics. Perhaps he was even more dangerous than Medway.

Quinn could feel himself shaking again. The image of Wilfred Thomas's mother came back to him. It was as if she was there in front of him, wailing uncontrollably, destroyed by grief and incomprehension, shaken undone by a pain that would never heal. Would Portman be able to utter such inanities if he had been there to witness her tears, her more than tears, her utter unravelling? If he had been the one who had broken the news of her son's murder to her?

Quinn tried to superimpose the writer's smug face into his memory of Elena Thomas. He fitted in surprisingly well, despite the incongruity of his comical hat. And in Quinn's imagination, the man's expression of contemptible complacency was transformed into shock as he at last understood raw human suffering.

'Now then, who's for lemonade?' Reg's voice was brittle rather than bright as she attempted to diffuse the tension that had suddenly arisen in the small garden.

Quinn watched in silence as she poured out the lemonade, the thin remnants of ice tinkling delicately against the Jugendstil ceramic jug. He took his drink eagerly and drained it in a few loud gulps, grateful for the biting, acerbic taste as it went down.

TWENTY-THREE

Quinn's body craved sleep. But it was too hot. He lay on top of his bedclothes in his underwear. Unmoving, tense, his senses unpleasantly alert.

The window was open but there was no breeze to disturb the curtains. Despite the stillness, he sensed the night invading his room. The sounds of the street were startlingly present with him.

A dog barking in a distant garden was tethered to the bottom of his bed, shrunken to the size of a shrew. A yowling tomcat was keeping up his indignant plaint from the top of the wardrobe. The footsteps that passed along the pavement took a momentary detour across his windowsill. A nightingale twittered as it looped through the dark spaces beneath the ceiling.

Often in this state, suspended between wakefulness and oblivion, some breakthrough would come to him. He would sit bolt upright in bed, snapping awake and completely focused. But not tonight.

Tonight he was haunted by the image of Elena Thomas. It annoyed him that his mind was stuck on it. As far as he could see, Elena Thomas had no connection to the deaths of the three young men he was investigating, other than through Timon Medway. Her face was an obstacle to the progress of his thinking. And yet for some reason his mind persisted in presenting it to him. To make matters worse, there looking on, chastened but still in his ridiculous hat, was W.G. Portman.

Quinn opened his eyes and closed his eyes and opened his eyes.

His whole body ached with exhaustion. The buzz and hum that filled his head seemed to originate in his bones, as if his entire body had become a peculiar resonating box.

If only he could stop thinking about how much he needed to sleep, then perhaps he might be able to drift off.

But now a new noise intruded on his consciousness: voices,

one female, one male, engaged in a low, intensely murmured dialogue. It seemed that the couple had decided to stop for their tête-à-tête immediately below Quinn's window. It felt as though they were under his bed, which accounted for the muffled quality of the sound.

Although he couldn't make out a word they were saying, he could tell from the tone and level of their voices that they were engaged in a discussion of the utmost urgency. Quinn had no idea what time it was. And he could not bring himself to find out. It wasn't just that he lacked the energy. It was almost as if the continued existence of the universe depended on his lying absolutely stock-still. But, God, if only they would shut up with their incessant whispering.

They would move on soon, surely, and leave him in peace. He strained to hear. If he could understand just one word, he might be able to relax, sleep even.

The two people speaking under his bed became embodiments of the figures who are sensed but not seen in every investigation, whose actions leave an unintelligible impact on the present.

Quinn wondered if the conversation he was almost eavesdropping on was the prelude to a murder.

And if so, who was the murderer and who the victim?

Or perhaps they were conspirators in the murder of a third party. The woman's husband, perhaps. Or his illegitimate older brother who stood in the way of an inheritance.

Strange how Quinn's mind was capable of solving cases that didn't exist but couldn't pull together the strands of the real case he was working on. It was always the same though. There was only so far your mind could take you. You reached the point where you had to wait for the next piece of the jigsaw to reveal itself.

He would need his wits about him tomorrow. Tomorrow, he sensed, would be a day of revelations. He had enough experience of this work to feel when the balance was tipping in his favour. There was a rhythm to these things.

If only he could just snatch a few short hours' sleep.

He heard the first stark notes of the dawn chorus begin to chitter and blurt. His room was filled with countless startled throats.

'Oh, why won't you let me be?' cried Quinn.

He hadn't meant to say the words out loud. He lay stiller than ever to gauge their impact on the world. The voices of the couple had now stopped, he noticed. He thought he heard their footsteps moving away down the street.

Or maybe he only dreamt it.

The following morning, Quinn was greased with sweat from the moment he woke up. A weight of exhaustion pulled at his body, as if his insomnia had conspired with gravity. It was an effort to move his feet and his arms ached as if he had been hefting dumbbells.

At the same time his body felt curiously unstable, on the verge of flying apart at any moment.

He was worn out on a molecular level.

Macadam and Inchball were already at their desks when he got to the department and he could tell by Macadam's face that there had been news. He had a look of barely suppressed excitement that Quinn knew well.

Even Inchball seemed buoyant.

Quinn waited until he had taken off his ulster and bowler before asking: 'Well?'

His two sergeants exchanged boyish grins to see who would be the one to tell him. In the end they broke the news between them.

'It's the fingerprints, guv.'

'The print on the card. It's Medway's, sir. As you suspected.'

Quinn nodded. It was the piece in the jigsaw that he had been waiting for. And yet he felt curiously numb, even deflated. The task ahead felt overwhelming. His sense of where it was leading was vaguer than ever. Nothing had come into focus. Yes, they had new information but it made no sense. If someone had advised him to give up the investigation, he would have done so without protest, gratefully even.

'Have we had anything from Pottinger yet?'

'The bastard's holding out on me,' said Inchball grimly.

Quinn was aware of his sergeants watching him anxiously. He knew that they must be disappointed by his subdued response. 'Anything else?'

'Miss Latterly called.' Macadam consulted a note he had made. 'Sir Edward wants to see you. Urgent, she said.'

Quinn felt the welling of emotion that had eluded him before.

Miss Latterly was at her typewriter. She hammered at the keys with an aggressive determination, and did not look up to inform Quinn: 'He's with someone.'

Quinn stared disconsolately at Sir Edward Henry's closed door. 'I shall come back then.'

'No. He specifically asked for you to wait. He won't be long, I'm sure. Do take a seat.'

A weight of disappointment settled on him. The last time they had spoken her tone had been softer, he felt sure. She had expressed a kind of exasperated affection for him, hinting at the possibility of something warmer developing between them. Or had he imagined it? Certainly, he had not acted on whatever encouraging moves she had made, so now of course, her demeanour had reverted to its earlier coldness. Exasperation won over affection. That was inevitable, and he only had himself to blame.

She had given him his chance and he had let it slip through his fingers.

But perhaps it was for the best. Perhaps they would both be happier if they never said another word to one another, other than those required by their duties. And yet that prospect saddened him unspeakably.

He sat down to wait.

Everything that he thought of saying to her sounded like an excuse. *I have been very busy . . . a friend died . . . I have not been myself . . . I think I might be coming down with something . . . I'm working on a very difficult case at the moment . . .*

Something came out of his mouth. He wasn't quite sure what. She heard it. 'Yes?'

'The weather has been quite . . .' He broke off and winced a smile at the difficulty of expressing accurately just how the weather had been. 'Well, at least it seems to be settling now. It has been stifling in the department.'

Miss Latterly gave vent to a despairing sigh. She might even have shaken her head, but Quinn was afraid to look.

To the relief of both of them, the door to Sir Edward's office opened. A man emerged whom Quinn had often seen coming out of that very door, the Whitehall mandarin Sir Michael Esslyn. As always, Esslyn ignored Quinn. He seemed to have obliterated from his memory the fact that they knew each other. Esslyn had once been involved in an investigation that Quinn had conducted, from which he had emerged technically blameless, although in Quinn's view at least, not entirely innocent.

Quinn waited for some sign from Miss Latterly that he should go in. But she was self-consciously intent on her work once more.

Sir Edward looked up from behind his desk. At the sight of Quinn, his features darkened. 'What the Devil are you playing at, Quinn?'

'I beg your pardon?'

'This latest investigation of yours. Who on earth gave you authorization to look into the deaths of these three unfortunate young men?'

'Details emerged about the circumstances of their deaths that led me to believe there was merit in an investigation.'

'What circumstances? That each of the poor wretches had spent some time in a lunatic asylum?'

'You know about that, do you?'

'Yes, I know about that. I know that that brute of a sergeant of yours has been disturbing a very important public functionary as he goes about his difficult work. Work that is done in the national interest, I might add.'

'Are you talking about Pottinger?'

'Dr Pottinger to you.'

'In what way, might I ask, is his work in the national interest?'

'Good grief, Quinn! Do you need to ask? You with your history! This isn't some personal grudge of yours I hope?'

'On the contrary. Nothing would give me greater pleasure than never to have to set foot in that place again. But you know, Sir Edward, that I must go where the evidence leads me. Just this morning . . .'

'Forget it. Do you hear me? Forget this whole thing. It's for your own good that I'm telling you this. But also I have to tell you, I have it on good authority that you are barking up the wrong tree. In fact, not only is it the wrong tree, there is no tree. You've imagined the tree, Quinn. It's not there.'

'I never said anything about a tree, Sir Edward.'

'Oh, you insufferable fellow! You know very well what I mean. I have as much sympathy for lunatics as the next man. More, in fact, as you well know.' This could have been a reference to Sir Edward's solicitude for a man who had once tried to kill him, who, it turned out, was in the grip of an extreme mental derangement.

'You do not wish me to continue the investigation?'

'There is no investigation!'

'I have reason to believe . . . that is to say, evidence has come to light that Timon Medway . . .'

'No no no no no! Not Timon Medway. Don't bring him into this. We don't want to give that man any attention again. Don't you realize that's just what he wants? To have us all buzzing around him like flies around . . .' Sir Edward broke off. Quinn realized that he had never heard Sir Edward swear. He put it down to his faith. 'We shan't give him the satisfaction. Especially as he can have nothing to do with these deaths. You do know that, Quinn, don't you? He was inside the asylum when the deaths occurred.'

'I believe that he may have planted the seeds of their deaths in their minds when he encountered them in Colney Hatch.'

'But you don't even know that he knew them!'

'But I do. I do now, as of this morning. I have certain proof.'

'I don't want to hear it. It's not important. It doesn't mean anything. You have certain proof of a coincidence, that's all.'

'Is this anything to do with Sir Michael Esslyn?'

'That's not a question you can ask, Quinn.'

'What would you have me do, then?'

'Haven't I made myself clear? Drop it.'

'Yes, yes, of course. That's understood. I just meant, instead. What would you have us investigate instead?'

'What is it that the Bible says, Quinn? Seek and ye shall find? Matthew, seven: seven. Do some seeking and finding. That's what I would advise you.'

'We were looking into a group of pacifists.'

'Pacifists?'

'Well, socialists and pacifists. That sort of thing.'

'Do pacifists do any harm?'

'I suspect these of being militant pacifists. I do not rule out the possibility of their using violent means to bring about world peace.'

'Good heavens! Who ever heard of such a thing? Very well . . . continue with the pacifists. But what about the Irish? It pains me to say it, being of Irish parentage myself, as you know. But the Irish situation is very troubling. So much anger on all sides. I can see no good coming from it. And if we are drawn into a war with Germany, it will be so much the worse.'

'We have been looking into them as well.'

'Excellent, Quinn. That's more like it. You see, you've got enough on your plate without bothering Dr Pottinger and his lunatics. Mad people kill themselves. That's all there is to it, I'm afraid. It's the ones that kill other people we need to worry about.'

Sir Edward gave a reflex smile that communicated nothing other than that the interview was at an end.

'If I may, one last question, Sir Edward. Am I to take it that Dr Pottinger will not be supplying the information that Sergeant Inchball requested from him?'

'No, he will not!'

The smile was gone from Sir Edward's face entirely when Quinn got up to leave.

'Shall I bring the car round, sir?'

'The car?'

'To take us to Colney Hatch.'

'We will not be going to Colney Hatch, Macadam. This line of enquiry is, I have been persuaded, fruitless.'

'What the . . .?' Inchball slapped his desk with his open palm in indignation. 'Just as we was bleedin' gettin' somewhere.'

'No. I am sorry. It is my fault. I led us down a blind alley. The fact is, we don't even know who two of the dead men are.'

'But if we had them names from Pottinger . . .' objected Inchball.

'Inchball's right, sir. It wouldn't take us long to identify them, if we had the information we were waiting for.'

'It won't be forthcoming.'

'So that's it? Even though we know Medway is behind it all?'

'We know nothing of the sort, Inchball.'

'His prints are all over them cards.'

'One thumbprint, I believe was found. All that indicates is he touched the cards. He may have distributed such cards to many in the asylum. Everyone perhaps. And so therefore, the presence of the cards, and the fact that he handled them, proves nothing.'

'This ain't you. This ain't you talking. You been got at.'

'With respect, sir, we will never get to the bottom of the cards if we don't go into Colney Hatch and investigate.'

'I am afraid, Macadam, we simply have no authorization to do that.'

'We can do what we bleedin' well want!' insisted Inchball with another slap of his desk. 'We're the Special Crimes Department. We have a special judicial warrant. Or have you forgotten that?'

'We can do nothing without Sir Edward Henry's approval. He wishes us to redirect our resources into investigating Irish agitators.'

Inchball gave a heartfelt groan. 'Not that again.'

'And also, we will be continuing to keep an eye on the pacifists. In particular, the Fellowship of the Gracchi.'

'Of which Timon Medway is a member!' cried Macadam delightedly.

'Sir Edward did not expressly forbid us from investigating him as a political agitator. Although we must tread carefully. I fear there is a direct line of communication between the superintendent of the asylum and certain powerful interests within the machinery of government.'

'There's something going on here,' observed Inchball. 'Something very fishy indeed.'

Quinn studied his sergeant's face closely, as if it was the first time he had seen it, or any face, and he was trying to make sense of it. And yet, if it held any meaning, it eluded him.

TWENTY-FOUR

S tanley Ince walked the first-floor corridor. He was tense and alert, his senses attuned to the moods of the inmates. They were all locked behind doors now, but he could feel their growing agitation. He stopped at a window and looked out over the gardens. The sky was darkening quickly, though not from the onset of night. It had been building to a storm all day. But the weather had still not broken.

Ince dreaded storms, indeed any extremes of weather. It was well known that a full moon disturbed lunatics. But the weather did it too, especially sudden changes. These last few days had been particularly changeable.

Howling winds were the worst. Nature screaming obscenities and befouling herself. And the way the trees rustled and trembled didn't help.

It always upset them.

In a lunatic asylum, emotion spreads like a highly contagious fever. It doesn't matter where that first emotion arises, or even if it is real. A shivering oak is as likely to spook a loony as a raving man. And once the first loony has been spooked, it's not long before they all are.

He had never encountered any other creatures who were as sensitive to barometric pressures. It was as if their bodies were filled with mercury. At the slightest increase in the air's density, they would go off on one.

He could hear them now. The massed whimpering. They were cowering in the corners of their cells and dormitories, arms clamped over their heads.

It would be worse when the storm broke. When the wind whipped up and rattled the windows in their frames. When the rain lashed down with Old Testament fury. The kind of rain that it was impossible to imagine ever stopping. Until the world was flooded and the sky drained.

Good God, he'd spent too long among these feeble-minded imbeciles. He was beginning to think like one of them now.

And now the first fat gobbet of rain crashed into one of the panes. There was an immediate answering shriek from somewhere behind him. The second drop followed soon after. The downpour began, drumming a tattoo upon the glass. Almost simultaneously the sky was lit up for one lurid instant, like a whore caught under a streetlight in her garish slap.

Something snagged at his vision in the flash. The sense of something awry. An object out of place. But now it was lost from sight. The darkness had come back, more impenetrable than before. Maybe he had imagined it. He had only an uncertain impression of it. Some fleeting thing glimpsed out of the corner of his eye. If there was a second flash of lightning and he looked for it, whatever it was, there would be nothing there.

And now, with the lightning, the shrieks began in earnest. And the heels pummelling the floor. The heads pounded against walls.

There would be blood to mop up tomorrow. Along with everything else.

He held his breath until it came. The first roll of thunder.

In answer, the sounds of the lunatics' distress grew into a roar.

There was nothing you could do but let their frenzy run its course.

A second flash of lightning – brighter, more startling than the first – showed the world to be a stranger place than he had ever imagined: wild, uncanny, misbegotten. In the brief illumination, he looked again to where he had sensed that something not quite right.

He saw now that he had been wrong. It did not try to flee his attempt to see it. Or rather, *he* did not. For Ince saw quite clearly that it was a man out there, standing in the middle of the lawn, alone, naked, his arms reaching up towards the lightning.

And though the man had his back to him, Ince knew immediately, and without a shadow of doubt, that it was Timon Medway.

TWENTY-FIVE

Hyde Park was sodden and littered with the debris of the previous night's storm. Clumps of battered clouds lingered in the sky, like a riotous assembly that had been broken up by the police.

On the ground, the air was fresh and eager, a breeze that came at you and wouldn't let you be. It even had a chill edge to it. The sun shone gamely, giving the dampness a pristine gleam. There was a sense of renewal in the air.

Quinn had arranged to meet Inchball and Macadam at Speakers' Corner at nine. The idea was that they would wander from speaker to speaker, mingling with the crowd, one eye open for anyone handing out Gracchi leaflets, and an ear cocked for Irish accents.

Look. Listen. Learn.

It might have seemed like a vague and even hopeless plan. Inchball had said as much, in his own blunt way. *Clutchin' at bleedin' straws!*

But you never knew what you might witness, and where it might lead.

Macadam was the first to turn up. They had agreed not to acknowledge one another, except by the briefest of signals: scratching the left ear with the right hand. Whereas scratching the right ear with the left hand meant that you had seen something of interest and so required support. Scratching the right ear with the right hand, or left ear with left hand, simply meant that the ear in question was itchy.

Inchball, when he arrived, made no attempt to conceal his disgruntlement. He had better things to do on a Sunday morning and he wasn't talking about going to church.

He became quickly confused by the ear signalling and simply shook his head in exasperation.

It seemed a good moment to split up.

So far, there were three or four speakers in evidence, positioned at a distance from each other, with varying numbers of listeners clustered around them. As always, the speakers had raised themselves above the crowds by standing on steps or portable platforms. These were adorned with placards promoting the cause that the speaker was arguing for.

A cursory glance was enough to identify their themes:
CHRISTIANITY
WOMEN
PEACE
SOCIALISM
The SOCIALISM speaker had attracted by far the biggest crowd. Without thinking, Quinn found himself drawn into it. He shouldered his way towards the front.

It was easy to see why this man had gathered so many people about him. It was not what he was saying, Quinn suspected, so much as the way he was saying it. In fact, Quinn guessed that there were as many who disapproved of his message in his audience, as those who applauded it. He heard as many jeers and boos as he did cheers.

The man was young, good-looking and impassioned. His hair was black and glossy and he was continually sweeping the long fringe up off his forehead, over which it continually fell. Despite this repeated distraction, his eyes blazed with a visionary fervour. But he was not without humour too. And though his accent betrayed a public school background, he had a knack for expressing himself in simple, down-to-earth expressions that spoke directly to his audience.

His gesticulations were precise and forceful. There was something of the actor about him.

Quinn looked into the faces of those listening. In some he saw detached amusement, in others, intent devotion, a fervour that was equal to the speaker's. After he had seen the same expression on a number of faces, he realized what it was: hope.

'Comrades!' cried the speaker. 'I see over there, to my right, a gentleman who is quoting verses from the Bible. From the New Testament, I believe. He preaches a message of brotherly love. Remember the story of the good Samaritan? That's what a socialist is! That's right. That's all it is. My message, the message of the socialist gospel, is not so different from his, you know. Except I want us to build a fair and just society – a paradise, if you will – in this world. Why wait for the next? I mean, we only have his word for it that there will be a next world! I believe in life before death. What is it that it says in the Bible? The Lord helps those who help themselves. In other words, you're on your own, mate. You can pray all you like, but you'd better not wait for God to come down from His heaven and smite the unjust. You've got to do your own smiting. Oh, yes! God is just. He's just not interested in our mundane affairs. Not as far as I can see, anyhow. So, it's up to you, it's up to all of us, to create a better world, a better life, ourselves. Can't leave it to anyone else, oh no! A good life, a better life, for everyone, that's all I'm talking about here. For all my brothers and sisters. Sisters, yes! Sisters! For over there, beyond the Christian gentleman, I see that one of my sisters – we are all brothers and sisters, you know – yes, one of my sisters is talking about the woman question. The woman question is resolved, is answered, in socialism. For the socialist holds that we are all equal. Men and women. There is no woman question, once you accept socialism. And there, to my left, another well-meaning gentleman argues the case for World Peace. Who could take issue with that? Not I. But how do you deliver world peace? Through universal, global socialism. Because it is the capitalists and the imperialists and the industrialists and the profiteers who cause wars. And they are the only ones who benefit from wars. There is a cabal – and I use the word advisedly – oh yes, I'm afraid so. It pains me to say it, but there you have it. Money is the root of all evil. I've read me Bible, you can see! If you want to know the guilty ones, just look where the money goes. Who has the most to gain from war? I'll tell you one thing. It's not the poor bloody foot soldier who'll end up dying in a ditch so some fat slimy kike . . .'

Was this what it always came down to? Whatever ideology you subscribed to, at some point it became simply the way you justified your hate.

Quinn felt suddenly exhausted, and hopeless.

Some of the audience began to drift away, but an equal number, perhaps more, replaced them. Quinn noticed that another speaker had set up his stall. He glanced at his banner and his eye was caught by the word UNIONISM. The speaker was a bowler-hatted gentleman in a dark suit, wearing an orange sash. The union flag was draped over his podium. Quinn pushed his way out of the socialist's crowd to hear what the newcomer had to say, blanking Macadam as they crossed paths along the way.

More people were arriving at Speakers' Corner all the time, swelling the ranks of each speaker's audience. The Christian gentleman was faring worst, drawing only a handful of listeners, presumably because if people wanted to hear a sermon on a Sunday morning, they would go to church.

The advocate of unionism, on the other hand, was pulling them in. Quinn suspected that many of those amassed there were supporters he had brought with him. They looked like him, with the same thickset body shape, and were dressed similarly, except for the sash. Their faces were twisted with the same expression of righteous rage. If Quinn had ever seen a group of men spoiling for a fight, this was them. They were, to a man, holding umbrellas. In their hands, the furled black sticks became unspeakably sinister.

They seemed to be the only ones who could understand the speaker's thick Ulster accent. It even struck Quinn that they had heard the speech before. They knew where to cheer so well that they sometimes jumped their cue, and drowned out the telling phrase.

He was cautious about looking them directly in the eye, in the way that you would not provoke a vicious dog if you could avoid it. And yet he found their anger fascinating. It was clear that they were outraged. As his ear attuned to the speaker's voice, he began to understand why. The country they pledged loyalty to had betrayed them. It had placed them in the most invidious position. They were being sorely, grievously provoked. There would be blood, the speaker declaimed. And it would not be on his hands.

The government of the day was a traitor to its own people. He would not hesitate to call upon all true and loyal defenders of the Union to take up arms and wage war on those Judases of Westminster.

'The blood will be on their hands! For they have brought this upon themselves by their perfidy.'

He urged his congregation to make no mistake. War was coming. It would be the worst kind of war. The bloodiest kind of war. A war of survival. There would be carnage and conflagration. God knew, they had not sought this fight. But neither would they shirk from it.

That roused his supporters. There seemed to be certain words that triggered their enthusiasm: conflagration, perfidy, shirk. It was as though they were applauding his vocabulary rather than his sentiments.

Quinn looked to his side to gauge the reaction of the bowler-hatted man next to him. Like his fellows, he held himself clenched with pent-up aggression. Quinn tried to affect a similar expression, as if he was trying on the other man's anger, as he might try on a suit at the tailor's.

The man next to him must have sensed Quinn looking at him, for he faced him with a hard stare. But then he took in Quinn's appearance and his expression warmed. He gave a terse nod, acknowledging him as one of his tribe. It was true, Quinn did not look so different from these men. He was wearing a bowler hat himself. And perhaps his famous ulster overcoat would be taken by them as a token of solidarity, an adequate substitute for an umbrella.

More in embarrassment than fear, Quinn averted his gaze and looked down. His eye was caught by a small enamel badge pinned to the man's lapel. A red hand raised in open-palmed salute.

His gaze shot up to the man's face again. 'I like your badge,' he shouted, pointing at the object in question. 'How would I get one?'

'Yoy must join the UVF.'

'UVF?'

'The Ulster Volunteer Force.'

'Thank you. Yes. Of course.'

'And you must be prepared to lay down your life for the defence of the Union.'

Quinn nodded and moved on. It was time to give the pacifist group some consideration. This time on the way he encountered Inchball, who engaged in some confusing and confused business with hands and ears, scratching every conceivable ear with every conceivable hand.

He does it to provoke me.

Quinn averted his eyes from his sergeant with a frown. He could not help giving a small disapproving shake of the head, though he contrived to make it appear a distracted, self-absorbed gesture, made to contradict his own musings. And nothing at all to do with the strange pantomime that was happening in front of him.

The speaker who stood beneath the PEACE banner was a tall,

wiry man of patrician bearing. He had a full head of silver hair, and a wayward moustache that seemed about to take flight from his face. The moustache might have been distracting, but there was a sort of no-nonsense briskness to his delivery and a direct-ness to his gaze that held you and made you take him seriously. There was clearly no doubt in his mind of the truth of what he argued, and as far as he was concerned that ought to be enough to settle the matter beyond dispute.

The full wording of his placard was STAND TOGETHER FOR PEACE! Quinn recognized the phrase from the Fellowship of the Gracchi flyer which he had found on the first dead man. Much of the man's speech echoed sentiments that had been expressed in that, although it might be said he went further in the practical action that he advocated. 'Don't enlist! Do resist!'

It wasn't long before one of the very same flyers was thrust into his hand by a young woman who was weaving her way through the growing crowd. Quinn held up a hand to stop her moving off. He pointed at the man addressing them.

'Who is he?'

'Oscar Villiers. Isn't he marvellous?'

'You're a member of this lot, are you?' Quinn pretended he was reading the flyer for the first time. 'The Gracchi?'

'Of course.'

Quinn scanned the text. He read out: '*Combine and conquer the militarist enemy* . . . How do you do that, if you're a pacifist? How do you conquer anybody if you're a pacifist?'

'We have to win the argument.'

'And how do you do that? I mean, surely the man who wins the argument is the man with the biggest army?'

Despite Quinn's cynicism, the young woman maintained her good humour. She smiled winningly. 'Well, then, we have to win over as many people as possible to our cause. We have to make sure that our army is bigger than any other army. Can we count on you?'

Quinn frowned. 'An army for peace?'

'That's right.'

'But what do you fight with?'

'Words. Reason. Right. Justice . . . Love!'

'Love?'

'Yes! Why not?'

'Love can't stop bullets.'

'Yes it can. It can stop them being fired in the first place. If we win everyone over to our side, there won't be anyone to fire the bullets.'

'There will always be someone to fire bullets.'

'Some *man*, yes. But you are forgetting that half the population are women. Mothers, daughters, sisters . . . wives. It is their love that will stop bullets. They will prevail upon their menfolk. Why, you yourself, when you think of your own mother . . .'

'My mother is dead.'

'Your sweetheart then . . .'

'I don't have a sweetheart.'

'Oh dear! No sister either?'

'No, nothing like that. There is no woman to prevail upon me.'

'But even from a man's point of view, war – if it comes – it will not be your war. You have nothing to gain from it. Why should you sacrifice your life for the sake of the military industrial complex?'

'Because there will be nothing I can do to stop it.'

'But there is something you can do! You can join us. If everyone joins us, if all men join us, there will be no one to fight the war.'

'Then we will be conquered. The nation will be conquered. The Germans will overrun us.'

'Except that all the German men will have laid down their arms as well!'

'Do you really believe this?'

'Yes.'

'Does he believe it?'

'Yes. It will happen. It must happen.' She looked adoringly up at Oscar Villiers. 'Oscar will make it happen.'

Quinn followed the direction of her gaze. There was no doubt that Villiers was a charismatic speaker. The crowd around him was growing all the time. Perhaps it was the combination of a message they wanted to hear delivered by a somewhat authoritarian individual – indeed, the kind of man one might normally expect to exhort young men to enlist.

But to achieve the utopian vision the young woman had described, Villiers would need something more than mere charisma.

TWENTY-SIX

The following morning, Quinn had Macadam drive him round to Bedford Square. They waited in the car and watched the three-storey, double-fronted house for half an hour, only getting out once they had seen a silver-haired figure glance out of one of the upstairs windows.

This time, the ageing butler who had previously barred Macadam was unable to slam the door in their faces before Quinn's boot intervened to wedge it open.

'If you open the door a little wider, I shall remove my foot.'

But, of course, he took the opportunity to shoulder his way in. The old butler tottered back on his heels, slumping against the wall to regain his balance. Quinn felt a brief pang of guilt but the man's readiness to lie dispelled it. 'His Lordship is not at home, I tell you.'

'It's *Mr* Oscar Villiers we have come to see.'

The hallway was decorated with that effortless good taste that spoke of money and privilege.

A door to the back of the hall opened and the young woman Quinn recognized as W.G. Portman's mistress Reg came out.

'What is it Menton? Oh, it's you.'

'Good day, Miss . . .?' Quinn realized he had failed to ascertain her name at their last encounter.

'I'm Regina Villiers.'

'Yes, of course. You must be Mr Villiers' daughter?'

'I suppose I must be. What do you want?'

'We'd like a word with your father.'

'I told them, Miss Regina, that his Lordship is not at home.'

'Now, now, Menton, you know you mustn't call him that any more. I'm terribly sorry, Inspector, Menton gets easily confused. Although, in a sense, he's perfectly right. His Lordship is no longer at home. But Daddy is. Would you come through? He's in his study. I'm sure he won't object to seeing you.'

Quinn frowned. Once again, she made it seem as though

the interview depended on some degree of condescension on her part.

The room was filled with tobacco smoke. Villiers was seated at a large colonial-style desk with a green leather top, puffing away on a calabash pipe which protruded from beneath his unruly moustache. He looked up from a copy of *The Times* open on the desk. There was no trace of alarm in his expression, merely mild curiosity.

'Daddy, these gentlemen are policemen. They have come to arrest you. But don't think of escaping. They have the place surrounded.'

'That's not quite true, Mr Villiers. I am Inspector Quinn of the Special Crimes Department. And this is Sergeant Macadam. We would simply like a word or two with you.'

Villiers signalled with his pipe for Quinn to go on.

Quinn resisted an urge to waft the smoke out of his eyes and crossed to the window hopefully. 'I was at Hyde Park yesterday. I heard you speak.'

'I think you will struggle to find anything criminal in what I said.' The charisma that Quinn had been willing to grant him yesterday seemed like simple arrogance now.

'You urged men to refuse the country's call to enlist, should it arise.'

'Why should I encourage healthy young men to volunteer for their own deaths?'

'You went further, I think. In the event of conscription being introduced, you argued that it was every man's duty to resist it. That sounds suspiciously like sedition.'

'There is a greater duty than that which our country demands of us. What is country anyhow? It is merely an accident of birth. Nationalism is the root of all conflict. I prefer to think of the greater duty that we owe to the human species. To the world. We are all citizens of the world.'

'That's all very well, but there are always those who would attack us. You cannot get the whole world to lay down its arms at once. That will take time, if it's possible at all. So in the meantime . . . we must have a strong army to defend ourselves against our enemies. Do you not see that your words will give encouragement to our enemies?'

'I hope they will. I hope they will encourage them to do the same.'

'Hope? Is that all you have to offer? You pin all this on hope?'

'Hope is a powerful force, Inspector.'

'Let's say that I agree with you. Let's say your aims are commendable. Let's say I share your goal of world peace. What is it you say in your leaflet? *War is madness . . . War is death . . .* Let's say I agree. I still don't see how you can stop it. Not by mere hope alone. You need something more powerful than hope to conquer the militarist enemy.'

'What do you have in mind, Inspector? It almost sounds as if you have come here with a proposal.'

'There is a member of your organization called Timon Medway. I spoke to Mr Portman about him.' Quinn glanced over to Reg. She raised an eyebrow provocatively, a wry indication that she knew what was coming.

Villiers' face flushed crimson. 'Portman! That scoundrel! He's a bad egg. A bad egg, I tell you. I told Manley Adams we should expel him. And now he's been talking to the police about confidential membership matters.'

'We already knew. We have a list of your members.'

'How the Devil did you get that?'

'The information is in the public domain. I expressed my surprise to Mr Portman that you would allow such a man as Timon Medway to be a member. You are aware of his history?'

'I fail to see the point you are making?'

'He is a murderer. A multiple murderer. Hardly the best qualification for a pacifist.'

'All that was very unfortunate, I grant you. But the fact that he has chosen to join us shows that he is no longer a man of violence.'

'Unless he wishes to use your organization to mask his own ends.'

'How on earth could he do that?'

'I don't know. All that I do know is that I do not trust Timon Medway.'

'Everyone deserves a second chance, Inspector.'

'That's what Mr Portman said to me.'

'Well, there you go. If even Portman can say that.'

'What do you mean?'

Quinn caught the warning shake of the head from Reg to her father.

'Well, you know Portman. Utter scoundrel. No respect. Utterly immoral. He'll say anything to get a woman into bed. There's no place for his kind in the Gracchi.'

'You would prefer a child murderer to a philanderer?'

'That's not the point, Inspector, and you know it. What I mean is, even Portman – who in many aspects of his life has no principles whatsoever – even he understands the principle of Christian forgiveness.'

'Have you ever had any direct communication with Timon Medway? Has he ever offered to help your organization in any concrete manner? Has he ever, for example, offered a more substantive method of bringing about world peace than simple hope?'

'What do you have in mind?'

'I don't know. That's why I'm asking you.'

'I don't see what he could do, given that he is locked up in a lunatic asylum.'

'But did he ever offer?'

'We would not have taken any such offer seriously, had it been made. Naturally, we value the support of all our members. Our cause does occasionally excite the enthusiasm of the more eccentric elements.'

'Timon Medway is not eccentric. He is evil.'

Villiers made light of Quinn's warning. 'We take such offers with a pinch of salt.'

'What was his offer?'

'He offered to form a cadre of militant pacifists who would carry out a series of acts.'

'What acts?'

'That was never specified. But I rather had the impression he was thinking of bomb blasts and other outrages. Standard anarchist activity. Not our kind of thing at all.'

'He wrote to you of these proposals?'

'Yes.'

'Do you still have the letters?'

Villiers rose from his seat and crossed to a filing cabinet. A moment later he handed Quinn a wad of folded papers. 'There was only one, that I was aware of. Mind you, one was enough.'

Quinn glanced down. He felt a jolt, as if from an electric shock. There was no mistaking the tiny handwriting. A sudden queasiness came over him. He felt the strength drain from him, as if the bundle of paper he held was immeasurably heavy. He was suddenly empty, and cold. He watched his hand begin to shake.

He did not need to read the letter to know that Timon Medway had not changed. Would never change.

Back at his desk, Quinn studied the letter. There were seven pages of it, filled on both sides with Medway's compact, obsessive writing. He wrote on squared mathematical sheets of foolscap. Although he did not adhere to the lines of the grid, he wrote in unerringly straight and uniformly spaced rows, except that some letters were off-set from the rest, either floating slightly above, or sitting slightly below the line. But there was a regularity to this off-setting. It was clearly deliberate, although the purpose behind it, if there was one, was at first sight difficult to guess. It formed an elusive, asymmetrical pattern that was oddly distracting.

As for the content, Oscar Villiers' judgement of it seemed to be accurate. It was a rambling, self-justificatory and frankly tedious document. It lacked the passion and the coherence to be called a diatribe.

The most striking aspect of it was the reference Medway made to his own crimes, although he did not call them crimes. *Certain bold acts brought me to the world's attention.*

He went on to propose that: *the Fellowship of the Gracchi be equally bold in its efforts to further its laudable objectives.*

Was he therefore proposing that they resort to child murder?

An act is neither good nor evil in and of itself but only when its repercussions and consequences are taken into account. If the effect of Act A is to propulgate the aims of the Fellowship, then Act A can only ever be deemed good.

We must learn from those whose objectives are diametrically opposed to our own, but whose methods are incontrovertibly effective. Let us grasp the sanguinary

*hand of the militarist. Nor shall we wash off the blood
that adheres to our own hands until we have made real
our vision of universal peace.*

Medway's handwriting itself had always struck Quinn as self-conscious, even arch, although he had never seen such curious upping and downing of the letters before.

Despite their almost minuscule scale, Medway executed the letters with precise consistency and control. It's true that he allowed himself the occasional excessive flourish: an extended bar on every t, or oversized loops on the gs and ys. Sometimes these flourishes were executed at the expense of other letters. But there was a mechanical repetitiveness to them which undermined any sense of spontaneity or flair. Timon Medway's handwriting was a peculiarly lifeless and depressing artefact.

And then there were the letters that he seemed to be drawing attention to by placing them with perfect consistency and control at exactly the same distance from the true every time. It gave the impression of randomness, but Quinn sensed the pattern behind it. More than that, he had a premonition of a meaning that was eerily personal to him.

He started to make a note of the letters pulled out: *a, i, n, l, a, u, l, s, a, n, i, n, l, l, s, i, a, i, q* . . .

His heart started to thump. His palms grew moist.

He rationalized the list to unique instances of its constituent letters: *a, i, n, l, u, s, q.*

They were the letters of his own name. *Silas Quinn.*

That night Quinn entered the house with his usual stealth. He could hear voices coming from the drawing room. The door was ajar. The mood inside struck his ear as jolly, excitable even. People were talking over one another. Laughter was quick and ready, though it had a nervy brittleness to it.

The volubility of the gathering drowned out the sound of his entrance.

Still he paused for a moment at the threshold, straining to listen, like a burglar breaking into his own home.

As usual, Appleby and Timberley were dominating the discussion. Quinn identified Miss Ibbott's tinkling laughter and her mother's rather indulgent chuckle. The new couple were there too. The husband's droning monotone piped up regularly with some no doubt boorish or asinine comment, which his wife was quick to contradict.

Was it wrong of Quinn to take pleasure in the evident tension between them? Did he imagine himself usurping Mr Hargreaves in the marital bed? He shook his head at his own absurdity. This was a dangerous path to go down.

'It was an absolute hoot, I tell you!' declared Timberley.

'You have never seen the like,' confirmed Appleby.

'Well, I am peeved that you two went to see him without me!' complained Miss Ibbott.

'Oh, it wasn't a suitable entertainment for young ladies.'

'Now, now, Mr Appleby, we are not quite as delicate as you imagine, you know,' put in Mrs Hargreaves.

'Oh, you'd be fine!'

There was much outraged hilarity at the unflattering implication of Appleby's remark.

'I meant *unmarried* young ladies,' he clarified.

'Well, I'm glad we've cleared that up!' said Hargreaves, lamely.

'Was it a horribly indecent show?' wondered Miss Ibbott. 'I'm not sure I approve of you two innocent boys being exposed to such shocking scenes.'

'Oh, as it turned out, it wasn't indecent at all,' insisted Timberley.

'More's the pity!' The ill-judged quip came from Hargreaves.

'It just sort of made you think that it could take an indecent turn at any moment,' Timberley explained.

'It was chaos! Utter chaos. He had one fellow believing he was a window cleaner up a ladder. And a woman believing she was in the tub, you know . . .!'

Suitably scandalized laughter greeted this revelation.

Appleby continued: 'There she was, merrily soaping away. The window cleaner chap climbs up his ladder . . . Or at least that's what he thinks he's doing. There's no ladder, no window, no bucket of suds nor chamois leather. Well, you can guess what happened, I'm sure.'

Just in case they couldn't, Timberley supplied the details: 'He looks through the window and sees her there in the bath, in the altogether. She screams and covers her privates. And he gives a filthy leer. That's the amazing thing. They both behaved as if she really was completely naked!'

'She wasn't though, was she?' asked Mrs Hargreaves, sweetly anxious.

'Of course not!' her husband scoffed. 'Oh do keep up, Cissy. It was all in her head.'

'He had another fellow convinced he was a pug or some kind of lady's lap dog or other. He had to sit up and beg for imaginary titbits from this rather common woman who was convinced she was the Duchess of Devonshire, or some such. And I can tell you, never was there a less aristocratic individual!'

'It was very funny. Especially when the pug jumped up on his mistress's lap.'

'The whole place was in uproar.'

'I've never laughed so much in my life. It was pandemonium.'

'That's what they call him. Professor Pandaemonium!'

Quinn was through the door before he had time to question his decision.

'What did you say?'

Mrs Ibbott must have been as startled as everyone, but she was quick to hide her surprise. 'Inspector Quinn! What an unexpected surprise. Come in, come in, take a seat. Join us, do.'

Quinn collected himself enough to say: 'I beg your pardon. I didn't mean to intrude. I was just passing, and I couldn't help hearing . . .'

'Not at all! Not at all! No need to apologize,' insisted Mrs Ibbott.

'You were talking about a show of some kind?'

'A stage hypnotist, that's right,' said Timberley, somewhat warily.

'What was his name?'

'Professor Pandaemonium.'

'And where did you see this show?'

'At the Camden Empire.'

'And do you recommend it?'

'Indeed I do. It is most entertaining.'

'Thank you. That's all I wished to know. Good evening.'

He gave a series of bows to each of them in turn, as if he had just performed a music hall act himself. But there was no applause. They sat in stunned silence as he backed out of the room, still bowing.

TWENTY-SEVEN

The next few days passed slowly. It was hotter than ever in the attic room. They opened all the windows but there was no relief. It was as if there was not enough air to go around all departments and, regrettably – perhaps because they had not completed the requisite forms in time – it had been denied them.

The slightest exertion, mental or physical, left Quinn short of breath. Once he had the sense that his lungs were failing him. That somehow they had fallen out of step with the rhythm that was needed to keep him alive. He began to panic. His breaths became progressively shorter and more ragged. He became convinced that the only possible outcome of this unpleasant experience was his death. How could a body that had forgotten how to breathe keep itself alive?

It was only Sergeant Macadam, suddenly by his side, whispering soothing words to him, encouraging him to count backwards from ten, that calmed him.

In general, Quinn was beset by a curious sense of everything coming together and falling apart at the same time.

When he was not crippled by panic, he was stymied by indecision.

The last thing he wanted was to find himself up against a conspiracy that went all the way up to the highest echelons of government. He was therefore inclined to do what he had been urged to do. To let it go. To look elsewhere. Without conviction. Without hope of success. To go through the motions until something else came along.

But even when he made a show of dropping the enquiry into Colney Hatch, and instead investigated the pacifists and Irish militants, it was curious how he was led back to that cursed place. First, the red hand of the UVF. And then the fact of Medway's membership of the Gracchi. Were they meaningless coincidences, or evidence of an emerging pattern – signs, in other words.

And what of the conversation he had overheard in the lodging house? He had checked the file relating to the first of the young men to kill himself and it was as he had thought. Professor Pandaemonium was listed on the Camden Empire playbill that had been found in the pockets of his suit.

There was another source of indecision plaguing him. A rather foolish, possibly insane notion had possessed him. It was the idea that he would ask Miss Latterly to attend the music hall with him. His mind justified it to him on the peculiarly illogical basis that it would *kill two birds with one stone*. As if this were a good thing. As if, were he to voice such a sentiment to Miss Latterly, she would approve of it.

Needless to say, he did not act on this preposterous inclination. He merely contented himself with indulging in a deeply consoling fantasy of the two of them taking their seats side by side in the theatre, and turning to each other from time to time to smile their appreciation of the show.

In the event, he went on his own. As he always knew that he would. Perhaps he might have asked Miss Dillard to accompany him, had she not been dead. But then he told himself that it was probably not her thing.

She would not have liked the leery crowd, the flashy young men and their raucous women, all of them intent only on their own pleasure. As if it were something urgent and sustaining, something they would kill for.

A woman like Miss Dillard would be trampled in the rush.

And yet, paradoxically, the smells of cheap perfume, sweat and alcohol reminded him of her.

He took his seat as the house lights went down. A band of dusty tail-coated musicians with glazed expressions scraped and thumped and blasted their way to the end of a ragged overture. This was much more, he thought, Mrs Hargreaves' kind of thing. He should have asked her! Why had he only thought of it now, when it was too late? Of course, there was the problem of the husband, but he was in no doubt that she would have welcomed the opportunity to get away from his tedious company for an evening.

There was a prolonged disturbance in the curtain, at the culmination of which a fellow in a garish mustard-coloured checked suit stumbled out, teetering precariously at the very edge of the stage as if he would fall off. He flapped his arms desperately to regain his balance.

His face was made up to draw attention to his eyes, which were held wide open and spectacularly crossed. Quinn could only assume this was Cross-Eyed Al.

'Ah, yes . . . now I see you!' Al announced to great hilarity and some applause, which the witticism did not seem to merit. Quinn could only assume it was some kind of catchphrase. 'I seem to have misplaced the key.' Al mimed turning a key, keeping his face deadpan, and his gaze unfocused all the time. He then mimed parting the curtains – or rather trying to part them. In his mime he became entangled in the imaginary curtains, as entangled as he had evidently been a moment before in the real curtains. For reasons Quinn could not explain, this was surprisingly funny. The audience lapped it up. Especially when he repeated the business of nearly falling off the stage, this time seeming to come even closer to disaster.

'Just had an argument with the wife. It happens a lot these days. We don't see eye to eye over anything.'

Despite himself, Quinn found himself laughing along with everyone else.

'"Al," she said, "Al."' Al mimed looking in various different directions. '"I'm over here."'

More laughter, as he mimed finally locating his wife. 'Ah yes . . . now I see you!'

There were cheers at the recurrence of the catchphrase.

'"Face the facts," she said.' His pitiful expression provoked pitiless laughter. '"That's easy for you to say," I said.'

And so it went on. Until he ended his act with a rendition of 'Always Leave Them Laughing When You Say Goodbye'.

The Legs Eleven Dancing Troupe turned out to be six dancers with eleven legs between them.

The costumes of the five female dancers left it in no doubt that they were in full possession of both their legs. And there was much whistling and cheering at the sight of these shapely limbs. The one final leg belonged to the only male member of the troupe. He was dressed in top hat and tails, with the trouser of his missing leg cut off and sewn up at the thigh.

He moved around the stage with surprising grace and agility. Admittedly, he carried a cane that he rather cleverly worked into his dance steps, without giving the impression that he relied on it. The elegance of his upper body movements and arm gestures made up for a lot. He knew how to extend a pose and hold it.

It was strangely impressive, but also unsettling. Quinn was glad when it was over.

The band struck up an arrangement of 'That Mysterious Rag'. A flash pot went off, and a cloud of coloured smoke filled the stage. As it cleared, a spotlight picked out a solitary figure centre stage, a rather dapper man with a pointed beard and a completely bald head. He was looking down at an oversized pocket watch which he held in his hand. At a given moment, he closed the lid of the watch decisively, pocketed it and looked up to face the audience at last.

'It is time,' he intoned, solemnly. He nodded once and the house lights came up. The audience shifted uncomfortably in their seats. There was some nervous laughter.

The man on the stage held out one hand in front of him. 'Some of you will feel, as I raise my hand, some of you will feel the urge, the desire, the need, the overwhelming imperative . . . to stand up. Could I ask you, if you do feel that, as I raise my hand, upon the count of three, could I ask that if you feel the need to stand up, that you do, please, indeed, rise to your feet. I will begin counting to three now, and at the end of counting to three I will raise my hand. One, two, three . . .'

The man slowly raised his hand, and at the same time approximately a quarter of the audience rose to its feet. Quinn was slightly disappointed to realize that he had no desire to join them. He briefly thought about faking it.

'Good evening, I am Professor Pandaemonium. And you, those of you who have risen to your feet, will be my devils tonight.'

The man punctuated his speech with little confirmatory nods of the head. Quinn remembered that Blackley's man Yeovil had shared a similar tic.

'Now I know that some of you who stood up are only pretending to be under my influence, simply because you want to be part of the show. Perhaps you want to make a fool of me. But I warn you that you will end up making a bigger fool of yourselves. The truth is you only think you are pretending. You began by being resistant to the idea of another person taking over your will. But you are not able to resist the reality of it. That's why you stood up. And why you made the excuse to yourself that you are only pretending. Very well. Tell yourselves that if you want. The truth is you will succumb more heavily than the others. In the light of that warning, if anyone wishes to sit down, now is your chance. No one will think any the worse of you.'

About half of those who had stood up took their seats again. One man seemed to waver between backing out and remaining standing. Professor Pandaemonium of course honed in on him. 'You, sir, you can't decide, it seems. Perhaps you would like some help.'

The professor pointed his extended arm at the man and lowered it. The man sat down. Then the professor raised his hand and the man stood up. He repeated the trick several times to the enjoyment of the rest of the audience. 'Perhaps you would care to join me on the stage. I think you would make an excellent devil. Give him a round of applause, please.'

The professor used similar means to select around a dozen people from those who remained standing. 'When I lower my hand, the rest of you who stood up can sit back down. On the lap of the person to your right. On the count of three. One, two, three.' He lowered his hand and it was exactly as he had said it would be. The audience laughed. 'Keep looking at my hand. On the next count of three, as I move my hand to the side, you will realize your mistake, and with some embarrassment resume your own seat. One, two, three . . .'

The act itself was as Appleby and Timberley had described it. The 'volunteers' who went up on stage were induced to perform a variety of bizarre actions, in the belief that they were engaged in some ridiculous scenario or other. Quinn retained a grain of scepticism, which allowed him to believe that the whole thing was a set-up. He simply couldn't see how Professor Pandaemonium's meagre prompts and directions could be enough to persuade any halfway rational person to humiliate themselves in this way. Though, of course, if it was genuine, those participating would have had no sense of their own humiliation.

It was also true that some of what he said was inaudible to

the wider audience. He would lean into them in an uncomfortably intimate way and whisper further commands into their ears. Quinn noticed that he had a habit of doing this with one 'volunteer' in particular, a young woman who just happened to be the most attractive of the females on the stage.

At any rate, the people around Quinn seemed to be in no doubt about the authenticity of the spectacle they were witnessing. He couldn't help wondering if they were the ones who were being hypnotized.

Part of the pleasure, Quinn realized, was the way that Professor Pandaemonium made them dance along a line of transgression and taboo. He played with the idea of nakedness. Of amorous encounters between unlikely couples. Of prurience and lust. No one came out of it well. Not the victims, nor the ones who laughed at them.

It was as if he was forcing them all to face up to the worst aspects of their humanity.

Quinn flashed his warrant card at a harassed looking theatre employee and asked to be directed to Professor Pandaemonium's dressing room.

'Oh, God, what's he done now?'

'What do you mean by that?'

The man thought better of any further indiscretion. 'Nothing. But you know, that power he has, it could get him into a lot of trouble, if he isn't careful.'

'I assumed they were stooges.'

'Good heavens, no! You saw his act?'

'Yes. I didn't see how it was possible.'

'Exactly.'

The man led him along a gloomy corridor and knocked at the last door on the right, which he opened without waiting for a response. 'Are you decent, love? There's someone to see you.' He nodded to Quinn and went on his way.

The hypnotist was sitting in front of a mirror removing his make-up. As he caught Quinn's reflection, his face seemed to register disappointment. 'Who are *you*?'

'My name is Inspector Quinn, of the Special Crimes Department.'

Professor Pandaemonium sat up in his seat to compose himself before rising to face Quinn. 'What's this about?'

'Where did you learn to hypnotize people like that?'

'It's a gift.'

'Can you hypnotize anyone?'

'Some people are more suggestible than others.'

'But if someone is highly suggestible, you can get them to do anything you want?'

'I . . . what are you getting at, Inspector?'

'You're not in any trouble. I just need to understand . . . how it works.'

'It's not a question of getting them to do what I want. It's a question of releasing them from the inhibitions that prevent them from doing what *they* truly want.'

'You mean, barking like a dog?'

'To some extent, yes. Even that. Civilized behaviour, the way we normally interact with one another, requires us to maintain a facade. A mask of humanity that deceives us into thinking that we are more than mere animals. But really that's all we are. Clever, talking animals, who can move around on our hind legs. There's a part of all of us that longs to return to a more primitive, a more honest state of being.'

'Could you – or another hypnotist – persuade someone to kill themselves? Is it theoretically possible, that's all I'm asking?'

'Theoretically. Though I can't see why anyone would want to do that.'

'What's your real name?'

'My real name?'

'Yes.'

'Ralph Clarke.'

Quinn took out from his inside jacket pocket the photograph of Malcolm. 'Have you ever met him? Could he have come to one of your shows and been hypnotized by you?'

'No, I don't recognize him. Who is he?'

'He was my brother. He died.'

'I'm sorry.'

There was little point showing Clarke a photograph of the first man to die, the one who had had the playbill in his possession. The face was lacerated beyond recognition. But he produced a photograph of the second man. 'How about him?'

'No.' As far as Quinn could tell, he did not seem to be lying.

'Have you ever been inside Colney Hatch Lunatic Asylum, either as a patient or a member of staff?'

Clarke's face darkened. He took a moment to reply. 'I used to work there.'

'In what capacity?'

'I used to be a doctor. A psychiatrist.'

'What happened?'

'It's a matter of public record, so I suppose there is little point trying to conceal it. I was struck off. It was said I behaved inappropriately with one of the patients. It wasn't true but . . . There were lies told about me. My account of what happened was not believed.'

'Did you encounter a patient called Timon Medway when you worked there?'

'Timon Medway! He was the one who spread the lies about me. And after all that I had done for him.'

'What did you do for him, Mr Clarke?'

'I trusted him. I believed him. I believed that he had changed. That he wanted to help people now.'

'I see.'

'He betrayed my trust.'

'You knew what he had done? What he was capable of?'

'You don't understand. In that place, he stood out. He was not just an extraordinary patient. He was an extraordinary human being. And he had a gift.'

'A gift?'

'I encouraged him. I taught him what I knew.'

'You taught him to hypnotize people?'

'He was helping the doctors. He is an incredibly intelligent and intuitive human being.'

'He is a murderer!'

'Has he done something? Has he . . .?'

'People have died because of what you taught Timon Medway.'

'It's not possible. It was a therapeutic tool. To help people.'

'You don't place something like that in the hands of a lunatic.'

'You don't understand. He could get you to do anything. He didn't need me. He could already do it.'

There was a knock at the door. Ralph Clarke appeared to grow agitated. He shifted nervously and made no move to answer. In the end it was Quinn who opened the door. He recognized the attractive young woman who had been the recipient of Professor Pandaemonium's most intimate commands on stage. Clarke blushed and averted his gaze.

'Go away,' said Quinn to the young woman. 'Go away, now!'

He shut the door in her face and turned back to Clarke. He gripped his throat with one hand, knocking a chair over and pushing him back against the wall.

Quinn leant all his body weight into the squeeze. Clarke's fingers came up to prise away his grip, but to no effect.

Clarke started to twitch, his arms and legs jerking uncontrollably. He reminded Quinn of an insect in an ether jar.

Quinn knew that if he carried on squeezing the man would soon be dead.

He also knew that he had never wanted to kill a man so much as he wanted to kill Ralph Clarke now.

For no reason that he could understand, Quinn became fascinated by his own hand, the hand that was strangling Clarke. His fascination turned to horror. He almost came to believe that the hand had a will of its own that he could not control. He released his grip and shook his fingers loose, as if he were a violinist preparing to play.

The hypnotist slumped to the floor, rubbing his neck and letting out short, laboured breaths.

TWENTY-EIGHT

The thing was to keep looking straight ahead. That was what Alf had taught himself over the years.

Don't look down. He'd been taught that his first day working for Larkins.

But don't look up either. He'd had to work that one out for himself.

Maybe it didn't get everyone the same. Maybe there were some steeplejacks who were spurred on by the dizzying sight of the open sky above their heads, pierced by the perspective of the stack they were climbing.

But the way it worked for Alf was to keep his attention focused unrelentingly on the rung of the ladder in front of him. Or if he was in a cradle, to concentrate on the square foot of masonry in front of his face, scanning for cracks, fingers tenderly exploring the weathered surface like it was a lover's face.

If you needed to know how close you were getting to the top, you could always count. Count off the rungs. Count the seconds spent swinging in the wind. Count your mates above you. It always paid to know where they were. And not to get directly underneath them. He'd known men drop hammers.

There were some jacks who never thought about accidents. Or so they said. He'd been like that once himself. When he was a younger man. And believed he would live forever.

Accidents were what happened to others.

You couldn't feel so alive. The kind of alive you only feel at 180 feet. You couldn't feel that alive and ever believe in the possibility of death.

As if just feeling alive was enough to keep you alive.

And then it came. The realization, one day, that he was the oldest man in the firm. He became something of a celebrity. Everyone had heard of Alf Roberts. They'd written newspaper pieces about him.

Fifty-four years of age and the oldest in his industry.

The men who had been there before him. The ones who had taught him the ropes.

They'd all gone to the floor.

He was the one who taught the others now.

He was still alive. He wanted to keep it that way. The older he got, the more he wanted it.

Like a cricketer who was on ninety-nine and wanted to stay at the crease for the century.

He was still light on his feet. And strong in his arms.

But he felt the distant tug of the earth beneath him all the time now.

It made him careful. Nothing wrong with that. But you had to be lucky too.

He'd been part of the crew that climbed Nelson's Column back in 1905, to get it ready for the Battle of Trafalgar centenary celebrations. To think they'd risk their necks to string a bit of bunting around the Admiral. You had to laugh.

Now here he was, nearly ten years later, back on the column. There'd been a lightning strike in the storm a few days ago. Several witnesses reported a direct hit to Nelson's bicorne. Though you could never be sure until you went up and had a look.

And so the firm of W. Larkins Ltd had been called in.

While they were up there they might as well take a wire brush to the layers of pigeon guano that had accumulated on the hero of Trafalgar.

It was laborious toil, tethering the ladders to the column. They were held in place by ropes, looped loosely around at base level so that they could be lifted into place and secured.

It was Alf's habit now to tie the knots himself.

Let the others ride their luck. He would put his trust in a firmly hitched builder's knot.

Course, a job like this always got the crowds out. That was to be expected.

People came to look at Nelson's Column anyway. But now there was the added attraction of a steeplejack clambering up the side of it.

These days there were always a few taunts when Alf took to the ladder. Cries of 'Oi, Granddad!' And laughter.

He was used to it. Lapped it up even. Because the doubters

were always silenced by his limber ascent. Sprightly didn't come into it. The jeers turned to cheers. His age transformed the spectacle from a feat of daring – a mere once-in-a-lifetime sighting – into something that simply shouldn't be. A miracle, in other words.

For all the clamour of approval, he never forgot the first rule. Don't look down.

No matter how much you were tempted to check the size of the crowd, or even wave to your admirers.

Keep your eyes ahead.

Soon enough you stopped hearing the noise anyhow.

So it was strange that now, suddenly, forty-four rungs up the shaft, not quite halfway by his reckoning, he heard an unaccountable roar from the floor.

Was the roar for him? It couldn't be. He had done nothing to merit it, other than cling on for dear life.

And now he felt it. The shake and tremble transmitted up the ladders. The slippage in the rigging.

Someone else was coming up behind him.

The fool was taking the ladders far too fast, judging by the rapid clatter of wood on masonry. At a faster lick than even Alf would risk.

And still the crowd was roaring. If anything, louder than before.

So it was that Alf broke the first rule. He looked down.

What he saw nearly caused him to let go with both hands.

Alf had never seen the like.

The fellow was naked as the day he was born. No doubt about it. Even though Alf was looking down on him from above.

He was coming up on Alf quickly. It wouldn't be long before he laid hands on the very same ladder.

'Go down! Go down, you!' shouted Alf, waving the man back.

But the man didn't seem to hear. He was like a clockwork automaton, a toy monkey climbing up a palm tree.

Alf shook his head in disbelief. There were so many things wrong here. Where do you start? In the end, Alf settled for yelling: 'Only one man on the ladders at once!'

It was his third rule of steeplejacking.

But it was evident that this individual didn't give a hoot for rules, whether of steeplejacking or anything else.

Now he was on the ladder directly below, the one lashed to

Alf's. Close enough for Alf to hear his laboured breathing. And something else. The man was talking to himself. Alf couldn't make out what he was saying but it sounded cracked. As if there could be any doubt about that!

Another roar from the ground. Against his better judgement, Alf looked past the man to see the crowd below. He had never seen so many people gathered to watch him climb, their faces all upturned.

Alf was numb with shock, frozen to the spot.

It was as if he was a spectator in the event, watching to see how it would unfold.

He took a particular interest in what his foot would do now that the man had his hand around its ankle.

He couldn't blame it for trying to shake itself free of that unwanted grip.

He felt the weight of the man pulling him down. He knew instinctively that he was being drawn into a life or death struggle. This man was intent on death. His own at the very least. And it seemed it didn't matter to him who he dragged down with him.

His very lack of clothing seemed somehow to indicate that he was desperately done with life.

Alf looked up, breaking the second of his steeplejacking rules. He moved hand over hand, lifted his free foot and then yanked hard to wrest the other out of the madman's grip.

The foot came loose surprisingly easily. From the ground rose a sound like the wind whipping through long grass, as several thousand people took in a sharp breath at once.

Alf looked down in time to catch the last flailing moments of the naked man's fall. The crowd parted. Pigeons scattered. There was a dull, disheartening crack. And now the man lay sprawled over Landseer's lions in a pose of languid, almost decadent abandon.

Alf's legs began to tremble uncontrollably. His palms were suddenly bathed in sweat. His grip faltered as the strength drained from him. Trafalgar Square began to spin, like water going round in a draining plughole.

He had to stop looking down, or he would go the same way.

But the sight was irresistible. And the earth sucked at him. As if gravity's power had multiplied, as a result of the sacrifice which had just been made to it.

TWENTY-NINE

The death of the unknown man who fell off Nelson's Column failed to make it on to the front page of any newspaper.

Another death, of an altogether more notable personage, was universally held to be the most interesting thing that had happened for a long time. And so the Trafalgar Square incident was not the only item of news that was relegated to the inside pages by the assassination of Archduke Franz Ferdinand in Sarajevo.

Quinn made enquiries and ascertained that a brown corduroy suit had been discarded at the base of the monument. And that in the pockets of that suit had been found a card printed with the motif of a red hand. As before, the letters F.J.U.S. were written on the reverse, together with the number 7 – details that he had considered it expedient to keep from the press. However grotesque it seemed, one could never rule out the possibility of so-called 'copycat' acts. And so it was always useful to withhold a detail or two, by which one always knew when the original perpetrator was at work.

What made this death different from the others was the presence of the steeplejack, who came close to sharing the fate of the dead man. Most likely he was inadvertently caught up in an insane act of self-destruction. But the possibility that the other man had been trying to bring him down with him could not be discounted. If nothing else, it indicated that whatever Timon Medway's intentions were, his activities were capable of endangering other people besides his direct victims.

For Quinn was now in no doubt that Medway was behind it all.

Quinn was possessed by a frantic nervous energy. He paced the confines of the attic room in New Scotland Yard, leaving his sergeants somewhat bemused, if not alarmed.

'In general terms I know how he did it.' A dim consciousness that he was producing more spittle than was normal threatened to inhibit Quinn's enthusiasm. But he decided that matters had reached a point where such niceties were no longer important.

He dabbed at his mouth with his cuff and pressed on. 'Not the specifics of it. I don't pretend to understand how the technique works. I dare say, Macadam, you can discover that. Doubtless there will be an appropriate periodical that you can subscribe to. Or it will turn out that you have a cousin who is a hypnotist.'

'A hypnotist?'

'That's right. He hypnotizes them. What I don't understand yet is why. Although I am not sure we can ever know why a man such as Timon Medway does anything. Except that he considers the rest of us to be his playthings. And if sometimes he breaks one of us, as a careless or an angry child might smash a toy, it is nothing to him.'

'What about the cards?' wondered Inchball. 'Where do they come into all this?'

'Oh, like many criminals of this kind, Medway is possessed by a monstrous arrogance. They are a sign of his great superiority over the rest of humanity.'

'You mean he wants to be caught?'

'Not exactly. He is confident that we – the police – will never catch him, monumental dullards that we are. And so he can taunt us with such clues, safe in the knowledge – so he believes – that we are far too stupid to solve them. His arrogance will be his undoing. It was before and it will be again.'

'Do you think we have enough to get Sir Edward to change his mind?' asked Macadam.

Quinn's pacing came to an abrupt stop. 'We cannot trust Sir Edward. We cannot trust anyone but ourselves.'

He caught the doubtful look that passed between his two sergeants at this dark pronouncement. But it was too late now for doubt or hesitation. What he must do was clear.

THIRTY

Mrs Ibbott heard the front door close. It could only be Inspector Quinn, even though the door was shut with more force than he usually employed.

All her other guests were at home already, enjoying a sociable evening in the drawing room. Mr Appleby, the Hargreaveses and her own daughter were playing a few hands of whist. Mr Appleby had tried to teach them bridge, but Mary complained that it was a bore. Mr Timberley, who famously had no truck with cards, was reading a detective novel while sitting sideways in an armchair, his legs draped over one arm.

She must say, she found it very gratifying the way everyone got along so well these days. Not to speak ill of the departed, but Miss Dillard had always been one for keeping herself to herself.

The Hargreaveses had slotted in nicely, she had to say. Like a breath of fresh air, they were. Mrs Hargreaves seemed very sensible, as well as thoroughly charming. Mrs Ibbott hoped she would turn out to be a good example to Mary. And Mr Hargreaves struck her as a steady, dependable sort. A nice counterbalance to the excitability of her two young men.

Neither of them were flashy, which was what Mrs Ibbott most liked about them.

If only she could persuade the Inspector to join them occasionally. She knew he had taken Miss Dillard's death heavily, more so than he cared to admit. And, granted, his work was a grave responsibility that must weigh heavily upon his shoulders. All the more reason to relax with friends now and then. But he was a tough nut to crack, and she was beginning to suspect that her attempts to draw him in were counterproductive. He had to find his own way into the drawing room, as it were. Though she would never tire of making sure he knew the door was open for him.

With that in mind, she started to rise from her seat. But there was no need. The door burst open without her intervention.

Inspector Quinn stood in the door frame. It took Mrs Ibbott a moment to realize that he was not quite himself. His face was flushed – had he been drinking? – and his necktie was awry, his collar sprung. In fact, she would have described his overall appearance as dishevelled.

His gaze was focused, however. Fiercely so. Quite frankly, his look frightened her.

The room fell silent at his entrance, all eyes turned towards him.

'I know you want me dead. All of you.'

He directed his gaze on each of them in turn, holding it at last on Mrs Hargreaves. His jaw trembled as he looked at her, as if he would burst into tears at any moment. It seemed as if he was waiting for something from her, some kind of denial perhaps. He shook his head in recrimination.

'You think I don't see it? I know what it means when you laugh behind closed doors.'

Mary couldn't help herself. She let out an audible snigger. It was nerves, of course. The poor girl was terrified out of her wits.

Mrs Ibbott wouldn't stand for that. 'Inspector Quinn, I don't know what's got into you. I can assure you that no one wants you dead. On the contrary, we all wish the very best for you and regret that you are not able to join us in the evenings more often for a little friendly conversation. I fear that you are spending too much time in your own company. And that your excessive dedication to your work has placed an undue strain upon your nerves. Perhaps you are in need of a holiday? One thing I will say, however, is that I will not have you speak to my guests or my daughter in this alarming manner.'

'You needn't worry. I won't stay in a house where people want me dead. Not a moment longer.' Again he turned to Mrs Hargreaves. Something about his look made Mrs Ibbott very uneasy. 'Will you come with me? Leave this . . . life. And come with me.'

His invitation provoked a shriek from Mrs Hargreaves, as well it might.

Mr Hargreaves sprang to his feet and squared up to Inspector Quinn. 'What the hell is going on here?'

'She despises you.'

Someone gasped. Mrs Ibbott had a strong suspicion that it was Mary.

Now Mr Timberley and Mr Appleby were on their feet too, interposing themselves between the two rivals. Mr Timberley made it his business to soothe the husband, while Mr Appleby tried to reason with the Inspector. 'I say, old man, that's a bit strong, you know. You can't just say things like that to a chap.'

'Come on, Hargreaves. Don't listen to him. He's not right . . . in the head. That's obvious. The poor fellow's having some kind of breakdown.'

Inspector Quinn must have heard this. He turned his ire on the hapless Mr Timberley. 'I won't be judged by you! You and your . . . Latin.'

'I think you need to . . .' But it seemed Mr Appleby couldn't think what the inspector needed to do. Except, perhaps, go. He had his hand on the policeman's shoulder and was gently pressuring him backwards out of the room.

But this only provoked a fresh outburst, as soon as Inspector Quinn realized what was going on. He swept his own arm upwards to bat away Mr Appleby's solicitous hand. 'Get your hands off me!'

Mrs Ibbott was suddenly terrified that the situation would turn violent. It seemed that there was nowhere else for Inspector Quinn's ugly anger to go.

Her worst fears seemed likely to be borne out when Inspector Quinn shouted: 'I have killed men! Many men! Dangerous men. I am not afraid of you.'

Mr Appleby backed off with both palms held up in placation. 'My dear chap . . . I am very glad to hear that you are not afraid of me. There's absolutely no reason why you should be. I think you really should, perhaps, lie down, have a rest, you know. Perhaps you've had a few to drink . . . we all do it. Sleep it off. In the morning, we'll all look back on this and have a jolly old laugh about it.'

But judging from the raw suffering evident in his eyes, it seemed unlikely that Inspector Quinn would ever be able to laugh about anything again.

He shot out a hand to point at Mrs Hargreaves. And tears now were streaming down his face. 'I *love* her.'

This was undoubtedly the most shocking thing he had said so far, the most shocking thing imaginable for him to say.

'Steady on!' came from Mr Appleby, while Mr Hargreaves bridled against the restraint of Mr Timberley's body, his face flushed with rage.

There was another shriek from Mrs Hargreaves, who was clearly not enjoying the attention, and appeared to be as surprised by Inspector Quinn's declaration as everyone else. Mrs Ibbott was in no doubt that the poor woman had done nothing to encourage him. This really was a most trying situation.

Mr Hargreaves was screaming at the Inspector now. 'You bloody bastard! How dare you!'

Granted, he had been sorely provoked. But as far as Mrs Ibbott was concerned, there was no need for language. 'Mr Hargreaves! Do not make a bad situation worse by indulging in the language of the taproom. My daughter is present, if you please.'

Regrettably, it was evident Mary was enjoying herself far too much. She appeared to be viewing the whole thing as a scene in a play.

It was enough to remind Mrs Ibbott of her maternal duty. 'Mary, go to your room!'

'Mother! I'm not a child!'

'Go to your room!'

Mary scowled at her mother but complied – at least to the extent of making her way towards the door of the drawing room. She gave a little yelp as she hurried past Inspector Quinn, her fists balled and held up to her face protectively.

'And you, Inspector, I think you should take this opportunity to retire too. I dare say things will look differently in the morning.'

'Oh, don't worry. I'm going.'

He pushed Mr Appleby away from him – rather unnecessarily, Mrs Ibbott thought – and fled the room. A high-pitched scream revealed Mary's presence lurking just out of sight.

Mrs Ibbott then heard the front door open and a howl of pain and rage as he flung himself out into the night.

'What an extraordinary . . .' began Mr Hargreaves.

'Oh, shut up,' cried Mrs Hargreaves, her nerves understandably on edge. For the first time, Mrs Ibbott wondered if, after all, there might be something in Inspector Quinn's bizarre outburst.

Mrs Ibbott shook her head as if to dispel the memory of an unpleasant dream. She found Mary cowering against the wall in the hallway. The front door was wide open.

She went out on to the top step and looked down the street in both directions.

There was no sign of him.

Mrs Ibbott closed the door quietly, stealthily, as if to honour his memory.

He was an unusual man, she had to admit.

THIRTY-ONE

The Dublin Castle pub on Camden's Park Street was, as its name suggested, frequented by a largely Irish clientele. Most of the men who drank there were workers brought over to provide cheap labour for the railways. Many of them worked in the nearby Chalk Farm goods yard.

It was a fair assumption that they were Catholics in their religion, nationalists in their politics, and Guinness drinkers in their saloons.

Tonight the talk was all about the trouble in the Balkans. Would there be war in Europe? Would the English be drawn in? And if so, where would that leave the Irish?

There was little enthusiasm for German militarism. The general feeling was that the Teutonic bullies should be taught a lesson. Fritz was a bloody menace, it was agreed, and someone had better stand up to him. The consensus was that if it came to war, the Irish would fall in step with the English, Paddy lining up behind Johnny to volunteer. Their own struggle would have to be set aside for as long as it took to defeat the common enemy.

Hadn't your man Asquith at least tried to do the right thing? It wasn't his fault if the pig-headed Proddies chose to scupper the agreement. And if the nationalists showed themselves to be stalwart allies at England's time of need, who could doubt that the Liberals would reward them with the great prize of independence once the war was over?

Of course, there were some who scoffed at this and were rather of the opinion that the English were as bad as the Germans, if not worse, and could be trusted no further than they could be thrown.

Which was all beside the point, as far as some young daredevils were concerned. They cared nothing for politics. They only craved adventure and weren't afraid to don British khaki to find it.

If it came to a scrap, they would not be found wanting.

The discussion at the bar had reached such a point when the door flew open with the force of an attack. Some even suspected a bomb blast, until they saw the swaying figure of a man in the doorway. Ah, it was only another clumsy drunk misjudging the force needed to open a door.

But there was something about this particular pish-head that didn't seem quite right. The men of the Dublin Castle regarded him warily. He was a stranger for one thing, and strangers usually meant trouble.

His eyes were the most unsettling thing about him. They were not, in all honesty, the eyes of a drunk. They did not wander and waver in the drunkard's usual scatter gaze. No, this fella's gaze was oddly focused and intense. He had the look of a fire and brimstone preacher.

Most of them hoped he would quickly realize he had stumbled into the wrong pub and quietly slip away. But there seemed little chance of that. His eyes said that he had come there with a purpose and the purpose was to make trouble.

The room fell silent and every head turned in his direction.

He held out an accusing finger and opened his mouth to declaim to the whole pub. As soon as he did, it was clear he was no Ulster Proddie as some had feared, but an Englishman. 'You are the key to it all! You unlock the whole mystery. I have been trying to work out how he did it, and it's you. I do not know whether you are willing accomplices or unwitting tools. I hope to God that it is the latter. But perhaps he has won you over to his side with inducements. He promised you the earth, I do not doubt. But you must know you cannot trust him! He is the Devil! Satan! Today, he is killing English boys, poor sick-in-the-head unfortunates. But tomorrow, who can say that he will not turn his powers against your people? The very flower of your nation. He uses you as some kind of conduit. There is a force at work here. The red hand made me think of it. The red hand is the symbol of the Ulster Volunteer Force. It was when I realized that that I knew the Irish must be involved in some way. The red hand is somehow of great significance to the Irish. It is either a great provocation or a rallying banner. It's all coming together in my head. Although . . . Can any of you explain the significance of the number seven to me? Is it a very Irish number?'

This puzzling tirade was received in stunned silence until one old fella at the bar gave voice to what everyone else was thinking: 'Will you shut the feck up, you crazy English eejit.'

This provoked an outburst of raucous hilarity and the rest of the man's words were drowned in laughter. He was soon dismissed as a harmless lunatic, as the regulars of the Dublin Castle turned back to their dark pints.

The man would not be discouraged, however. He continued to give voice to his obscure ravings, even though no one was listening.

Eventually, the landlord came out from behind the bar and frog-marched him off the premises, giving him an unceremonious shove out the door, to loud cheers from his customers.

Enough was enough, he declared. 'I wouldna minded, but the cunt didn't buy a single fecking drink.'

This was universally held to be the wittiest remark of the evening.

Over the next several days a strange and solitary figure was repeatedly sighted around the environs of Camden.

His appearance became increasingly unkempt as his behaviour grew more unpredictable and chaotic. Of course, not everyone noticed this; most people preferred to look the other way when he hove into view.

There were those who had their eye on him, however.

Most frequently he was encountered in one or other of the locality's public houses. He attempted to enter the Dublin Castle on a number of further occasions, only to discover that he was now barred from the premises. And so he tried his luck in the other Castles around there, the Edinboro, the Pembroke and the Windsor, frequented by Scots, Welsh and English railway workers respectively. It wasn't long before he was barred from those too.

His message to each of these nationalities was similar to that he had delivered to the Irish. He believed them to be complicit in the crimes of an unnamed individual, whom he considered to be an incarnation of the very Devil. It fell each time on equally deaf ears. He took to accosting people in the street, demanding of them if they knew the meaning of the number seven, or had ever seen the sign of the red hand.

Those who had their eye on him noticed that his demeanour appeared increasingly frantic, as he was met with repeated incomprehension and rebuff. The residents of Camden began to cross the street to avoid him. There was something dangerous about the mad vagrant who had suddenly appeared in their midst. He threatened not simply their civic peace, but also their personal sanity. He had brought the prospect of madness into their lives, revealing it as something frighteningly close to home.

'He's bloody good at this,' one of those watching him observed to his companion.

'Too bloody good.'

It was getting close to the time for them to intervene.

As far as anyone could tell, he was sleeping in the open, on the towpath by the canal. Often he was seen standing at the side of the canal, shouting argumentatively at the water. At these moments he was not concerned with the unnamed criminal, or the mysteries of the number seven and the red hand. His beef with the canal seemed to be over a woman. 'She doesn't love you!' he screamed, while making a wild gesture with one hand.

Other times he would be found huddled beneath one of the bridges, weeping for hours at a time.

Anyone who had the misfortune to get close to him could smell how far gone he was in degradation. His face was dark with stubble and grime. His hair matted, his clothes soiled and torn. His fingernails were long yellow claws.

One night he took off his shoes and threw them at the moon.

Each of his shoes fell with a discreet plop into the canal. Even though he had not disturbed the perfect, infuriating circle of the moon, he must have found some relief in the act. He laughed about it for a long time afterwards.

From then on he went about barefoot. Soon his feet were filthy and blooded. He stopped roaming the streets, and spent almost all his hours camped out on the towpath, without even a newspaper to shelter him from the elements.

He often relieved himself where he stood, or sat, or squatted, or lay. Like a baby, he had no understanding of what he was doing.

A signal passed between the two men who kept an eye on him. 'I'll get the doctor,' one of them said.

'Find a bobby, too,' the other answered with a nod. He then started to move towards the vagrant, who at that moment lay on the ground, soaked by a light but persistent drizzle of which he seemed to have no inkling. His body shook with great, heaving tremors, as if he was lying on top of a small earthquake. His eyes stared straight up into the grey sky. His mouth gaped open to gulp down the rain.

As fast as he drank the liquid in, it leached from his eyes.

The man who had been keeping an eye on him crouched down. The stench of the other man hit him, bringing tears to his eyes. He had to force himself to lean closer to the other man's face to whisper: 'It's Macadam here, sir. Can you hear me? We're going to take you in now.'

Silas Quinn stared into his sergeant's face but gave no indication of recognizing him. 'Bubble. I popped him like a bubble.' He stabbed a finger weakly in the air.

THIRTY-TWO

He had never been away.

That life he thought he had lived, just a dream.

A strange dream. As absurd as all dreams are.

And now he was trying to remember it. He was in that first moment of waking, in the moment when you pass from one life to another, from a life of bizarre wonders and uncomfortable truths, a life that makes perfect sense while you are caught up in it, a life that grips you with its urgency and moves you with its pathos and shocks you with its terrors.

But a life that begins to fade the moment you open your eyes.

What details he could remember only convinced him of its unreality. Had he really believed himself to be a policeman of some kind? Employed where? In something called the Special Crimes Department?

Ha!

The tricks the mind plays on us.

And what were they called, the two men who worked there with him? Such odd names they had.

No . . . gone.

It would come back to him.

Or perhaps not.

Perhaps he should let it go. Stop trying to remember.

It was too exhausting. All he wanted to do was sleep. He would sleep and dream another life, and the life he dreamed this time would fade on waking just the same.

It didn't matter. He could dream as many lives as he liked.

And with each successive life he dreamt, that one life, the life that had felt more real than the others, receded further from his mind's grasp.

And had he really stood beneath a full moon and thrown his shoes into a canal? What had he been thinking?

There were more Jews in here than he remembered. As if each time he fell asleep – each time he lived another life – they brought more Jews in. All he could say was it must be especially stressful to be a Jew today, particularly injurious to one's mental health.

There were so many of them now that they had their own wards, one for Jewish men, and one for Jewish women. Another patient, a man with deep-set eyes and a face as pale and round as the moon, told him that the Jews had all been placed in wooden huts. One night, the huts had been set on fire while the Jews slept. All the Jews had been killed. It had been done deliberately to keep the numbers down, according to his informant. But there were so many mad Jews in the world that it wasn't long before numbers were up again and they had to build more huts for them.

Some of the people he encountered he remembered from the last time he had been here. If it was right to speak of a last time, and it was not, as he suspected, one continuous stay interrupted by a long and peculiarly intense dream.

He learnt to recognize those who expected nothing of him, whether staff or fellow inmates. It was not that he consciously sought them out. But some natural affinity drew them together; he expected nothing of them either.

They did not chide him if he sat all day in the same chair, quietly weeping.

At times it was suggested that he should play cards with some of the others. Or go outside into the gardens. Or help on the farm. But there was never any real expectation that he would. No approval was given if he did, nor disappointment registered if he didn't. It was all the same to them.

One of those who fell into this category was a young man called Henry Hicks.

Hicks was an undernourished individual, whose brown corduroy suit, several sizes too large, hung loosely off him. He had a permanently frightened face, an expression that was exacerbated by unruly straw-like hair that stood up in all directions. Henry Hicks never looked anyone in the eye and responded to any stimulus like a timid kitten.

How he knew that the young man was called Henry Hicks, he couldn't say, for the young man himself had never volunteered his name. Indeed, Henry Hicks rarely said anything, and when he did speak it was in a strange incomprehensible language, which sounded suspiciously made-up.

'Ackle pash, capple maddle hash,' was no language he recognized. And yet, somehow he had a sense, if not of meaning, then certainly of an emotional content.

There were times when he almost convinced himself that these pronouncements were the most profound utterances that any human had ever made. They represented the decay and redundancy of language and seemed to be the only rational reaction to the situation they found themselves in.

They usually came at the climax of a crisis, and invariably eased whatever tension had been building.

There was always something both inevitable and utterly unexpected about them. They were almost redemptive. He found their concise, aphoristic certainty particularly satisfying.

'Malakit por danakit.'

And it was only when he spoke that Henry Hicks seemed to break free of his fear.

There were those who clearly did expect something of him, who had some purpose in which he played a part. It goes without saying that he did not understand either their purpose or his part in it. It was never explained to him. It was some kind of test, a game to them perhaps, in which he had to work out what to do based on the reactions that his behaviour provoked. For example, if he did something that resulted in pain, then he must try to make sure that he did not do that thing again. Although first he had to work out what he had done that had provoked the pain, which was not always easy.

It was a confusing and frustrating game, and he was not very good at it. As much as he was able, he tried to avoid these people. But the purpose that they entertained towards him was so strong that they often came looking for him.

Foremost among these was Mr Ince, but there were others to whom he delegated his dispensations. With so many patients in the asylum needing his attention, he could not always be expected to administer his treatment to every lunatic personally.

It was hard to know what Mr Ince wanted from him. He always strived to comply with whatever command he issued, and was never wilfully disobedient. Even so, he would feel the brunt of his custodian's key fob.

Mr Ince took umbrage at his very existence, it seemed.

A seemingly more benign presence, who nonetheless entertained expectations towards him, was Dr Pottinger. That first day,
after he had been cleaned and dressed and fed, he was taken to
Dr Pottinger's office. The superintendent had greeted him if not
warmly then certainly eagerly. Not so much as an old friend, as
a *bon viveur* returning to a favourite restaurant.

'Well, Silas, here you are again! We have been following your
career with some interest, you know. It has been quite remarkable
to see your rise to celebrity, when I think back to the young man
who came to us all those years ago. Not to put too fine a point
on it, you were a nervous wreck, my friend!' Dr Pottinger beamed
indulgently. 'Afraid of your own shadow, you were. And yet, you
left this place to become a fearless and famous police detective,
did you not?'

Silas frowned doubtfully, although he did not say which part
of Pottinger's assessment he was unsure about.

'We are quite looking forward to getting to work on you. Dr
Leaming – I don't think Dr Leaming was here the last time you
visited us – yes, Dr Leaming is doing some outstanding work with
nervous men. That is to say, men who are crippled by their fears
and anxieties. Most of the subjects he works with are somewhat
younger than you, but I think he might be persuaded to add you
to his programme. Your work as a policeman has surely strength-
ened your constitution to a robustness that could withstand the
rigours of his therapy. It is physically demanding, but entirely safe.
And I feel that it could benefit you enormously. You were
always a very responsive patient, Silas. I have high hopes for you.
We put you together once before. I am sure we will be able to do
it again. I shall talk to Dr Leaming. Would you like that? Excellent.'

Some days he was dogged by the sense that there was something
he should do. A reason he was there.

There were moments when it nearly came back to him. He
would glance down at his own implausible body and the brown
corduroy suit he had been dressed in. Something would stir in
his memory.

As he groped to remember he realized it was something to do
with that other life, the life he had dreamt.

The life of the man called Silas Quinn.

It made no sense and wearied him unspeakably.

He could not hold on to his train of thought. And so he let it go.

But it would always come back to him. He would be wandering along the endless corridors, beneath the honeycombed tiles of the ceiling. He would be gripped by the sense that he was looking for something – for the answer to a question he had forgotten. It was not a pleasant sensation, both urgent and elusive at the same time.

As if everything depended on him solving a mystery that had not been revealed to him.

Then one day, minutes, hours, days, weeks after his admittance, a man sat down next to him on a bench overlooking a gently sloping lawn. The man was dressed in a loose gardener's smock over his brown corduroy suit. He stared straight ahead as he spoke. 'You came. I knew you would. After all, I summoned you.'

THIRTY-THREE

The voice. He knew the voice immediately. It was not so different from any other adult male voice. Quite neutral, in fact. The kind of voice that a man who hailed from Woking, or Basingstoke, or even Godalming, might speak with. At the same time there was nothing ordinary about it.

It was the voice of a madman.

There was more to it than that. A quality that unsettled him. Something personal, a malice directed against only him.

He turned to view the man's profile. He had the high forehead of an intellectual and wore wire-framed spectacles. His hair was dark and curly with flecks of silver here and there. He was smiling. His eyes shone with a dark glitter.

The shock of hearing that voice brought everything back.

'I know you.'

'Of course you do. It's your fault that I'm here.'

'No. If it was down to me you wouldn't be here.'

'Oh? Where would I be?'

'You'd be dead.'

The other man's laughter was weightless and empty, like the shaking of a gourd filled with husks. 'That's not very nice, Inspector. Not when you consider all that I have done for you.'

'What have you done for me?'

'I gave you the solution.'

'The solution to what?'

'To the mystery.'

'What mystery?'

'The mystery of those poor young men who died, naked and alone.'

'You killed them.'

'No I did not. I was – and remain – most vehemently opposed to their deaths. I am a pacifist now, you know.'

'I know.'

'Of course you know. I made sure that you did.'

He was silent now, as he thought about what the man had said.

The man turned his face towards him. His smile deepened into an expression of loathsome complacency. 'Go on, say it.'

'Say what?'

'Say "I don't understand!" Because you don't, do you?'

'You killed them. You planted the seeds of their own self-destruction in their minds.'

'No no no! You've got it all wrong! I'm very disappointed in you! Did my clues mean nothing to you?'

'The cards?'

'Yes, that was me! Well done. But really, it's not such a remarkable thing to work out. You were meant to work it out, in fact. I made sure that my fingerprints were on them. And I expect that even you were capable of cracking that elementary numerical code.'

'Seven.'

'Just stating the number doesn't prove that you've cracked it.'

'It's a simple numerical cypher, the letters of your name replaced by a number between one and nine. You write the alphabet in a grid, nine across. A, B, C, D, E, F, G, H, I on one row and then so on, filling the rows until you have assigned every letter to a number. Take the numbers from your name, Timon Medway, and add them up. Eight plus eight equals sixteen. Then, one plus six equals seven.'

'No no no! You've got it all wrong! Timon Medway is not my name.'

'Very well. Isaac Newton. Let's say that you are Isaac Newton. It's the same. You get the same result.'

Again the gourd was shaken. 'That's better! You see, it's not too hard. I made sure of that.'

'I see. And why the red hand? What was the significance of the red hand?'

'Can't you work it out?'

'It has something to do with the UVF?'

'The what?'

'The Ulster Volunteer Force.'

'Whatever gave you that idea?'

'We were pursuing a line of enquiry that the deaths were something to do with the struggle for independence in Ireland.'

'Oh dear. It's not that at all. No, the red hand is there, Inspector, simply because I like the picture. I find it speaks to me. And I hoped it would speak to you.'

'So it has no significance?'

'Everything has significance, Inspector. The red hand had a twofold significance. In the first place, it was there to protect them. It is a symbol of strength and fury, is it not? And by writing my number, the number seven, on the reverse, I had imbued it with magical properties. It became a talisman, if you will.'

'It didn't work.'

'Not in its primary function, alas. But there was always a chance that the magic would not be powerful enough. I knew that. I'm not a fool. Which was why I gave it a secondary significance. You worked out the letters of course?'

'J.S.U. stands for Jeova Sanctus Unus. Isaac Newton's alchemical pseudonym.'

'*My* pseudonym, you mean! What about the F?'

It was a question he could not answer.

'Oh, Inspector! I'm disappointed in you!'

'Force?'

'Don't guess! Why would it be *force*? It makes no sense. The rest of it is Latin. Why would that one word be English? Come on! Use your brain! I know it's small and ineffectual, but I know you, Inspector Quinn. You're not uneducated. You once studied medicine, did you not? There are many Latin words in medicine I believe.'

'It's Latin?'

'"It's Latin", he says. You're such a dullard these days, Silas.'

'My Latin is a little rusty.'

'I will help you out then. What do they all have in common? The ones who died?'

'They all were here, in Colney Hatch?'

'Oh, Inspector Silas! Can you really be so very stupid? Have you forgotten already what the other letters stand for?'

'You. They stand for you.'

'Quite so. So, try again. Show your working out. You will get marks for that.'

'The *F* represents, somehow, a link, a relationship, between you and the young men who died.'

'Better! Now . . . The young men who died. I'll ask you again, what did they have in common?'

'They were all naked?'

'Don't try to be too clever, Inspector! It doesn't suit you.'

'They were all . . . young men.'

'That's it. He's got it. Young men, yes. They were all my . . .?'

'Friends?'

'*Friends?* That's not a Latin word! The Latin for friend is *amicus*. If I had wanted to say they were my friends I would have written A.J.S.U. Amicus Jeovae Sancti Uni. I said instead F.J.S.U. Is your knowledge of Latin really so lamentable?'

'This hasn't been an easy time for me. I . . .'

'Don't make excuses! I didn't summon you here so that you could make excuses. I need you to be stronger than that. A Latin word beginning with *F* that expresses a relationship of one male to another. Is it really so hard?'

'Filius.'

'At last! Yes! They were my sons.'

'In what sense were they your sons?'

'I had adopted them. So you must see that I would never have caused their deaths.'

Silas closed his eyes, wishing the other man into oblivion. His presence there next to him on the bench was suddenly an unbearable persecution. And he was overwhelmed by a sense of futility. His whole life had been leading to a moment of utter absurdity.

He must salvage something from it. 'Who were they? We know the identity of only one of them. Malcolm Grant-Sissons.'

'Your brother.'

'How did you know?'

'Malcolm told me.'

'Is that why you killed him?'

'I told you, I was not responsible. And I also told you, he was my son. I adopted him. Which means that we must be related too, you and I. We're family now.'

'Who were the others?'

'Don't you know? I would have thought that was relatively straightforward to discover. All you would have to do is apply to the asylum authorities.'

'We did that.'

'And?'

'The information was not forthcoming.'

'Could you not insist?'

'I was warned off by my superiors.'

'And that did not make you wonder?'

It was galling to be the brunt of a child murderer's righteous indignation.

'You don't deserve to know their identities. You gave up at the first hurdle.'

'There are some things you cannot fight.'

'But those are the very things you must fight!'

He looked again at the man next to him. A messianic glint burnt in his eyes. For all that he knew about this man, his personality was strangely seductive. He could see how others could be persuaded to believe in his reformation.

'What did it tell you? The fact that they blocked your investigation?'

'They were protecting Colney Hatch?'

'Yes, but why would they do that?'

'Because Dr Pottinger asked them to. He has friends in high places.'

'But why would he ask them to, unless . . .'

'He had something to hide?'

'Don't you see? The state killed them. My sons. Your brother. The state murdered them and attempted to cover it up. And you let them get away with it.'

'I have to trust those who are in authority over me. And besides . . .'

'You thought I was responsible?'

It seemed almost bad manners to insist on that now. 'I spoke to Ralph Clarke. He told me that you are capable of getting anyone to do anything.'

'Did he also tell you how he used to molest the female patients that he hypnotized? It was I who caught him at it. He bears me a grudge.'

'*You* murdered children.'

'No! I *saved* them. I saved them from the misery and disappointment and corruption of this world.'

'You murdered children.' Silas insisted on it.

Timon Medway gave a deep sigh. 'I see that we must agree to disagree on this point. There is something far more important at stake here. We must put aside our difficulties for the greater good.'

'What on earth can you mean?'

'We must work together, Inspector. To stop them. That's why I brought you here, after all. The cards were designed to draw you to me.'

There was a long moment while he thought how to respond. 'Tell me who they were and I will help you.'

'First there was Harold. Harold Walker. He died in the bear pit. There was very little wrong with him when he came here. Except that he was an orphan. His family had been killed in a gas explosion while he was at work. Mother, father and three junior siblings. The experience had a somewhat shattering effect on his nerves. He became understandably morose and unreliable and as a consequence lost his employment. He had not the means to keep up the rent on the family home, nor even to bury his family. He was nineteen years old when the accident happened. It was a lot for a young man to contend with. I tried to help him as much as I could. But I knew that he was doomed. I saw what they did to him.'

'What did they do to him?'

'They sought to embolden him.'

'I don't understand.'

Medway raised a hand, urging patience.

'Next came Cedric. Sad Cedric. Cedric Glynn, that is. The young man who threw himself off Suicide Bridge. Another orphan, of course. They always pick orphans. The truly lost and forgotten, whom no one visits. Cedric lost his mother to consumption and his father to alcoholism. He had looked for the answer in religion. But had taken it too far. Angels spoke to him. And God, and the Devil, of course. The usual suspects. The voices became confused in his head. He was no longer able to distinguish good from evil, God from the other one. He became fearful of doing anything at all and was reduced to a virtually catatonic state. Malcolm you know about. Another orphan. Although he was not entirely alone in the world, was he? He had you. But you had abandoned him.'

'That isn't fair.'

'Like many mortals, you are weak and cannot bear the truth.'

'What about the other one? The one who fell off Nelson's Column?'

'Ah, yes. Peter. Poor Peter. Peter Clement was not an orphan, but he might as well have been. His family had abandoned him. Cast him out like a leper. And why? What was his sin? To have loved. We cannot choose where the heart will lead us. We can only open ourselves up to love. And Peter opened himself up all right. He was what some would call a pansy. His family run a butcher's shop in Highbury. Very respectable. Very stupid. Can you imagine how disgusting the smell of butchered meat must have been to a young man of delicate sensibilities? At any rate, he was discovered *in flagrante delicto* with a friend. Perhaps it was the sight of all those sausages every day that did it to him. Who can tell? His brute of a father threw him out. He did it quite literally, and publicly. Picked him up by his collar and the belt of his trousers and hurled him out into the street. Well, it wasn't long before Peter was destitute. He was forced to sell his arse to keep a roof over his head. That brought him to the attention of the authorities. Oafs like you. After serving a six-month prison sentence, he appealed to his father. You would have thought with a name like Clement . . . Alas, the old man was more hard-hearted than he was before. He simply looked through his son as if he wasn't there. It was up to his mother to say, "You'd better go. And mind you don't come back again." His own mother turned her back on him. That was worse somehow than the father. Worse even than a brother, which was what Malcolm had to endure with you.'

He didn't have the energy to protest.

'He fell apart completely. A total nervous collapse. Destitute, distraught, deranged, he was eventually brought here. Mr and Mrs Clement were informed. They wrote back to Pottinger. Words to the effect, *We have no son by that name.* Very sad for Peter. But Dr Leaming rubbed his hands with glee.'

'Dr Leaming? What about him?'

'Dr Leaming wanted him for his programme.'

'What programme?'

'Dr Leaming is conducting an experimental programme, the purpose of which is to eradicate fear.'

'Excuse me?'

'Leaming has a theory – and as far as it goes it is a perfectly valid theory. It's certainly better than Pottinger's tonsil theory. According to Leaming, all nervous and mental disorders have a single cause. Fear. If you can eradicate fear, you will be able to cure every conceivable mental illness. Dr Leaming is not a bad man. He is much worse. He is an idealist. And like all idealists he is dangerous. He has no conception of the rule of unintended consequences. Even now, after four deaths, he won't accept that it has anything to do with the work he is doing.'

'How does the state fit into this? Why would they protect Leaming and Pottinger? Why wouldn't they just close down the programme?'

'Not everyone who has been on the programme has died. There have been some spectacular successes. News of these reached certain individuals in the War Office.'

'Sir Michael Esslyn!'

'That I cannot say. At any rate, there is a war coming, you know. Or haven't you heard? Our government has been preparing for it for longer than you know. Imagine the usefulness of an army of fearless soldiers. It would be the ultimate secret weapon.'

'How do you know so much about this?'

'Because . . . I work with Leaming on the programme.'

'So it's true then? What Ralph Clarke said? You hypnotize them?'

'I told you, you can't believe *him*. I don't *do* anything. They use me. Leaming uses me. I'm like a tool in his hands. A therapeutic tool.'

'What is it you do?'

'Nothing. Very little. Barely anything.' Medway sniggered unpleasantly. For the first time in their conversation, something of the monster Silas knew him to be revealed itself.

'But you're an inmate?'

'The patients help out with all manner of tasks here. There are those who work on the farm. Or in the dairy. Yes, we have a number of dairy cows, as well as pigs and over two hundred head of sheep. We farm chickens for their eggs and meat. There are the crops to sow and harvest, the wheat, the potatoes, all manner of vegetables. And then there's our orchard. Then again, some of us work in the kitchens. We have a print shop – which was where I had the cards done up, by the way. And a tailoring workshop. A carpentry shop. A hairdresser. An upholsterer. We even have a tattoo parlour, which I can personally recommend. I myself work in the gardens, as well as helping Dr Leaming with his programme. Without the involvement of patients, this place could not function.'

'Yes, but to employ you in their treatment? A lunatic treating lunatics?'

The other man shrugged. 'I didn't want to do it. I had no choice. At first, I will admit, I believed in Leaming's ideas. I shared his ideals. But you know I am a pacifist now. When I learnt that the programme was being sponsored by the War Office, I determined to subvert it from within. And now, after what has happened to my boys, I cannot permit it to continue. And I need your help to stop it.'

Silas looked at the other man and wondered if he could trust him. In the context of a tale told in the garden of a lunatic asylum on a pleasant sunny afternoon, what Timon Medway had told him made perfect sense. But the only thing he knew for sure about Medway was that he was insane. If he held on to that one certainty, he could trust nothing that the man ever said.

It was almost as if Medway had read his mind. 'Besides, I cannot be held responsible for any of this. I am insane, remember.'

The gourd full of husks was given one final shake.

THIRTY-FOUR

The life that he had thought to be just a dream turned out to be real after all.

He began to take a more conscious note of his surroundings. He noticed the permanent odour of ammonia that hung in the air, masking other scents that were even more unpleasant.

He could now taste the food that was given to him, although he might have wished he couldn't. For the most part, it was shockingly bad. He could well believe that it was prepared by lunatics.

They received three meals a day, seated on benches at long bare tables in the vast patients' dining hall. It required four sittings, segregated by sex, to serve everyone. The staff ate in their own dining room. Presumably they were served different meals.

In the morning the porridge was lumpy and cold, almost impossible to swallow. The bread was more palatable, and there was always jam and butter to spread on it. It still required a lot of chewing. He washed them both down with over-sweetened cocoa. They were also offered half a pint of beer with breakfast. It was held to have a calming effect on some of the patients, although too much made others unruly. Silas invariably left his untouched. There was always someone to drink it for him.

Such transactions had to be conducted furtively. If Mr Ince caught you playing games like that, you'd feel the heavy end of his key chain and no mistake.

Lunch was more often than not some kind of stew, made from an indeterminate meat. It was served either with or without dumplings or a pie crust and potatoes. As the potatoes came from the asylum's own plantation, they were often the best part of the meal. There was fish on Fridays, served with rice. It should have made a welcome change. But it invariably had a bitter, slightly tainted taste.

What the food lacked in flavour it made up for in heaviness. If you could bring yourself to eat it, you did not feel hungry afterwards.

Supper was always bread and cheese, again served with beer. He was more inclined to drink it now, in the hope that it would help him sleep.

Mr Ince and his subordinates patrolled the tables making sure that order ruled. A certain level of quiet conversation was permitted, although most patients showed little inclination to talk to their fellows.

Most mealtimes, therefore, went by in silence, apart from the clatter of spoons on the tin pannikins. They were not allowed knives and forks, and had to learn to spread their butter with spoons.

Of course, there were those who could not control themselves.

He could always feel it building, the tension in the air. It was like a storm breaking. And the first yipping shriek was like the first roll of thunder. Mr Ince would come down heavy on the perpetrator. Especially those who turned the air blue with obscenities, or who hurled their food across the table.

Sometimes, in severe cases, violence alone could not quell the agitation. One lunchtime, Silas witnessed three orderlies close in on a mountain of a man, a real prizefighter by the look of him. The man had tipped his dining companions from their bench, which he had smashed against the wall. He was now swinging a bench leg to ward off any attempt to subdue him.

Even Mr Ince with his chain could not get close to him.

The dining hall was in uproar. The orderlies blew their alarm whistles. The inmates shrieked in panic.

It was left to the medical staff to resolve the situation.

There was always a nurse on hand with a trolley of meds. On the day of the incident it was Drummond. He was brandishing a hypodermic needle. The difficulty was getting close enough to use it.

The man was backed into a corner. Anyone who dared a frontal approach would no doubt receive a solid clout around the head.

Nurse Drummond conferred for a moment with the orderlies. Then moved to one side.

At a signal from Drummond, the orderlies ran at the man, stopping short about three or four paces in front of him. This was enough to draw him out. He committed to a defensive lunge. Drummond seized his opportunity and nipped up behind him, stabbing the needle into the side of his neck.

The man let out the howl of a wounded animal. A cry that was picked up and echoed by the other inmates.

The man wielded the bench leg weakly behind him to ward off his unseen assailant, but he seemed to know that he was beaten. A moment later, he thudded to his knees and then collapsed with a roll on to his side.

It was all over in a matter of minutes. Naturally, attention had been focused on the violent lunatic. It was only Silas's developed policeman's instincts that made him think about the meds trolley, left unattended all the while.

He caught Timon Medway's eye just as he turned away from apparently contemplating the contents of the trolley. Medway granted him the privilege of a sly wink. For all Silas knew, Medway may even have taken something off the trolley.

He preferred to be outside if he could. For one thing, he escaped the pervading smell of the interior. But it was good, too, to be reminded that there was a world beyond the asylum, even if it was a cruel delusion to think that he might ever one day rejoin it. On a simple animal level, he liked to feel the sun on his face and a fresh breeze disturb his beard. For, yes, he let his beard grow. And kept his head cropped short. Like almost every other man in there. He welcomed the anonymity.

He asked to work in the vegetable garden.

He found the work both exhausting and soothing. He knew nothing about horticulture but discovered that he was a quick learner and a willing labourer. A few words of encouragement or praise was enough to sustain him for days. What pleased him most were the honest, wholesome dirt under his fingernails and the gentle twinges in his back.

When he was not at work, he often found himself gravitating towards a small building about 150 yards from the main building, at the far north-west corner of the grounds. From a distance it might be taken for a strangely austere, brick-built bandstand. It was in fact the pump house, where the water that supplied the asylum was drawn up from its subterranean source.

The throb of the steam-driven engine was strangely comforting, more so than any brass band playing strident marches would have been.

It was here that he would sometimes meet Timon Medway. It was strange. He came to think of this man – a man he had once hunted down as the incarnation of pure evil – he came to think of him as something like a friend. Indeed, he hardly spoke to another soul, other than when he was required to address a member of staff. It's true that he also spent time with Henry Hicks. He enjoyed the young man's company. But trying to talk to Henry was a largely unrewarding experience.

Silas and Medway would walk around the pump house, as if they had gone there for the exercise. They would converse all the time in low murmurs, their voices inaudible to hidden eavesdroppers over the noise of the engine.

On every circuit of the pump house, he was granted a view of the weird twisted tree whose limbs seemed to be frozen in the midst of a violent seizure. He had the impression that each time he progressed to the other side of the building, and the tree was out of view, it would begin to thrash its branches wildly, holding its petrified pose only when he could see it, like a variation of the children's game of statues.

Thus they laid their plans.

At night he slept in a dormitory with around fifty other men. The beds were closely packed in, some almost touching, others crammed in at right angles to the rest so that no space was wasted. Silas's bed was along the wall, beneath a window. There were bars, but no curtains or blinds. On a moonlit night the dorm was flooded with an eery silver brightness. And, except for the catatonic patients, who never stirred from their beds, they generally all woke with the dawn.

He made no effort to become acquainted with the men nearest to him, nor they with him. Their enforced proximity made any such intimacy an affront.

They slept so close to one another that if you turned in your bed there was a danger you would roll into the bed next to you. It was a wonder their dreams did not become contaminated with each other's terrors. Perhaps they did.

For Silas, the nights were the worst. The constant snoring and farting did not trouble him much, nor even the frantic thumping tremors of masturbation; such sounds had to be expected in any large congress of sleeping men, and were in their own way comforting. What shook him was the whimpering and sobbing, the screams of terror, the panicked gasps for air, and most of all the meek, fearful whispering of names – *'Mildred!'*, *'Mother!'* – by those who had been abandoned by their loved ones.

He slept on a narrow horsehair mattress as solid as a seam of clay. The trick was to make sure that he was physically exhausted by the time he lay down.

His work in the vegetable garden helped. As did the tumbler of cloudy, brackish-tasting liquid he was given to drink before retiring.

He had heard nothing more about the possibility of Dr Leaming treating him.

He had mentioned Pottinger's suggestion to Timon Medway, who had welcomed it as an opportunity for Silas to infiltrate the programme. Though what he would be able to achieve by this was not clear.

Then one morning as he was making his way out of the dining hall after breakfast, Mr Ince appeared from nowhere to block his way.

'Where do you think you're going?' It was the kind of question Mr Ince specialized in. Every conceivable answer that could be given to it would inevitably be the wrong one. Silas felt his stomach knot with anxiety.

'Outside. I'm due to work in the vegetable garden this morning.'

'Oh no you're not.'

'Am I not?'

Mr Ince smiled with satisfaction. 'No. You're coming with me.'

'W–where are we going?' Silas regretted his slight stammer, which felt artificial, as if he was deliberately trying to signal his weakness.

Mr Ince lapped it up, of course. 'That's for me to know and you to find out.'

Mr Ince led him at a brisk pace along the endless corridor.

Every now and then Mr Ince would stop and wait for Silas to catch up, with a chivvying: 'Keep up now! We ain't got all day!'

And he would treat him to a cheerful cuff about the ear with the back of his hand as he drew level.

At least he did not brandish the key fob.

After ten minutes or so, they came to a door at the far end of the East Wing. Mr Ince barged in without knocking.

It was a small treatment room, dominated by a large, elaborate chair, something like a dentist's chair, in the centre. Dr Leaming was seated at a narrow desk against one wall, reading through some notes. He looked up when they came in, and took in Silas with an avid gaze.

'Here he is,' said Mr Ince. There was something insolent about the way he dallied there, as if he was checking up on the psychiatrist. He pursed his lips critically.

'Oh, right, very good.' Dr Leaming spoke with a slight Yorkshire accent. The homely incongruity of this no doubt did much to throw patients off their guard, even if it did not quite put them at their ease. From the moment he saw him, Leaming could not take his eyes off Silas. He was drinking in his distress. And it seemed he wanted it all to himself. 'Thank you very much, Mr Ince. That'll be all.'

'You want me to leave you alone with him?'

'I'll be fine, don't you worry. I wouldn't want to keep you from your duties.'

'On your own head be it.' Mr Ince stomped from the room with ill grace, slamming the door behind him. Silas was in no doubt that someone – most likely he himself – would bear the brunt of Ince's displeasure later.

Dr Leaming gestured towards the massive chair in the centre of the room. 'Take a seat, won't you.'

Silas eyed the chair uneasily. It looked comfortable enough, upholstered in green leather, with a headrest, arm rests and even an extension at the bottom which could be lifted up to support the legs. But there was something undeniably sinister about it all the same. Small circular metal discs, about the size of a penny, were attached to various points around the chair, by what seemed to be adjustable bars.

A control panel stood on a podium to one side of the chair, apparently connected to it by wires.

Dr Leaming noticed Silas's reluctance. 'There's nothing to be afraid of. On the contrary.'

Silas lowered himself gingerly into the chair. Dr Leaming sprang up from his seat and busied himself over the controls. At the push of a button, the chair began to throb gently. There was then a series of alarming noises, a strident screeching followed by clanking and knocking and the sound of gears grinding. The whole chair shuddered violently as some kind of hidden machinery went into operation. He felt his legs raised and straightened by the trembling leg rest, at the same time as the back reclined.

Finally, after what could have been as long as ten minutes, he was almost horizontal.

As if all that wasn't unnerving enough, he now saw himself reflected in a full-length mirror set into the ceiling.

'There! You see? Very *comfy*, isn't it?'

Silas nodded his head tensely. 'Comfy' was not quite the word he would have chosen.

But it was the word that Dr Leaming insisted on. 'Yes, that's right, isn't it? It's very *comfy*. The most *comfy* chair you've ever sat in, that's what it is. You're feeling incredibly *comfy*, aren't you? And relaxed. So relaxed. That's good. That's very good. Right. Now, today, we're just going to have a little *chat*, you and me, that's all. So that we can get to know each other a bit better. I always like to have these *chats* in here, in the treatment room, so patients can get used to the surroundings.'

Dr Leaming paused and gave a confirmatory nod. 'Don't look at me. You don't have to look at me. Look up at the ceiling. Straight above you. What do you see?'

'Myself.'

'Yes! Yes, indeed. For, after all, that is what we are here to consider, is it not. Silas Quinn. So let us keep the image of Silas Quinn before us.'

'I would prefer not to look at myself.'

'I know. I know. It's strange at first. But you'll get used to it. After a while, you won't even notice it.'

'It seems rather . . . egotistical.'

'Do you not like to look at yourself in the mirror, Silas?'

'It's not that. I don't have much cause to.'

'An interesting answer. Good. I like that. Good man. Now, it says in your notes that you're a policeman?'

Silas saw himself nod.

'Do you like being a policeman?'

Silas was startled by the question. 'It's all I know.'

'Well, that's not true, is it? Because it also says that you trained to be a medic.'

'No, I . . . I didn't complete my studies. I couldn't.'

'Ah yes, that was the first time you were admitted to Colney Hatch, wasn't it?' Dr Leaming didn't wait for an answer. 'Now Silas, I'm going to ask you a *question*. And I want you to think about it very carefully before you answer that *question*. I want you to be as honest as you can. I'll warn you, it's a difficult *question*, but only because it requires complete honesty. Are you ready for the *question*?'

Leaming's voice was a strange combination of authoritative and soothing. Silas recognized the techniques and constructions of hypnotism, the repetition and the inexplicable emphasis. The way, almost, of talking about talking, of laying the ground for what is to come, of slowly, subtly aligning the will of the person listening with that of the person speaking. *Soon I will say this. And when I say this, you will do this.*

It did not surprise him, therefore, to hear himself say, 'Yes.' He saw himself raise one eyebrow.

'Good man. Good *man*.'

Dr Leaming must have pushed a button on the control panel, because the chair began to vibrate pleasantly.

'The question is this, Silas. What are you most afraid of?'

He had not expected to. He had had no inkling of it coming. But as soon as he was asked the question, Silas began to sob violently, uncontrollably, as if a valve had been opened inside him.

And he could not tear his eyes away from the sight of his tear-streaked face.

THIRTY-FIVE

His tears must have been taken by Dr Leaming as an honest answer. He found himself admitted to the programme.

His treatment took place every weekday morning after breakfast. Each session lasted no longer than an hour, sometimes a lot less. He had the sense that Dr Leaming invariably brought the consultation to an end at a moment of crisis or breakthrough, which were often the same thing.

He found himself looking forward to the sessions during the other hours of the day.

To begin with the treatment consisted of him staring up at his reflection, as he listened to Dr Leaming's authoritative but soothing voice, while the chair thrummed gently.

At the start of the second session, Dr Leaming began: 'Do you remember the question I asked you last time? I will ask you it again. And this time you will answer. What are you most afraid of?'

'Myself.'

Silas saw an expression of surprise on his own face looking down at him, which settled into a look of mild reproach.

The answer seemed to satisfy Dr Leaming, not to say excite him. He made some adjustments to the control panel and the intensity of the vibrations in the chair increased.

'Exceptional. Ex-*cep*-tional! You show great insight by that answer, Silas. You should be proud of yourself. It usually takes many more sessions before we get to that. Fear of the self is the greatest block to a therapeutic breakthrough. Being able to admit it is the first step towards overcoming it. And if you can overcome your fear of yourself, you can overcome all your fears.'

The following day, he was about to get into the chair as usual when Dr Leaming held out a restraining hand. 'One moment please. Given the progress that we made yesterday, I feel that we are ready to take the treatment to the next level. Kindly remove your clothes and place them on the chair over there.'

'Remove my clothes?'

'Oh, yes. It's not possible for you to confront yourself – the root of all your fears – through the barrier of clothing.' Dr Leaming said it in his usual down-to-earth Yorkshire accent. Silas found it difficult to object. 'Don't you want to carry on with the therapy?' And in that bland question he laid the threat of depriving Silas of all the consolations that he had so far experienced, as well as the promise of future redemption.

The leather upholstery grew uncomfortably hot next to his skin.

Dr Leaming was kneeling down beside the chair. Silas felt something cold touch the underside of first one thigh and then the other.

'What's that?'

'It's nothing to worry about,' Dr Leaming reassured him. 'You may feel a slight tingling sensation emanate from each of these contact discs. It is simply a small electrical current designed to reinforce the work that we are doing here.'

Dr Leaming was on his feet again, at the control panel. He pressed a button and the chair adjusted itself to the usual near horizontal position with the same industrial din as before. Silas was shocked to see himself naked in the mirror. He hardly recognized himself.

'So. This is it. Your worst fear.'

'I suppose it is.'

Dr Leaming made some adjustments to the control panel. The lighting in the room dimmed and modulated, so that all Silas could see now was the reflection of his own nudity exposed. It was as if his ghost had left his body and was hovering above him.

'What do you see?'

'A man.'

'Do you recognize him?'

'I suppose it's me. It's a mirror, after all. That's how mirrors work.'

'And it frightens you, what you see?'

'It's not *that* that I'm frightened of. It's what's in here.' Silas watched himself tap the side of his head.

There was a heavy clunk of gears and the chair began to vibrate.

'Everything bad that happens to you is your own fault. You cause it. You make it happen. It's punishment for something bad you did long ago.' There was a beat before Dr Leaming added: 'Is that what you think?'

'Yes.'

'You're not the only one to have such thoughts, you know.'

'I don't suppose I am.'

'But in your case, you have more reason to entertain them than most.'

'Do I?'

'You've killed people.'

'In the line of duty. If I hadn't killed them, they would have gone on to commit worse crimes.'

Silas felt the first jolt in his right thigh. It was not exactly the pleasant tingle that Dr Leaming had led him to expect. He cried out and saw the grimace of shock distort his features. And then laughed. It really hadn't been as bad as all that. It was just that he wasn't expecting it.

'That's what you tell yourself. But you don't believe it. You killed them because you wanted to. Because it gave you satisfaction to do so. Because you are a killer.' The strange thing was, there was nothing disapproving or judgemental in Dr Leaming's voice. 'That's what you're afraid of.'

'Yes.'

'It started with your father's suicide.'

'Yes.'

'You wanted your father dead.'

'No.'

Dr Leaming made some further adjustments to the control panel. This time Silas was ready for the jolt of electricity in his thigh. His reaction was limited to an involuntary twitch of the leg.

'You see, it isn't so bad. You don't have anything to fear from the chair. Your fear is up there, above you.'

'What if I hadn't said "myself"? What if I'd said "spiders"?'

'Where does the fear of spiders come from?'

'Some kind of primitive survival instinct? It seems irrational now. But perhaps it began as a tactic for protecting us from poisonous spiders.'

'No, but where does it come from, really? The fear? All fear?'

'From ourselves?'

'Exactly. So whatever you had said, eventually you would have had to confront yourself.'

Silas frowned, self-consciously creating a thoughtful expression. It was hard not to be self-conscious confronted by a reflection of himself naked.

'Why do you blame yourself for your father's death? You couldn't possibly be responsible. Why do you feel guilt over that? Over something you played no part in?'

'Perhaps if he had been able to talk to me . . .'

He felt another jolt of electricity through the muscle of his thigh.

'Don't lie to yourself, Silas. You must be honest, otherwise this won't work.'

'I don't know what you . . . what you're driving at.'

'*You* don't feel guilt at your father's death. *Your* guilt is because you *wanted* him dead.'

Silas shook his head in denial of Leaming's suggestion. But he saw in the eyes that looked down at him an acknowledgement of its truth.

After Silas began the treatment, he and Timon Medway no longer sought each other out at the pump house. From now on, they were never alone in each other's company. Whenever their paths crossed, they stared blankly ahead.

They were aware that their unlikely friendship had not gone unnoticed. Mr Ince made no secret of watching them; he meant them to know that he was on to them.

It seemed they both intuitively felt that their plans were entering a crucial phase. Silas was astonished to discover that he missed Medway's company. Although he accepted that they were wise to let this distance grow between them, he suspected that Medway had turned from him, possibly because of some unwitting offence that he had committed. He felt himself cast adrift.

To compensate him for this loss, he spent as much time as he was allowed in Henry Hicks' undemanding company. Mr Ince saw this too. Silas had to accept that he was one of the two most interesting individuals in the asylum as far as Mr Ince was concerned. The other being Timon Medway.

*   *   *

A rectangle of tremulous light floated in the darkness above him. Framed within it was the naked body of a man. Freakishly pale and thin, the man lay as still as a corpse laid out on a mortuary table. As if the thing he most feared was movement.

The man was strangely familiar, like a figure in a dream whom you take to be a close friend, but who turns out to be a phantom invented by your sleeping mind.

The room, and the world that contained it, had been swallowed by the darkness.

They were alone now, he and this man who watched him with a detached and slightly quizzical expression, as if none of this was anything to do with him.

They were suspended high above the void, with nothing but the void above them.

Out of the void, a voice spoke to him: 'What do you fear, Silas?'

For the first time, he found himself at a loss how to reply. Perhaps there was nothing he feared any more.

He looked into the eyes of the only other man in existence and at last recognized his fear.

'Him.'

He felt a sharp punch in the back of his thigh, as if he had been struck with a hot hammer. He saw the man shift his leg uncomfortably, as if he had felt it too.

'Who is he?'

Of course, he had always known. That is the way with dreams. If this was a dream. 'It's me.'

'Good. Very good. And why do you fear yourself so much, Silas?'

'Because of what's inside me.'

'What's inside you?'

'Horrible, horrible things.'

'You have to confront what is inside you. You have to confront your fears.'

The void was suddenly filled with a screech of grinding machinery. Whatever was supporting him began to quake violently. He saw the man – the man that was himself – tremble as if gripped by a fit of the chills.

'We must shake the fears out of you.'

The darkness folded in on itself, then shimmered and shifted and rippled as if something was being unfurled in it. There was a change to the soft glowing rectangle, a subtle transformation in the light that illuminated it.

And something happened to the body that was contained in it too. It flickered and faded and then came back into view. But now it was covered in black markings, almost every inch of it inked and scrawled with dark graffiti.

He scanned the markings with a mixture of horror and wonder. A whole world of pain and cruelty was depicted on that body now – on *his* body, for it was still his face that confronted him. He saw decapitated corpses and corpses pierced with knives and needles, corpses bent over and obscenely violated, corpses bound and bloody, bodies dismembered and rotting. He saw the mutilated corpses of women and children, and even babies.

'What do you see now?'

'Death.'

'The death that is in you. That *was* in you. The death that is the source of your fear. Death is the fear that brings all other fears into focus. It's what gives fear its stringent taste.'

The noise of machinery intensified. There was another adjustment of the darkness and he felt himself slowly lifted higher in the void.

'What's happening?'

'You're going to meet your fears. Head on.'

It must have been a trick of the light – or rather a trick of the dark. But he had the sense that the markings suddenly came to life, twitching and writhing with an unnatural animation. Not that he was looking at them directly. It was like the tree near the pump house, thrashing its branches about when he couldn't see it, only to freeze into a rigid pose whenever he was looking at it.

The cranking and ratcheting stopped abruptly and the rising void juddered to a standstill. He was inches from his own face.

Then his face, too – like the rest of his body – had flickered and faded. Another face appeared where his had been. This face was familiar to him, yet still he could not prevent himself from gasping when it was revealed to him.

'What do you see?'

But the other man's face had vanished as soon as it had appeared. His own was staring back at him.

'Timon Medway.'

There was another stabbing punch in the back of his thigh. This time he had expected it. Even so, his knee jerked up, hitting something solid and setting it rattling.

'You saw the face of evil. The face of your own evil. There is a Timon Medway inside you. That's why you have killed so many men. You are trying to kill what there is of them inside of you. That is the only way you know to overcome your fears. But you cannot overcome your fears that way. Because there will always be another Timon Medway. Someone else to remind you of the evil inside yourself.'

'What can I do?'

The question went unanswered, except for the heavy grinding of machinery. He felt himself lowered once more in the void. The rectangle of light in which his body was framed flickered one last time and then went black, its negative imprint shimmering for a moment on his retina.

THIRTY-SIX

S ilas breathed in the sticky heat of the greenhouse. It reminded him of another place, a hot, airless room in the roof space of a high building. Except the air was fuller here, bursting with moisture and rich, clammy smells. A cloying vegetal sweat mingled with the tang of fertilizer.

He had managed to recruit Henry Hicks into the gardening detail. Silas thought it would do the young man good not just to get outside now and then, but to put his back into some honest toil. He found the work gave him purpose, and he hoped it would do the same for his strange friend.

To plant and tend and harvest the food that they all ate – it simply felt like a good thing to do. It made him feel less hopeless, somehow. It connected him to life, to all the lives that were lived there. Once, he might have shunned any bonds of community with these suffering people. Now he welcomed them.

And just to watch a plant grow from a seed, to measure its sprouting shoots with his gaze, to support those shoots with canes, to pick the parasites from its leaves, to watch the burgeoning fruit upon its stems – all this was a privilege, wherever it was experienced.

Henry's passivity made it difficult to know whether he was a willing participant. Wherever you placed him, whatever you asked of him, it seemed to be all the same to Henry.

They were sowing spring cabbage in planting trays. Silas plunged a forefinger into the compost. It was Henry's job to drop one or two seeds into each hole, which Silas then covered over. It was undemanding and absorbing. They worked in companionable silence.

Silas heard the scrape of the greenhouse door opening. He straightened his back and looked around.

The man whose body and face had replaced his own in the darkness was approaching.

They had not spoken since the treatment began. There was an

urgency now to their exchange, as if they were not sure how long they would have together.

'How does he do it?'

Timon Medway had reached the bench where they were planting the cabbage seeds. Henry Hicks seemed to have an instinctive fear of Medway. He backed away, leaving Silas and Medway together.

Medway affected a wounded expression and waved a sarcastic farewell with the fingers of one hand, bending them lamely at the knuckle. He glanced distractedly at the contents of the bench, picking up an empty terracotta pot which was on a slate tile.

Medway stared into the plant pot, as if he expected something to emerge from it, a white rabbit perhaps, or a dove.

'Oh, simple stage craft. There is a two-way mirror in the ceiling. I am lying behind it, on a glass platform raised a few inches above the mirror. By carefully changing the way the light falls on the mirror he is able to make parts of me appear and disappear.'

'And the markings on your body? Are they . . .?'

'Tattoos.' Medway put the pot down with extraordinary delicacy, as if he believed it to be an ancient Ming vase. With typical perversity, he did not put it back where he had found it and now noticed the slate tile it had been sitting on. He touched it lightly with a finger, as if he doubted its reality. Once that was confirmed, he turned his full gaze on Silas.

'Permanent?'

'I am life. The bringer of light. But I am also death. It is right that I should be marked as such.'

'How can you bear to have those monstrous designs on your skin? Forever!'

Medway frowned as if he did not understand the question. 'It is necessary,' he insisted.

'Is that what he does to everyone?'

'The timing may vary. But the essentials are the same.'

'Is it always you?'

'Yes. I appear to be most people's idea of evil incarnate. Even lunatics'.'

'But what if they don't know who you are?'

Timon Medway was indignant at this suggestion. 'Everyone

knows me! And even, let us say, for argument's sake, someone does not recognize my face, they recognize what is *in* me. That's what matters. Besides, I usually make some efforts to get to know them before the treatment begins.'

'As you did with me?'

Medway smiled. 'Well, in your case it wasn't necessary, was it? We already knew each other. You know full well why I renewed our acquaintance.'

But Silas suddenly felt that he didn't know anything any more.

Medway must have seen the wariness in his eyes. 'You do trust me, don't you?'

'I would be insane to trust you.'

Medway found this inordinately funny. The gourd of husks was briskly shaken.

'How does it work? How does it make them fearless?'

'Don't you feel it working on you?'

'I don't know. I . . .'

'You haven't tested it. Perhaps we should.' He turned back to the bench, picked up the slate tile and held it in front of him by both hands, as if to shield himself from a blow to the solar plexus. 'What do people fear most?'

'Don't start that!'

'Pain, I would say. Wouldn't you?'

'I suppose so.'

'If Leaming has been successful then you will have no fear of pain. You will not hesitate, for example, to clench your hand into a fist and punch this slate with all your strength.'

'Why should I do that?'

'You will learn from it.'

'I will break my hand.'

'I thought you trusted me?' Medway pouted reproachfully and gave the slate a brandishing shake, meant to show how firmly he was holding it. 'Aim at the tile with all your might. Everything will be fine. Trust me.'

The tile was about half an inch thick, perhaps a little less. A substantial enough object not to shatter at a blow from him. It was fair to say that his hand would come off worse in any altercation.

But whatever else he was feeling – bemusement, annoyance,

and even boredom – Silas had to admit fear was not among his emotions just then. How could it be? He was entirely in control of what he was doing.

And so he clenched his fist, tensed the muscle of his forearm as he drew it back.

'Ankanchankan!' They had forgotten Henry Hicks.

Silas looked up to reassure him. 'It's all right, Henry. Nothing bad is going to happen.'

He clenched his hand even tighter. He felt the energy building in the tension of his biceps.

Timon Medway's reflexes were admirably quick. He whipped up the slate and jumped to one side. But he was not quite quick enough. Silas caught his knuckles on the abrasive tile as it was swept away. He hardly felt it, but there was an almost musical ping as he made glancing contact.

'Sorry!' said Medway, grinning in a way that suggested he was not sorry at all. He dropped the tile carelessly to the floor. 'That wasn't supposed to happen. Let me see it.'

Silas held out his outstretched hand, showing specks of blood drawn through the grazed skin.

'You'll live.'

'I trusted you.'

'And you were right to. Did you break your knuckles?'

Silas frowned at his wound, as a delayed pain started to make itself felt. He shook his hand vigorously to ward it off.

'Sattass dass?' wondered Henry.

'It's all right. It's nothing.'

The rusty squawk of the greenhouse door sounded its alarm again. All three turned to see Mr Ince approaching, his stride curiously assertive and wary at the same time. He walked with his pelvis thrust out, but his shoulders drawn back. As if he was hastening towards something which repulsed him.

'What's going on here?'

'We're sowing cabbages,' said Silas.

Mr Ince squared up to Silas, but found himself to lack a couple of inches on the other man. To compensate for this, he took out his key fob and jangled it in his hand, as if he was considering giving it a good swing on its chain, the way you might take out a dog for exercise.

All of this proved too stressful for Henry. He gave a high-pitched whine and then cried: 'Aldan sandantarn.'

Mr Ince snapped. 'I'm sick of your fucking gibberish!' He spun on his heels away from Silas and in one motion swung the key fob, now at the full extent of its chain, lashing it across Henry's face.

Silas rushed at Mr Ince with his shoulder down, pushing him into shelves of brassica seedlings. The shelves clattered apart, bringing all their contents crashing to the ground. But the two men were left standing. Silas had one hand at Mr Ince's throat. Mr Ince's face darkened. He eyed Silas with a steady hatred.

'Leave Henry alone.' Silas said it very quietly, almost whispering it into Mr Ince's ear. And then he released his grip.

Mr Ince drew the key fob in. There with all the keys was a gleaming silver whistle. He raised it to his lips and blew with all the force he could muster.

He kept his eyes on Silas all the time.

THIRTY-SEVEN

They had the straitjacket on him now, his arms strapped tightly across his front.

There were four of them marching him along the corridor. Mr Ince to the front, one orderly on either side, another behind, penning him in with a diamond formation. They kept a meticulous distance from him and handled him impeccably now. No brutality, no swearing, not even the occasional shove to hurry him along.

They had won. He was defeated. There was no need to assert their dominance over him. It went without saying.

And strangely, perversely even, he was content. He had felt the fight go out of him as soon as the shrill piercing blast of Mr Ince's whistle had drawn the other orderlies crashing into the greenhouse. He had not resisted as they wrestled him to the floor. He had even welcomed their assault, and welcomed the hard, sharp bite in his cheek as they ground his face into gravel.

He had surrendered willingly.

His struggle was over. And it was a relief.

He sensed a buzz of excitement in the air. It was always the same when there was an incident. The inmates picked it up and transmitted it through every ward and common area. The staff grew more than usually on edge.

He had been told that there were six miles of corridor in the Colney Hatch asylum. It seemed that they were intent on making him walk the full extent, as if they were taking him on some kind of procession. It was a public display of their power.

At last they came to a metal-reinforced door, into which was set a panel with a T-shaped slot. While Mr Ince found the key for the cell, Silas had time to read the writing on the panel.

POCOCK BROTHERS LTD
235 SOUTHWARK BRIDGE ROAD
LONDON, S.E.

THIS ROOM IS FITTED WITH IMPROVED INSPECTION
REGISTERED NO. 812993
ALSO IMPROVED SANITARY LEAD GUTTERS
REGISTERED NO. 812994

The heavy door swung open and the inside of the cell was revealed. A pungent stench rushed out, as if it had been long cooped up and was making a bid for freedom. It was the smell of blocked lavatories. Silas looked down at the drain that ran around the edge of the floor, the improved sanitary lead gutters. They were clear of any solid matter for now, but stained with dubious residue here and there. However effective they were at carrying away the secretions of those who were locked in the cell, something of their accumulated misery lingered.

The walls and floor were lined with what looked like the leather mats used by gymnasts. They did not strike Silas as scrupulously clean. What the lead gutters did not drain, the padding no doubt absorbed.

'Take off his shoes,' Mr Ince directed one of the orderlies.

Silas maintained his passivity as his laces were undone and his feet lifted out of his shoes.

'In you go,' said Mr Ince. His voice was chipper, as if there was a great treat in store for Silas.

Silas complied with a nod.

Mr Ince shared a joke with the other orderlies, but it was cut off by the door slamming shut.

A moment later, he heard the lock turn with a crisp finality.

He was alone with the stench.

There was a small window high in one wall, which there was no way of opening. A single bare lightbulb was fixed to the ceiling, surrounded by a wire frame.

He took a few paces across the cushioned floor and slumped down against one wall.

He closed his eyes and let his head fall back, gently touching the leather padding.

He had no future but this room. And it was hard to believe he had ever had a past before it.

He felt strangely calm.

*   *   *

The stench was inescapable. But necessary.

It was the reality of his situation forcing itself on him. Otherwise he might be lulled into thinking this was just another dream that he would wake from.

But there were no dreams any more. There was nothing other than this cell and its insistent, hectoring stench.

Nothing else mattered now. It was his only reality.

And the only way to survive it was to accept it.

He allowed it to envelop him, connecting him with every other suffering soul who had ever been confined in that space.

It was so palpable that he felt it soaking into his hair, tickling his scalp and layering itself over his face.

Was it the effect of Leaming's treatment? By rights, he ought to have been afraid. His life was closing down. Parading him through the asylum like that had been done as much to taunt him as to warn the other inmates. As if to say: *This miserable existence – this is the only freedom that you are allowed and you are about to lose it. You are going to a place worse than this. And you will only come out when we decide you can.*

He ought to have raged. He ought to have been distraught. He ought to have wept tears of panic and impotence.

But he was content instead to sit and wait to see how things would turn out. He had become a spectator in his own life.

Nothing could get to him. Not even the smell, or the tears it induced. They were not tears of self-pity or remorse. They were a simple physiological reaction. He could not wipe them away, of course, as his arms were bound by the straitjacket. But he had reached a state of such passivity that even that did not trouble him. He simply let the tears cascade from his eyes until they were done.

And the stench no longer disturbed him, because now it was in him.

The cushioned floor yielded beneath his bony backside.

Nothing could harm him.

And he couldn't harm anyone.

It was difficult to know what he could do about anything anyway. He couldn't stop Leaming.

He was not sure he wanted to any more.

To relinquish all ambition, to relinquish all will, to relinquish desire – there was a kind of freedom in that.

Who am I to question my government?

I am sick. My perspective on everything is distorted. I cannot rely on myself. Whatever I think about something is inevitably wrong.

And I was drawn into this by a lunatic. A murderer. The last man I should trust about anything.

He had caught sight of Medway's face as he had been led away from the greenhouse. What had he read in his expression? There was certainly no sympathy there. A faint smile even curled on Medway's lips, as if he were enjoying Silas's plight.

For the first time, Silas chafed at his confinement.

As if in response to his change in mood, he heard the peephole cover slide open and felt himself observed. A moment later, the cover was slammed closed again and the lock to his door turned.

The door opened and Dr Pottinger came in. His normal priestly look had hardened into something steely. He was a priest whose faith had been questioned and who did not take it well. 'I must say, this is very disappointing, Silas. And just when Dr Leaming tells me you were beginning to respond to his therapy.'

Silas considered giving his side of the story, but the idea of speaking wearied him.

'Do you not have anything to say for yourself?'

Dr Pottinger waited. Silas tried to shrug, but the straitjacket made even that difficult.

'Perhaps you were provoked? Or you were trying to defend yourself? Or someone else?'

Silas looked Pottinger in the eye. He thought he detected there a softer look than he had first suspected, perhaps even something imploring about his gaze. Had Medway told him what happened? The idea that the asylum superintendent might be guided by the most notorious lunatic in his care was absurd. But no more absurd than using Medway in a therapeutic programme.

Or was it simply that Pottinger knew exactly what Mr Ince was like?

'It's all right, you can speak freely.'

Silas couldn't suppress a bitter, sardonic bark of laughter. He made to pull his arms apart, testing the ties that restrained him.

'Ah, yes. I see. Of course. I think we can dispense with that. Mr Drummond?'

The nurse must have been waiting just outside the cell. He presented himself instantly. His face signalled a solicitude that was more than professional.

'Remove Silas's straitjacket, please.'

Drummond's eager nod suggested he approved of the instruction. He gently encouraged Silas to lean forward so that he could reach the straps behind his back. With each buckle that was undone, Silas felt a welcome easing of tension. At last he was able to raise his arms above his head, allowing the straitjacket to be lifted off him. Nurse Drummond whisked the humiliating object out of the room with exemplary tact.

Silas looked down at his newly restored hands as he flexed them. Blood had dried into a coppery stain across the knuckles of one.

Silas rewarded Dr Pottinger by finding his voice. He knew how these things worked. 'What do you want me to say? Ince is a brute.'

'Is that why you tried to kill him?'

'I just wanted him to stop.'

'To stop what?'

'He was attacking Henry.'

'Mr Ince maintains that Henry Hicks was behaving in a threatening manner and had to be forcibly restrained.'

'Henry threatening? That's ridiculous. And how is swinging a key fob in his face restraining him?'

'Mr Ince is called upon to do a very difficult job. Sometimes he has to use whatever tools come to hand.'

Silas instantly knew that he had misread the situation. He certainly should not have let the accusation that he was trying to kill Ince go by unchallenged.

Silas shook his head wearily. *Let them do whatever they will do.*

'I see that you are still agitated. It will be hard for you alone in here tonight.' Dr Pottinger sniffed distastefully and winced. 'A mild sedative will help. In the morning, we can talk more about what has happened. Perhaps you would benefit from a tonsillectomy and full teeth extraction.'

Pottinger turned and moved to the doorway, where Nurse Drummond was again waiting. Silas didn't catch the murmured conversation between them but Dr Pottinger returned with a tumbler of what appeared to be his usual bedtime medication.

'What is that? No one has ever told me.'

'Potassium bromide. It's nothing to worry about. Just something to help you sleep, that's all.'

Silas looked around the cell. 'There is no bed in here.'

'Yes, I am sorry about that. Unfortunately, that is how it has to be. There are some patients who would hurt themselves on a bed. Or would use it to hurt the staff who are trying to help them. For that reason, we cannot allow a bed in here. However, with this sedative, you should be able to sleep on the floor. Indeed, you will be able to sleep anywhere.'

Dr Pottinger held the tumbler out to Silas. 'Drink up, there's a good chap.'

Silas downed the draught in two swallows to diminish the foulness of its taste. He shuddered as he handed the tumbler back to the psychiatrist.

As soon as the door was closed on him once more, he leapt to his feet. He stood with his head bowed against the cushioned wall, leaning over the improved lead gutter.

Then he inserted a finger into his mouth and pushed hard, probing the softness at the back of his mouth. His finger tasted of the greenhouse. The fingernail scraped his soft palate, rapidly stimulating the gag reflex.

Two retches – the same number of gulps it had taken to swallow it – and the liquid was out of him, warmer and thicker and cloudier than it had gone in. His vomit hit the wall with some force. He felt its backsplash in his face and watched its viscous descent towards the gutter.

He swallowed down the salty after-burn, a lumpy ache lingering in his throat.

He would have welcomed the oblivion that the sedative offered but there were too many unanswered questions nagging him. He needed to think.

But mainly it was instinct that was driving him.

He settled down on the floor, his back against the padded

wall, watching the last embers of the day burn out in the high window.

At some point he lay down, consigning his bones to the floor's meagre comfort.

There were times in the long hours of absolute darkness that he regretted vomiting up the sleeping draft.

The clarity that he had hoped for eluded him. His head buzzed and ached. And instead of rational thoughts progressing towards a deductive breakthrough, he experienced a flickering motion picture show of disjointed images. His mind replayed the crucial incidents of the day just gone. Over and over. But with gratuitous distortions that he knew to be false. And so the seeds he planted with Henry sprouted instantly, pushing forward writhing shoots. And Henry spoke not his usual gibberish but perfectly formed and coherent sentences, in a surprisingly plummy accent. And this time when he punched the slate that Medway held, the tile shattered into countless pieces. And this time he felt no pain. And this time he squeezed Ince's throat until the life went out of him. So that when he let go, Ince fell limply to the floor. No, no, that wouldn't do. His mind replayed the encounter again. This time, when he let go, Ince apologized and promised to mend his ways. No, no . . . This time Silas didn't grab his throat but merely reasoned with him. And the encounter ended with Ince saying, 'I suppose we'll just have to agree to disagree.'

It was all nonsense. Perhaps he was even dreaming.

If so, these were deeply unsatisfactory dreams, for they never once transported him to anywhere outside that stinking cell. And he was all the time acutely, painfully aware of the floor.

When he saw Henry Hicks standing in the centre of the room, he knew that he was hallucinating. It was the exhaustion, he supposed. All the same, he appreciated the company. Henry's presence was as reassuringly undemanding as ever.

'What's going on, Henry?'

But it seemed that Henry had lost the power of speech entirely.

THIRTY-EIGHT

He must have drifted off eventually. Because he was aware of being wrenched back into the reality of being in the cell, most likely from a dream of being in the cell. Or perhaps it was the other way around.

What had roused him was the click of the lock mechanism.

The first light of dawn flared softly in the high window.

Silas hauled himself to his feet and went over to the door. It was an inch or so ajar. The door yielded heavily, with a resistant groan.

He peered around it, out into the corridor. No one there. He could think of no reason not to leave the cell.

As the door swung to behind him, he noticed the key was still in the lock. It was part of a large fob of keys, attached to a long chain.

This must be the dream, after all.

The clamour of the birds as he crossed the lawn was almost deafening. Were they startled by his presence, or was the breaking of every day such a shock to them? Their alien voices made him feel more alone than he had ever felt before.

As dawn expanded overhead, the writhing tree appeared frozen in the act of warning him off. *If this is a dream*, he was aware of thinking, *its branches would be moving. And I would not feel the damp grass against my bare feet.*

He started to call out when he got within ten yards of the pump house. 'Medway? Timon?'

No answer. Thousands of frantic beaks swallowed his cries.

And then he remembered that Medway refused to answer to his own name.

'Isaac! Sir Isaac Newton! Jeova! God!'

He picked up his pace and began a trotting circuit of the pump house.

He had not gone more than five paces when a formless shape

on the ground pulled him up short. He had seen enough dead bodies in his career to know immediately what it was.

The body was face down, half on the floor of the colonnade, its legs protruding stiffly on to the grass.

Silas bent down and put a hand under one shoulder to lift it. His second hand came down to complete the turnover.

The face was oddly dark and glistening. There was enough light now for him to make out that the features were pulped to a bloody mess.

Even so, from the size and shape of the body, and the orderly's uniform, he recognized the dead man as Stanley Ince.

He heard footsteps on the concrete and looked up to see Timon Medway standing over him.

'My my, what have you done?'

'I have done nothing, as you well know.'

'It doesn't look that way. You have blood on your hands.'

Silas looked down. It was true. 'I just turned his body over. It's covered in blood.'

'That's a nasty wound on your knuckles there. Consistent with beating a man to death, I would say.'

'You know how I got it.'

'Do I?'

'I see. Your word against mine.'

'You'll find my word carries a lot of weight in here.'

'You're forgetting there was a witness.'

'Old Henry Shabbadabbalabba, you mean?' The gourd of weightless husks was shaken.

Silas stood up. 'You killed Ince. And I will prove it.'

'Oh, but I didn't. How many blows must it have taken to make that mess of his face, do you think?'

Silas looked back down at Ince. It was a curious question, but typical of Medway. Typical of his mad obsessions and his arrogance. Silas sensed that he was playing with him. Some instinct urged Silas to pursue it. 'I don't know. How many would you say?'

'Perhaps a thousand? Or maybe fewer? Shall we say seven hundred and sixty-three?'

There had to be some reason why Medway had chosen this number. 'Seven plus six plus three is sixteen. Six plus one is seven. The number on the back of the cards.'

'I'm impressed.' Medway held out his own spotless hands. 'So I ask you, does it look like I've landed seven hundred and sixty-three blows?'

'You could have used a weapon.'

'I think you'll find the blows are consistent with manual impact. Fisticuffs. A good pathologist will be able to tell you that. Besides, if there was a weapon used, you will first have to find it. And find my fingerprints on it. And I can assure you that you never will.'

'Is this what this has been all about? This is why you drew me here?'

'You will never leave this place alive, Quinn.'

Silas recognized the silver whistle which Medway now produced from a pocket. 'Listen to me carefully, listen very carefully. When I blow this whistle, you will remain exactly where you are. You will not attempt to move. You will not attempt to escape.'

The piercing note of the whistle drowned out the birdsong. Medway kept the blast going for what could have been a full minute. And even when he threw the whistle down, Silas felt his eardrums thrumming.

He heard shouts coming from the direction of the asylum building. When he next looked, Medway was nowhere to be seen.

In truth, Silas had no intention of making a run for it. He found Medway's half-baked attempt to hypnotize him – if that's what it was – deeply irritating. Of course, he would wait for the orderlies. He was a police officer.

Medway's plan to incriminate him was risible. It could only have been conceived by a madman who had spent too much time in the company of other lunatics. No sensible person would entertain it for a moment.

At fifty yards he recognized the two orderlies running towards him as the men who had taken him down in the greenhouse yesterday. He had never seen them except in Mr Ince's company.

As they drew level with the pump house, he watched their expressions change from alert trepidation to dawning horror.

'You've done it now,' said one of them, a young man with flaring acne. The other one, tall, thin and red-haired, glared with angry conviction at Silas.

'I haven't done anything.'

'There's blood on your hands,' pointed out the red-headed one.

'I had to turn him over. As you can see, he's covered in blood. It must have happened then.'

'And your hand's injured. There.' The two orderlies took it in turns to display their stupidity.

'This is ridiculous. Medway did this. Timon Medway.'

'Where is he?'

'He was here a moment ago. He blew the whistle.'

'Mr Ince's whistle.' The whistle had landed close to Ince's body.

'I suppose it must be. Look, I can't have killed Mr Ince, I was locked up in a cell. You know that.'

'But you got out.'

'How did you get out?'

'Someone opened my cell door.'

'Oh, yeah? Who would do that?'

'Mr Ince's keys were in the door,' Silas explained. 'Which suggests he was dead already and his keys taken off him.'

'Or Mr Ince let you out, you overpowered him and killed him and left him here.'

'No, it doesn't make any sense. Why would Mr Ince let me out?'

'Because he felt sorry for you,' said the red-head.

Even his spotty mate looked sceptical at this. 'Maybe not that. We all know what he was like. Maybe he took it into his head to teach you a lesson. He was going to give you a good whipping with his keys, then you got the better of him.'

'That's not what happened.'

'That's what it looks like.'

'To you perhaps. But not to any . . .' Silas broke off. He had been about to say 'sane person'.

'We all know you've been on Leaming's programme. We all know what that does to people.'

'What does it do?'

'It makes you capable of anything. At least, it makes you think you are.'

Tall Redhead blew on his own alarm whistle. Then the two men seized Silas by the arms, as more attendants ran across the lawn towards them.

THIRTY-NINE

He put up no resistance as they walked him back to the padded cell. This would all be cleared up soon, he had no doubt. Though he was not much reassured by the look Tall Redhead gave him when he saw Ince's chain hanging from the key, as if it somehow proved Silas's guilt.

Still, there was nothing else he could do but sit it out.

An hour later the cell door opened again. The same two orderlies came in. 'You're to come with us,' Angry Acne announced.

Most of the inmates were up and about now. He detected a strange excitement among the men. The rumour must have got around that the hated Ince was dead. Perhaps they believed that Silas was responsible. There was something celebratory in their evasive glances as he passed them: it could even be a shy admiration. One or two of them balled a fist which they seemed to cradle in the other hand, as if to say: *What must it have felt like to land the blow that killed him?*

The orderlies took him to Dr Pottinger's office. Pottinger was there with Leaming. There, too, were a number of other men. Policemen, by the looks of them. Local coppers, Silas guessed, but his heart bounded to see Sergeant Macadam and Sergeant Inchball in among them.

There was one other copper there. A man who seemed to be compensating for the smallness of his bald head by growing an enormous drooping moustache.

'What's he doing here?' The words were out before Silas could calculate the damage they might do.

Macadam attempted a brave smile. 'DCI Coddington has taken over the SCD in your absence, sir.'

This was the greatest lunacy that he had encountered in his time in Colney Hatch. DCI Coddington had been the chief investigating officer in the Blackley case earlier that year. As far as Silas was concerned, the man had proven himself to be a flagrant idiot. But the worst kind of idiot, the sort who thought himself a signally clever fellow. Silas had solved the Blackley case, but it was no thanks to Coddington, who had hampered and irritated him at every turn.

And of course, the worst thing about the man was the fact that he too wore a herringbone ulster. He had made them both look ridiculous.

There was only one officer in the whole of the Met who might fall for Timon Medway's absurd attempt to frame Silas Quinn.

And that was DCI Coddington.

'Good to see you again, Quinn. I only wish that it were under better circumstances.' To make sure his point was not missed, Coddington gestured vaguely at their surroundings. As if there was a danger Silas might have forgotten he was an inmate in a lunatic asylum.

'But you know why I'm here, don't you?'

'You're here because you suffered a mental collapse.'

'No no no. My sergeants must have briefed you.'

'*My* sergeants now.'

'I am here on an undercover operation. I am investigating the deaths of four young men at various locations around London. They were all patients here at Colney Hatch, involved in a therapeutic programme run by that man, Dr Charles Leaming.'

Leaming frowned at being pointed out. He looked down at the floor and shook his head, in dismay rather than denial.

'Did Sir Edward Henry approve this operation?' demanded Coddington.

'I couldn't tell him.' Silas knew how irrational this made him sound, even as he was saying it.

Coddington smoothed the ample whiskers of his moustache. 'So this was an unauthorized operation?'

Silas remembered how much he hated the man. '*I* authorized it. That was all the authorization it needed. Macadam, Inchball . . . tell him.'

But Coddington held up a restraining hand. 'I have already spoken to Sergeants Macadam and Inchball. They have told me all about the details of your . . . *plan*.' Coddington gave the word contemptuous emphasis. 'They have also told me of their own reluctance to go along with it and their fears for your sanity. I must say I agree with them. Anyone who thought this was a feasible plan of action really does need their head examining.' Coddington's moustache was momentarily exercised by his mirth.

'It was the only way I could get in here without arousing suspicion. And it allowed me to discover what was happening here from the inside.'

'Hadn't Sir Edward forbidden you from pursuing this line of enquiry?'

'That was exactly why I had to do it this way.'

'You suspect the commissioner of the Metropolitan Police of conspiring to commit a crime?'

'No, it's not . . . it's not Sir Edward. It's the people who are giving him his instructions. He is acting out of the best motives, as always. It goes without saying. He is a good man.'

'I am sure he will be gratified to hear *you* say it!' Coddington's sarcasm provoked a burst of appreciative laughter. Only Macadam and Inchball shook their heads in disapproval. 'Let me put to you an alternative hypothesis. Your nerves have always been your weak spot. I am informed that you have been a patient here once before. You have a history of mental derangement. And so your admittance here was not as the result of some clever plan you had cooked up, but because, well, to put it bluntly, you went mad.'

'I was feigning my symptoms.'

'I hear you shat yourself.'

'It was important to make it convincing.'

'Oh, I would say you certainly did that.' There was more laughter, this time a little muted. 'But, tell me, why was it so important that you infiltrate the asylum?'

'Timon Medway was here! Timon Medway was the key to it all! In fact, as it turned out, I was right. Timon Medway had deliberately drawn me here. He had given the cards to the men who died. The cards with the red hand. He made me believe that he had drawn me here to help him close down Leaming's programme. But all the time it was to get his revenge on me. He wanted to frame me for the murder of Mr Ince. He had planned it all along.'

'How very clever of him.'

'You don't understand. He is very clever.'

'For a lunatic, perhaps.'

'Yes, exactly. For a lunatic. He is clever, but his thinking is often flawed. His arrogance trips him up. He tried to frame me for this attack, but I couldn't possible have done it. I was locked up in a padded cell.'

'Except that Stanley Ince let you out. You repaid the act by brutally murdering him.'

'No. That's impossible. You must see!'

DCI Coddington clearly objected to being told what he must or must not do by Silas Quinn. 'Must I? What I see is your hand. First there's the wound. And that's his blood on your hands. You don't deny that?'

'I turned the body over. Look, you know it couldn't have been me. You can't do this just to pay me back for whatever humiliation you think I may have once subjected you to.'

'Humiliation? You think you could ever humiliate *me*?'

'Please, you're making a terrible mistake. This will fall apart in a court. I *cannot* have killed Ince.' Silas held up his injured hand. 'And as for this injury, which seems to be so significant to everyone. Timon Medway caused me to sustain it. It was a foolish, stupid thing . . . that he encouraged me to do. I punched a slate. I was showing off. I thought it was some kind of game, but I see now it was part of his plan.'

'You punched a slate? Are you mad?' Coddington waited for the hoots of hilarity from the local coppers. He rolled his moustaches as he basked in their appreciation. 'Oh, sorry, old chap. I forgot. So, let me see, were there any witnesses to this incident?'

'Henry Hicks.'

'And this Henry Hicks will vouch for you? He will confirm that this is how you sustained the injury on your knuckles?'

Silas hung his head. 'I don't know. He may . . . we may be able to get him to confirm it. Henry . . . Henry does not communicate in the normal way. He speaks in a language of his own devising, and only when he chooses to.'

Coddington made a rather overdone expression of confusion. 'I beg your pardon? I don't quite follow your drift.'

'It's part of his affliction.'

'Ah, I see! A lunatic! It all hangs on the word of a lunatic.

Who incidentally does not speak English, if I understand
correctly.' Coddington shook his head incredulously. 'Very well,
bring this mad person, Hicks or whatever his name is. We may
as well have one more.' He turned to his audience, while preening
his massive moustaches with anticipatory glee. 'I don't doubt it
will be entertaining, gentlemen. If not particularly elucidating.'

An orderly was dispatched to find Henry.

Silas flashed a desperate appeal towards first Macadam and
then Inchball. His two sergeants nodded encouragingly to him.
'When was Stanley Ince last seen?'

'He completed his shift at five o'clock yesterday afternoon,'
confirmed Dr Pottinger.

'And was he seen leaving the asylum?'

'I cannot say.'

'The fact is, the attack could have taken place at any time
between five o'clock yesterday, and whatever time it was this
morning when I found his body. A post-mortem should be able
to give you a more precise time of death. Until you have that,
you cannot draw any definite conclusions as to the identity of
his murderer. I was in the cell all night. Until just a few minutes
before I found the body. I cannot possibly have committed this
assault in that time. And who do you think blew the whistle?'

'But we don't know what time Stanley Ince let you out of the
cell,' objected Coddington. 'He could have come back at midnight
and released you. As for the whistle, that could have been Mr
Ince before he died. Or you.'

'How many times do I have to say it? Timon Medway let me
out. Timon Medway killed Ince. Timon Medway had Ince's keys.
Timon Medway blew the whistle. Here's what I think happened.
Medway must have stolen some medication, a sedative of some
kind. I once saw him behave in a suspicious manner around the
meds trolley. Make sure that the pathologist does a toxicology
test on the cadaver.'

'I don't need you to give me lessons in procedure!' Coddington
gave his moustache a complacent pat, as if to say he would rather
take advice from his whiskers.

Silas shook his head impatiently. 'Medway injected Ince with
the stolen sedative and then was able to overpower him. He didn't
beat him with his hands, because his hands were, as far as I

could see, undamaged. He might have worn gloves. Gardening gloves, perhaps. He works on the gardening detail. Look for a pair of bloody gardening gloves. He must have discarded them somewhere. Either that or he used some kind of weapon. The medical examination will tell you more.'

'Look, old chap, we all know what this Ince fellow was like. Something of a brute from all accounts. It's understandable. You lost your temper with him, your mind being unbalanced as it is. A moment of uncontrollable rage. We all get those. You hit him harder than you intended. Perhaps it was even self-defence. A witness has testified that the reason he took you out of the cell was to bully you in some way.'

'No! There is no witness to that! You don't know the basic difference between speculation and evidence!' Silas turned first to his own sergeants, then to the other policemen in the room. Surely someone there besides himself could see the man's incompetence?

'Now now, Quinn. You're not doing yourself any favours here, losing your temper like this.'

Just then the door opened.

The mood in the room changed dramatically when Henry Hicks was led in. The air of jocularity that Coddington's posturing had encouraged evaporated. Perhaps some of the local coppers were beginning to be persuaded by the points Silas had made. Even so, the fact remained that Coddington was the lead officer. It would take a bold subordinate to stand up to him and bring this farce to an end.

Henry surveyed the room with the frightened face of a very young child brought before a room full of strange adults. A fresh wound glistened on his cheek.

Silas tried to reassure him. But he suspected that his own smile was as tense and alarming as a baboon's rictus. 'It's all right, Henry. You're not in trouble. We just want to ask you a question. About what happened yesterday. You remember yesterday when we were in the greenhouse?'

Henry gave a tense nod. This was good. If he could communicate without speaking, the chances were they could get an intelligible answer out of him.

But Silas hadn't reckoned on Coddington.

'Whoa, whoa, whoa! You're the bloody suspect here, Quinn! Or have you forgotten?'

'But . . . Henry knows me. He doesn't know you. He's more likely to speak to me.'

'That's not how it works, chummy.'

Henry's anxious expression flitted between mute appeal and terror, as he glanced from Silas to Coddington.

Coddington began to address him in a loud voice, as if he believed the underlying cause of all mental illness was deafness. 'It's very simple. There's no need to be afraid. You won't get into trouble if you tell the truth. Did you go to the greenhouse yesterday?'

Henry's head bobbed up and down rapidly, as if the faster he nodded, the sooner the ordeal would be over.

'Who was there?'

'Nyaaaaa . . .'

Silas reached out a hand to reassure his friend. 'It's all right, Henry.'

'This is hopeless,' decided Coddington. 'We're never going to get any sense out of him.'

Silas knew that Henry's difficulty was in articulating his emotions through the spoken word. 'Henry, could you write down a statement? Would that be easier?'

A look of relief came over Henry. He nodded excitedly.

'Please,' said Silas. 'Can we have a piece of paper and a pen? Can you let him sit down?'

A space was made at the edge of Pottinger's desk and Henry was supplied with writing materials.

He passed his statement to Silas, who had it snatched out of his hands by Coddington.

A frown settled on Coddington's face as he read. After he had finished, he avoided looking at Silas.

Macadam took the statement from Coddington's limp grasp and read it out:

'I was in the greenhouse with Mr Quinn. We was planting cabbage seeds. You make a hole and then put one seed in each hole. Sometimes I put two in by mistake but Mr Quinn said it doesn't matter. I like being with Mr Quinn. Then Mr Medway came in. I don't like being with Mr Medway. He makes me feel all churned up. I don't know what will happen when Mr Medway is there. Usually something bad happens. Mr Medway makes bad things happen. He had a square and he told Mr Quinn to punch it. I didn't want Mr Quinn to punch it because it would hurt his hand. But Mr Quinn said it would be all right. Mr Quinn punched the square. There was blood on his hand. Then there was blood on the square. Mr Medway laughed. I don't like the sound of Mr Medway laughing. It is like mice scratching behind the wall. Then Mr Ince came in and whipped me with his keys and Mr Quinn stopped him. Signed Henry Hicks.'

Silas let out a deep sigh. 'The square is the slate tile he had me punch. Yes, Henry is right. There will be blood on it. That will prove that I did not sustain this wound . . .' He held up his splayed hand. 'Pounding Ince to death, for all that I might have liked to.'

'It proves nothing,' insisted Coddington desperately. He must have sensed he'd lost his audience. From their mutterings, even the local coppers were turning against him. 'You and this halfwit are in cahoots, that's obvious.'

With that, he proved how badly he had misjudged the mood. For all their burliness and brusqueness, the policemen had been moved by Henry's evident distress. They showed a level of human sympathy that DCI Coddington lacked. His authority over the other coppers drained from him in that moment.

Silas Quinn was there to assume it, even though he was barefoot and dressed in the brown corduroy suit of an asylum inmate. He cradled his beard in one hand, thoughtfully, as if he were weighing its value. He showed his authority by voicing the one question that needed to be asked. 'Where is Timon Medway?'

The question was addressed to no one in particular. And no one answered it.

FORTY

Wilfred George Portman looked down over the side of the Grahame-White Type XV at the rolling land below. The mighty Gnome 80 HP pusher engine clattered and roared behind him.

It was hard to think with that din going on. But in truth, he had done all his thinking already.

Now was the time for action.

He felt curiously numb. Emptied of emotion.

He felt an icy chill inside him. It was colder than the blast of wind on his face. His bones vibrated. It could have been the thrum of the engine. Or it could have been he was shivering at his own cold-bloodedness.

He had laid the groundwork over the years. Cultivating a correspondence, feigning a friendship even, with that man. The man he hated more than any other.

It was arguably the greatest work of fiction he had produced. At times, he had almost believed it himself. That he, W.G. Portman, was such an exemplar of socialist, free-thinking principles that he would forgive – and even befriend – a man like that.

The man who had murdered Wilfred.

Portman had read the news that morning, 5 August, 1914. England had declared war against Germany.

It seemed fitting, somehow. If he got out of this alive, he would volunteer as a pilot. He had no doubt there would be a need for men with his skills.

The truth was that before now he had not given any thought to what he might do after today. Today had been the end point of all his plans.

For the first time, he was flying solo. He missed having Claude Grahame-White in the seat behind him. The firm touch on the shoulder, reassuring him of his mentor's presence.

But today, he was on his own.

Severed from human contact, a thousand feet above the nearest hope of fellowship.

With only the wind whipping around him and the engine's drone for company.

'Where do you think he is, guv?'

It felt good to be called 'guv' again. Especially by Inchball. Quinn shook his head. 'He could be anywhere. We need more resources.'

A pair of shoes had been found for him. He was walking the entourage of coppers around the asylum, a guided tour, as if they might be interested in taking up residence there. Leaming and Pottinger were also in tow, though they were somewhat subdued, not to say sheepish.

The visiting party went from bathroom to day room, to ward, to dining hall, to dormitory. Medway's bed showed no sign of having been slept in.

At last they came to the door of Leaming's treatment room. Quinn paused, before turning on Leaming. 'Where did you hide him? For the purposes of the therapy?'

'The room above this one. The floor has been modified – a two-way mirror sunk into it.'

'Take us to it.'

Leaming led them at a run. The room was bare and curiously unprepossessing, hardly sinister at all. There was just the oddness of the window on to the room below. If Medway had been there, he was no longer. Quinn took the opportunity to peer down at the oversized mechanized chair in which he had experienced such strange sights and sensations. He half-expected to see himself naked there.

On his way out of the room, he said to Leaming: 'You will answer for this. In due course.'

'You won't know this, Inspector, but according to this morning's newspapers, war has been declared. The War Office has already confiscated all my papers. They sent someone round first thing. My work is protected by the Official Secrets Act. You will be made to sign. There will be nothing you can do. There's nothing I can do. Even if I wanted to.'

'Four men died,' said Quinn. 'Five if you count Ince.'

'That was never the intention.'

'No. You intended many more to die. And I have no doubt they will.'

Leaming offered no denial.

'Where to now, sir?' wondered Macadam.

'The pump house.'

Something began to intrude on Quinn's consciousness with each patient they rushed past. The curious excitement that he had detected among the male inmates was still there. Only now, instead of cradling their right hands, they were openly showing them to him. It was a signal. And when he realized what they were signalling, his heart began to pound.

'Look! Look at their hands!'

He went over to one patient, a scrawny, bent-over man weakened by poverty, drink and destitution. The man allowed Quinn to take his hand and hold it up. There across the knuckles, a bloody graze not dissimilar to his own. He pointed to another man. 'There! He's the same. They're all the same. Dr Pottinger, how many male patients are there in Colney Hatch?'

'Around nine hundred.'

'*Exactly!* I want the exact number.'

'I shall have to consult the registry. I believe it's around nine hundred. Eight hundred and fifty, something like that.'

'And when you discount those who are permanently incapacitated? Or in secure confinement?'

'I would have to check.'

'Seven hundred and sixty-three perhaps? No, I should think the exact number is seven hundred and sixty-six. And when you deduct three – myself, Henry and Medway – you get seven hundred and sixty-three. That's how many blows he said it must have taken to kill Ince. Don't you see? He had every available male patient hit Ince once. They all played a part in killing him!'

'How could that be?' wondered Dr Pottinger.

'Ince was already sedated. No one blow was the death blow, so in that sense, no single man is guilty – except for Medway, who used them all as a weapon. But they all hated Ince equally. And each one had an equal hand in his death.'

'How could you allow this to happen?' one of the police demanded of Pottinger.

'It's impossible to keep an eye on everyone. And, if they are not causing trouble, then we tend to leave them to their own devices. We are woefully under-resourced here, I will have you know. We do the best we can.'

Quinn offered an alternative explanation. 'Perhaps you knew, and turned a blind eye?'

'No!' The vehemence of Pottinger's denial was undermined by the evasiveness of his gaze. 'We gave him too much latitude, I will accept that. Sometimes, in here, it is possible to . . . I will not say overlook . . . but to make allowances for the terrible things that our patients have done outside. We begin to trust men whom we should not. He is a very persuasive man, you know. And quite engaging, in his own way.'

'He is a child murderer. Never forget that. I made that mistake myself.'

They had reached the pump house when the buzz of an aircraft engine had them swivelling their heads back towards the main building.

The flimsy two-seater craft looked like it was constructed out of a number of large boxes glued precariously together. It was making a sharp descent. They could be forgiven for thinking the pilot was intent on crashing into the asylum.

Just at the last minute they saw something unfurl from the side of the cabin. A rope ladder now trailed in its wake.

It was then that they saw him. The figure on the roof. Medway, it could only be.

He was clambering towards the highest point, the dome above the main entrance. Following some repair work after the recent storm, a workman's ladder had been left in place. Medway manoeuvred it to the side of the dome and began to climb.

Quinn held his breath as he watched.

Medway clung to the side of the dome, and then somehow turned himself around so that he was facing out. He wasn't able to reach the summit, but this was undoubtedly high enough.

The aircraft was flying dangerously low now. Just a score or so feet about the roof tops. The pilot steered a course towards Medway. Medway held out one hand to grasp the rope ladder as it brushed past him.

Despite his hatred for Medway, Quinn could not help admiring the daring of the act. A part of him even wanted it to succeed, just because he knew that there would never again be an opportunity to witness something so athletic and outrageous.

The ladder was within an arm's reach now. Medway swung out and held on.

And was borne aloft.

He climbed a few rungs before waving triumphantly to those watching him below.

The pilot put the aircraft into a steep climb. The engine strained under the additional load.

Quinn's admiration of a moment before turned to an icy despair, as he realized that Medway was escaping.

But then, at a height of around three hundred feet, the rope inexplicably detached itself from the aircraft.

And Medway plummeted, his arms and legs flailing in a desperate attempt to fly.

FORTY-ONE

Sir Edward Henry observed him across his desk with a look of silent reproach. The commissioner's face was drawn and colourless. Quinn thought he detected a slight tremor beneath the eye.

'You sent for me, sir?'

Sir Edward's jaw shook as he spoke. 'You . . . are quite something, Quinn.' Knowing Sir Edward as he did, Quinn was under no illusions. This was meant as the fiercest invective.

'I beg your pardon?'

'It was unforgivable – *unforgivable!* – of you to involve Macadam and Inchball in your preposterous plan.'

'It wasn't preposterous.'

'Were you investigating me? Is that why you kept me out of it?'

'I didn't trust Sir Michael Esslyn. I still don't. I believe I have been vindicated in my suspicions.'

'You have no idea! You have simply no idea, I tell you.'

'What will happen to me, sir?'

'I ought to send you back into that place.'

Quinn gave a measured sigh.

'There's a war on now, of course.'

'I was thinking of volunteering.'

'You'll do no such thing. You're in a reserved occupation, don't you know that? We'll need men like you even more in the coming days.'

'What will happen to Leaming?'

'Write a report. File it. Then put it out of your mind.'

'Nothing will happen.'

'The programme has been closed down, I can tell you that.'

'Well, yes. They don't have Timon Medway any more.'

'It's not for the likes of you or me to understand these things, Quinn. We must trust the experts.'

'Men died.'

'But who can say what advances their sacrifice enabled?'

'They didn't *make* a sacrifice! They *were* sacrificed.'

'Mistakes were made. The government acknowledges that.'

'To whom?'

'Do you want me to say sorry, is that it?'

There was a long moment of silence before Quinn said: 'Will there be anything else, sir?'

'What about the pilot? Have you tracked him down?'

'W.G. Portman, the writer. It turns out he was the father of Wilfred Thomas, Elena Thomas's son, who was murdered by Medway. We have him in custody, while we decide what to charge him with.'

'It sounds like premeditated murder to me. Motive: revenge.'

'It could have been an accident. He may have been trying to help Medway escape.'

'Is that what he says?'

'He has been advised to say nothing. We must interpret the events as best we can.'

'I'll leave that to you. Just get rid of the beard, will you. It makes you look like an old testament prophet.'

Silas weighed the beard absently in one hand. 'I hadn't thought.'

'I don't think Miss Latterly likes it.'

'Miss Latterly?'

'Go away, Quinn. I have had enough of looking at you.'

He paused on his way out beside Miss Latterly's desk. He considered for a moment saying something about his beard, specifically her alleged dislike of it. But he had the sense to realize this might put her at a disadvantage.

'Yes?' she said sharply, without looking up from her typing.

'I was only wondering,' he began. He hadn't known until now what he was going to say. 'If you would be interested in accompanying me to a concert perhaps, or a tea dance, or a moving picture show. Or perhaps we could go for a walk one evening along the river.'

At last she stopped what she was doing and looked at him.

'About bloody time,' she said.